Dear Reader,

You don't know me. I'm Chris Cleave's editor, and I'm
writing to tell you how extraordinary *The Other Hand*
is. As publishers, naturally we only publish books we
love, but every now and then something comes along
that is so special it gives us goosebumps. This is one of
those books – just as David Mitchell's *Cloud Atlas* and
Thomas Keneally's *Schindler's Ark* were. These had a
massive impact on readers worldwide, and I am very
proud that *The Other Hand* now sits beside them on the
Sceptre list. It's an amazing novel – horrifying but
hilarious, tragic but uplifting, hugely entertaining and
highly intelligent.

I hope you love this book as much as I do.

Yours sincerely,

Suzie Dooré
Senior Editor

Also by Chris Cleave

Incendiary

the other hand

CHRIS CLEAVE

SCEPTRE

First published in Great Britain in 2008 by Sceptre,
An imprint of Hodder & Stoughton
An Hachette Livre UK company

1

A CIP catalogue record for this title is available from the British Library

Hardback ISBN 978 0340 963401
Trade Paperback ISBN 978 1444 705621

Typeset in Sabon by Hewer Text UK Ltd, Edinburgh
Printed and bound by Clays Ltd, St Ives plc

Hodder & Stoughton policy is to use papers that are natural, renewable
and recyclable products and made from wood grown in sustainable forests.
The logging and manufacturing processes are expected to conform
to the environmental regulations of the country of origin.

Hodder & Stoughton Ltd
338 Euston Road
London NW1 3BH

www.hodder.co.uk

For Joseph

Britain is proud of its tradition of providing a safe haven for people fleeting [sic] persecution and conflict.

From *Life in the United Kingdom: A Journey to Citizenship* (UK Home Office, 2005)

1

Most days I wish I was a British pound coin instead of an African girl. Everyone would be pleased to see me coming. Maybe I would visit with you for the weekend and then suddenly, because I am fickle like that, I would visit with the man from the corner shop instead – but you would not be sad because you would be eating a cinnamon bun, or drinking a cold Coca Cola from the can, and you would never think of me again. We would be happy, like lovers who met on holiday and forgot each other's names.

A pound coin can go wherever it thinks it will be safest. It can cross deserts and oceans and leave the sound of gunfire and the bitter smell of burning thatch behind. When it feels warm and secure it will turn around and smile at you, the way my big sister Nkiruka used to smile at the men in our village in the short summer after she was a girl but before she was really a woman, and certainly before the evening my mother took her to a quiet place for a serious talk.

Of course a pound coin can be serious too. It can disguise itself as power, or property, and there is nothing more serious when you are a girl who has neither. You must try to catch the pound, and trap it in your pocket, so that it cannot reach a safe country unless it takes you with it. But a pound has all the tricks of a sorcerer. When pursued I have seen it shed its tail like a lizard so that you are left holding only pence. And when you finally go to seize it, the British pound can perform the greatest magic of all, and this is to transform itself into not one, but two, identical green American dollar bills. Your fingers will close on empty air, I am telling you.

How I would love to be a British pound. A pound is free to travel to safety, and we are free to watch it go. This is the human triumph. This is called, *globalisation*. A girl like me gets stopped at immigration, but a pound can leap the turnstiles, and dodge the tackles of those big men with their uniform caps, and jump straight into a waiting airport taxi. *Where to, sir?* Western civilisation, my good man, and make it snappy.

See how nicely a British pound coin talks? It speaks with the voice of Queen Elizabeth the Second of England. Her face is stamped upon it, and sometimes when I look very closely I can see her lips moving. I hold her up to my ear. What is she saying? *Put me down this minute, young lady, or I shall call my guards.*

If the Queen spoke to you in such a voice, do you suppose it would be possible to disobey? I have read that the people around her – even Kings and Prime Ministers – they find their bodies responding to her orders before their brains can even think why not. Let me tell you, it is not the crown and the sceptre that have this effect. Me, I could pin a tiara on my short fuzzy hair, and I could hold up a sceptre in one hand, like this, and police officers would still walk up to me in their big shoes and say, *Love the ensemble, madam, now let's have quick look at your ID, shall we?* No, it is not the Queen's crown and sceptre that rule in your land. It is her grammar and her voice. That is why it is desirable to speak the way she does. That way you can say to police officers, in a voice as clear as the Cullinan diamond, *My goodness, how dare you?*

I am only alive at all because I learned the Queen's English. Maybe you are thinking, that isn't so hard. After all, English is the official language of my country, Nigeria. Yes, but the trouble is that back home we speak it so much better than you. To talk the Queen's English, I had to forget all the best tricks of my mother tongue. For example, the Queen could never say, *There was plenty wahala, that girl done use her bottom power to engage my number-one son and anyone could see she would end in the bad bush.* Instead the Queen must say, *My late daughter-in-law used her feminine charms to become engaged to my heir, and one might have foreseen that it wouldn't end well.* It is all a little sad, don't you think? Learning the Queen's English is like scrubbing off the bright red varnish from your toenails the morning after a dance. It takes a long time and there is always a little bit left at the end, a stain of red along the growing edges to remind you of the good time you had. So, you can see that learning came slowly to me. On the other hand, I had plenty of time. I learned your language in an immigration detention centre, in Essex, in the south-eastern part of the United Kingdom. Two years, they locked me in there. Time was all I had.

But why did I go to all the trouble? It is because of what some of the older girls explained to me: to survive, you must look good or talk even better. The plain ones and the silent ones, it seems their paperwork is never in order. You say, they get repatriated. We say, *sent home early*. Like your country is a children's party – something too wonderful to last forever. But the pretty ones and the talkative ones, we are allowed to stay. In this way your country becomes lively and more beautiful.

I will tell you what happened when they let me out of the immigration detention centre. The detention officer put a voucher in my hand, a transport voucher, and he said I could telephone for a cab. I said, *Thank you, sir, may God move with grace in your life and bring joy into your heart and prosperity upon your loved ones.* The officer pointed his eyes at the ceiling, like there was something very interesting up there, and he said, *Jesus.* Then he pointed his finger down the corridor and he said, *There is the telephone.*

So, I stood in the queue for the telephone. I was thinking, I went *over the top* with thanking that detention officer. The

4

Queen would merely have said, *Thank you*, and left it like that. Actually, the Queen would have told the detention officer to call for the damn taxi himself, or she would have him shot and his head separated from his body and displayed on the railings in front of the Tower of London. I was realising, right there, that it was one thing to learn the Queen's English from books and newspapers in my detention cell, and quite another thing to actually speak the language with the English. I was angry with myself. I was thinking, You cannot afford to go around making mistakes like that, girl. If you talk like a savage who learned her English on the boat, the men are going to find you out and send you straight back home. That's what I was thinking.

There were three girls in the queue in front of me. They let all us girls out on the same day. It was Friday. It was a bright, sunny morning in May. The corridor was dirty but it smelled clean. That is a good trick. Bleach, is how they do that.

The detention officer sat behind his desk. He was not watching us girls. He was reading a newspaper. It was spread out on his desk. It was not one of the newspapers I learned to speak your language from – *The Times* or the *Telegraph* or the *Guardian*. No, this newspaper was not for people like you and me. There was a white girl in the newspaper photo and she was topless. You know what I mean when I say this, because it is your language we are speaking. But if I was telling this story to my big sister Nkiruka and the other girls from my village back home, then I would have to stop, right here, and explain to them: *topless* does not mean, the lady in the newspaper did not have an upper body. It means, she was not wearing any *garments* on her upper body. You see the difference?

– *Wait. Not even a brassiere?*

– *Not even a brassiere.*

– *Weh!*

And then I would start my story again but those girls back home, they would whisper between them. They would giggle behind their hands. Then, just as I was getting back to my story about the morning they let me out of the immigration detention centre, those girls would interrupt me again. Nkiruka would say, *Listen, okay? Listen. Just so we are clear. This girl in the newspaper photo. She was a prostitute, yes? A night fighter? Did she look down at the ground from shame?*

– *No, she did not look down at the ground from shame. She looked right in the camera and smiled.*

– *What, in the newspaper?*

– *Yes.*

– *Then is it not shameful in Great Britain, to show your bobbis in the newspaper?*

– *No. It is not shameful. The boys like it and there is no shame. Otherwise the topless girls would not smile like that, do you see?*

– *So do all the girls over there show them off like that? Walk around with their bobbis bouncing? In the church and in the shop and in the street?*

– No, only in the newspapers.

– Why do they not all show their breasts, if the men like it and there is no shame?

– I do not know.

– You lived there more than two years, little miss been-to. How come you not know?

– It is like that over there. Much of my life in that country was lived in such confusion. Sometimes I think that even the British do not know the answers to such questions.

– Weh!

This is what it would be like, you see, if I had to stop and explain every little thing to the girls back home. I would have to explain linoleum and bleach and soft-core pornography and the shape-changing magic of the British one-pound coin, as if all of these everyday things were very wonderful mysteries. And very quickly my own story would get lost in this great ocean of wonders because it would seem as if your country was an enchanted federation of miracles and my own story within it was really very small and unmagical. But with you it is much easier because I can say to you, look, on the morning they released us, the duty officer at the immigration detention centre was staring at a photo of a topless girl in the newspaper. And you understand the situation straight away. That is the reason I spent two years learning the Queen's English, so that you and I could speak like this without an interruption.

The detention officer, the one who was looking at the topless photo in the newspaper – he was a small man and his hair was pale, like the tinned mushroom soup they served us on Tuesdays. His wrists were thin and white like electrical cables covered in plastic. His uniform was bigger than he was. The shoulders of the jacket rose up in two bumps, one on each side of his head, as if he had little animals hiding in there. I thought of those creatures blinking in the light when he took off his jacket in the evening. I was thinking, Yes sir, if I was your wife I would keep my brassiere *on*, thank you.

And then I was thinking, Why are you staring at that girl in the newspaper, mister, and not us girls here in the queue for the telephone? What if we all ran away? But then I remembered, they were *letting* us out. This was hard to understand after so much time. *Two years*, I lived in that detention centre. I was fourteen years of age when I came to your country but I did not have any papers to prove it and so they put me in the same detention centre as the adults. The trouble was, there were men and women locked up together in that place. At night they kept the men in a different wing of the detention centre. They caged them like wolves when the sun went down, but in the daytime the men walked among us, and ate the same food we did. I thought they still looked hungry. I thought they watched me with ravenous eyes. So when the older girls whispered to me, *To survive you must look good or talk good*, I decided that talking would be safer for me.

I made myself undesirable. I declined to wash, and I let my skin grow oily. Under my clothes I wound a wide strip of cotton around my chest, to make my breasts small and flat.

8

When the charity boxes arrived, full of second-hand clothes and shoes, some of the other girls tried to make themselves pretty but I rummaged through the cartons to find clothes that hid my shape. I wore loose blue jeans and a man's Hawaiian shirt and heavy black boots with the steel toecaps shining through the torn leather. I went to the detention nurse and I made her cut my hair very short with medical scissors. For the whole two years I did not smile or even look in any man's face. I was terrified. Only at night, after they locked the men away, I went back to my detention cell and I unwound the cloth from my breasts and I breathed deeply. Then I took off my heavy boots and I drew my knees up to my chin. Once a week, I sat on the foam mattress of my bed and I painted my toenails. I found the little bottle of nail varnish at the bottom of a charity box. It still had the price ticket on it. If I ever discover the person who gave it then I will tell them, for the cost of one British pound and ninety-nine pence, they saved my life. Because this is what I did in that place, to remind myself I was alive underneath everything: under my steel toecaps I wore bright red nail varnish. Sometimes when I took my boots off I screwed up my eyes against the tears and I rocked back and fro, shivering from the cold.

My big sister Nkiruka, she became a woman in the growing season, under the African sun, and who can blame her if the great red heat of it made her giddy and flirtatious? Who could not lean back against the doorpost of their house and smile with quiet indulgence when they saw my mother sitting her down to say, *Nkiruka, beloved one, you must not smile at the older boys like that*?

Me, I was a woman under white fluorescent strip lights, in an underground room in an immigration detention centre forty miles east of London. There were no seasons there. It was cold, cold, cold, and I did not have anyone to smile at. Those cold years are frozen inside me. The African girl they locked up in the immigration detention centre, poor child, she never really escaped. In my soul she is still locked up in there, forever, under the fluorescent lights, curled up on the green linoleum floor with her knees tucked up under her chin. And this woman they released from the immigration detention centre, this creature that I am, she is a new breed of human. There is nothing natural about me. I was born – no, I was reborn – in captivity. I learned my language from your newspapers, my clothes are your cast-offs, and it is your pound that makes my pockets ache with its absence. Imagine a young woman cut out from a smiling Save the Children magazine advertisement, who dresses herself in threadbare pink clothes from the recycling bin in your local supermarket car park and speaks English like the leader column of *The Times*, if you please. I would cross the street to avoid me. Truly, this is the one thing that people from your country and people from my country agree on. They say, *That refugee girl is not one of us. That girl does not belong.* That girl is a halfling, a child of an unnatural mating, an unfamiliar face in the moon.

So, I am a refugee, and I get very lonely. Is it my fault if I do not look like an English girl and I do not talk like a Nigerian? Well, who says an English girl must have skin as pale as the clouds that float across her summers? Who says a Nigerian girl must speak in fallen English, as if English had collided with Ibo, high in the upper atmosphere, and rained down into her mouth in a shower that half drowns her and leaves her choking up sweet tales about the bright African colours and the taste of fried plantain? Not like a storyteller, but like a victim rescued from the flood, coughing up the colonial water from her lungs?

Excuse me for learning your language properly. I am here to tell you a real story. I did not come to talk to you about the bright African colours. I am a born-again citizen of the developing world, and I will prove to you that the colour of my life is grey. And if it should be that I secretly love fried plantain, then that must stay between us and I implore you to tell *no one*. Okay?

The morning they let us out of the detention centre, they gave us all our possessions. I held mine in a see-through plastic bag. A Collins Gem Pocket English Dictionary, one pair of grey socks, one pair of grey briefs, and one United Kingdom driver's licence that was not mine, and one water-stained business card that was not mine either. If you want to know, these things belonged to a white man called Andrew O'Rourke. I met him on a beach.

This small plastic bag is what I was holding in my hand when the detention officer told me to go and stand in the queue for the telephone. The first girl in the queue, she was tall and she was pretty. Her thing was beauty, not talking. I wondered which of us had made the better choice to survive. This girl, she had plucked her eyebrows out and then she had drawn them back on again with a pencil. This is what she had done to save her life. She was wearing a purple dress, an A-line dress with pink stars and moons in the pattern. She had a nice pink scarf wrapped around her hair, and purple flip-flops on her feet. I was thinking she must have been locked up a very long time in our detention centre. One has to go through a very great number of the charity boxes, you will understand, to put together an outfit that is truly an *ensemble*.

On the girl's brown legs there were many small white scars. I was thinking, Do those scars cover the whole of you, like the stars and the moons on your dress? I thought that would be pretty too, and I ask you right here please to agree with me that a scar is never ugly. That is what the scar makers want us to think. But you and I, we must make an agreement to defy them. We must see all scars as beauty. Okay? This will be our secret. Because take it from me, a scar does not form on the dying. A scar means, 'I survived'.

In a few breaths' time I will speak some sad words to you. But you must hear them the same way we have agreed to see scars now. Sad words are just another beauty. A sad story means, this storyteller is alive. The next thing you know, something fine will happen to her, something *marvellous*, and then she will turn round and smile.

The girl with the purple A-line dress and the scars on her legs, she was already talking into the telephone receiver. She was saying, *Hello, taxi? Yu come pick me up, yeh? Good. Oh, where me come? Me come from Jamaica, darlin, you better believe that. Huh? What? Oh, where me come* right now? *Okay, wait please.*

She put her hand to cover the telephone receiver. She turned round to the second girl in the queue and she said, *Listen, darlin, what name is dis place, where we at right now?* But the second girl just looked up at her and shrugged her shoulders. The second girl was thin and her skin was dark brown and her eyes were green like a jelly sweet when you suck the outside sugar off and hold it up against the moon. She was so pretty, I cannot even explain. She was wearing a yellow sari dress. She was holding a see-through plastic bag like mine, but there was nothing in it. At first I thought it was empty, and I thought, Why do you carry that bag, girl, if there is nothing in it? I could see her sari through it, so I decided she was holding a bag full of lemon yellow. That is everything she owned when they let us girls out.

I knew that second girl a bit. I was in the same room as her for two weeks one time, but I never talked with her. She did not speak one word of anyone's English. That is why she just shrugged and held on tight to her bag of lemon yellow. So the girl on the phone, she pointed her eyes up at the ceiling, the same way the detention officer at his desk did.

13

Then the girl on the phone turned to the third girl in the queue and she said to her, *Do yu know the name of dis place where we is at?* But the third girl did not know either. She just stood there, and she was wearing a blue T-shirt and blue denim jeans and white Dunlop Green Flash trainers, and she just looked down at her own see-through bag, and her bag was full of letters and documents. There was so much paper in that bag, all crumpled and creased, she had to hold one hand under the bag to stop it all bursting out. Now, this third girl, I knew her a little bit too. She was not pretty and she was not a good talker either, but there is one more thing that can save you from being *sent home early.* This girl's thing was, she had her story all written down and made official. There were rubber stamps at the end of her story that said in red ink this is TRUE. I remember she told me her story once and it went something like, *the-men-came-and-they-*

burned-my-village-
tied-my-girls-
raped-my-girls-
took-my-girls-
whipped-my-husband-
cut-my-breast-
I-ran-away-
through-the-bush-
found-a-ship-
crossed-the-sea-

and-then-they-put-me-in-here. Or some such story like that. I got confused with all the stories in that detention centre. All the girls' stories started out, *the-men-came-and-they-*. And all of the stories finished, *and-then-they-put-me-in-here*. All the stories were sad, but you and I have made our agreement concerning sad words. With this girl – girl three in the queue – her story had made her so sad that she did not know the name of the place where she was at and she did not want to know. The girl was not even curious.

So the girl with the telephone receiver, she asked her again. *What?* she said. *Yu no talk neither? How come yu not know the name dis place we at?*

Then the third girl in the queue, she just pointed *her* eyes up at the ceiling, and so the girl with the telephone receiver pointed her own eyes up at the ceiling for a second time. I was thinking, Okay, now the detention officer has looked at the ceiling one time and girl three has looked at the ceiling one time and girl one has looked at the ceiling two times, so maybe there are some answers up on that ceiling after all. Maybe there is something very cheerful up there. Maybe there are stories written on the ceiling that go something like *the-men-came-and-they-*

brought-us-colourful-dresses-
fetched-wood-for-the-fire-
told-some-crazy-jokes-
drank-beer-with-us-
chased-us-till-we-giggled-

15

stopped-the-mosquitoes-from-biting-
told-us-the-trick-for-catching-the-British-one-pound-coin-
turned-the-moon-into-cheese-

Oh, and then they put me in here.

I looked at the ceiling, but it was only white paint and fluorescent light tubes up there.

The girl on the telephone, she finally looked at me. So I said to her, *The name of this place is the Black Hill Immigration Removal Centre.* The girl stared at me. *Yu kiddin wid me,* she said. *What kine of a name is dat?* So I pointed at the little metal plate that was screwed on the wall above the telephone. The girl looked at it and then she looked back to me and she said, *Sorry, darlin, I can not* ridd *it.* So I read it out to her, and I pointed to the words one at a time. BLACK HILL IMMIGRA-TION REMOVAL CENTRE, HIGH EASTER, CHELMSFORD, ESSEX. *Thank you, precious,* the first girl said, and she lifted up the telephone receiver.

She said into the receiver: *All right now, listen, mister, the place I is right now is called Black Hill Immigration Removal.* Then she said, *No, please, wait.* Then she looked sad and she put the telephone receiver back down on the telephone. I said, *What is wrong?* The first girl sighed and she said, *Taxi man say he no pick up from dis place. Then he say, You people are scum. You know dis word?*

I said no, because I did not know for sure, so I took my Collins Gem Pocket English Dictionary out of my see-through bag and I looked up the word. I said to the first girl, *You are a*

16

film of impurities or vegetation that can form on the surface of a liquid. She looked at me and I looked at her and we giggled because we did not understand what to do with the information. This was always my trouble when I was learning to speak your language. Every word can defend itself. Just when you go to grab it, it can split into two separate meanings so the understanding closes on empty air. I admire you people. You are like sorcerers and you have made your language as safe as your money.

So me and the first girl in the telephone queue, we were giggling at each other, and I was holding my see-through bag and she was holding her see-through bag. There was one black eyebrow pencil and one pair of tweezers and three rings of dried pineapple in hers. The first girl saw me looking at her bag and she stopped giggling. *What you starin at?* she said. I said I did not know. She said, *I know what you tinking. You tinking, now the taxi no come for to pick me up, how far me going to get wid one eyebrow pencil an one tweezer an three pineapple slice?* So I told her, *Maybe you can use the eyebrow pencil to write a message that says HELP ME, and then you can give the pineapple slices to the first person who does.* The girl looked at me like I was crazy in the head and she said to me: *Okay, darlin, one, I got no paper for to write no message on, two, I no know how to write, I only know how to draw on me eyebrows, an tree, me intend to eat that pineapple meself.* And she made her eyes wide and stared at me.

17

While this was happening, the second girl in the queue, the girl with the lemon yellow sari and the see-through bag full of yellow, she had become the first girl in the queue, because now she held the telephone receiver in her own hand. She was whispering into it in some language that sounded like butterflies drowning in honey. I tapped the girl on her shoulder, and pulled at her sari, and I said to her: *Please, you must try to talk to them in* English. The sari girl looked at me, and she stopped talking in her butterfly language. Very slowly and carefully, like she was remembering the words from a dream, she said into the telephone receiver: *England, Yes please. Yes please thank you, I want go to England.*

So the girl in the purple A-line dress, she put her nose right up to the nose of the girl in the lemon yellow sari, and she tapped her finger on the girl's forehead and made a sound with her mouth like a broom handle hitting an empty barrel. *Bong! Bong!* she said to the girl. *You already is in England, get it?* And she pointed both her index fingers down at the linoleum floor. She said: *Dis is England, darlin, ya nuh see it? Right here, yeh? Dis where we at all-reddy.*

The girl in the yellow sari went quiet. She just stared back with those green eyes like jelly moons. So the girl in the purple dress, the Jamaican girl, she said, *Here, gimme dat,* and she grabbed the telephone receiver out of the sari girl's hand. And she lifted the receiver to her mouth and she said, *Listen, wait, one minnit please*. But then she went quiet and she passed the telephone receiver to me and I listened, and it was just the dial

18

tone. So I turned to the sari girl. *You have to dial a number first*, I said. *You understand? Dial number first, then tell taxi man where you want to go. Okay?*

But the girl in the sari, she just narrowed her eyes at me, and pulled her see-through bag of lemon yellow a little closer to her, like maybe I was going to take that away from her the way the other girl had taken the telephone receiver. The girl in the purple dress, she sighed and turned to me. *It ain't no good, darlin*, she said. *De Lord gonna call his chillen home fore dis one calls for a taxi*. And she passed the telephone receiver to me. *Here*, she said. *Yu betta try one time.*

I pointed to the third girl in the queue, the one with the bag of documents and the blue T-shirt and the Dunlop Green Flash trainers. *What about her?* I said. *This girl is before me in the queue. Yeh*, said the girl in the purple dress, *but dis ooman ain't got no mo-tee-VAY-shun. Ain't dat right, darlin?* And she stared at the girl with the documents, but the girl with the documents just shrugged and looked down at her Dunlop Green Flash shoes. *Ain't dat de truth*, said the girl in the purple dress, and she turned back to me. *It's up to yu, darlin. Yu got to talk us out a here, fore dey change dey mind an lock us all back up.*

I looked down at the telephone receiver and it was grey and dirty and I was afraid. I looked back at the girl in the purple dress. *Where do you want to go?* I said. And she said, *Any ends*. Excuse me? *Anywhere, darlin.*

I dialled the taxi number that was written on the phone. A man's voice came on. He sounded tired. *Cab service*, he said.

The way he said it, it was like he was doing me a big favour just by saying those words.

'Good morning, I would like a taxi please.'

'You want a cab?'

'Yes. Please. A taxi-cab. For four passengers.'

'Where from?'

'From the Black Hill Immigration Removal Centre, please. In High Easter. It is near Chelmsford.'

'I know where it is. Now you listen to me—'

'Please, it is okay. I know you do not pick up refugees. We are not refugees. We are cleaners. We work in this place.'

'You're cleaners?'

'Yes.'

'And that's the truth, is it? Because if I had a pound for every bloody immigrant that got in the back of one of my cabs and didn't know where they wanted to go and started prattling on to my driver in Swahili and tried to pay him in cigarettes, I'd be playing golf at this very moment instead of talking to you.'

'We are cleaners.'

'All right. It's true you don't talk like one of them. Where do you want to go?'

I had memorised the address on the United Kingdom driver's licence in my see-through plastic bag. Andrew O'Rourke, the white man I met on the beach: he lived in Kingston-upon-Thames in the English county of Surrey. I spoke into the telephone.

'Kingston, please.'

The girl in the purple dress grabbed my arm and hissed at me. *No, darlin!* she said. *Anywhere but Jamaica. Dey mens be killin me de minnit I ketch dere, kill me dead.* I did not understand why she was scared, but I know now. There is a Kingston in England but there is also a Kingston in Jamaica, where the climate is different. This is another great work you sorcerers have done – even your cities have two tails.

'Kingston?' said the man on the telephone.

'Kingston-upon-Thames,' I said.

'That's bloody miles away, isn't it? That's over in, what?'

'Surrey,' I said.

'Surrey. You are four cleaners from leafy Surrey, is that what you're trying to tell me?'

'No. We are cleaners from near by. But they are sending us on a cleaning job in Surrey.'

'Cash or account, then?'

The man sounded so tired.

'What?'

'Will you pay in cash, or is it going on the detention centre's bill?'

'We will pay in cash, mister. We will pay when we get there.'

'You'd better.'

I listened for a minute and then I pressed my hand down on the cradle of the telephone receiver. I dialled another number. This was the telephone number from the business card I carried in my see-through plastic bag. The business card was damaged by water. I could not tell if the last number was an 8 or a 3. I tried an 8, because in my country odd numbers bring bad luck, and that is one thing I had already had enough of.

A man answered the call. He was angry.

'Who is this? It's bloody six in the morning.'

'Is this Mr Andrew O'Rourke?'

'Yeah. Who are you?'

'Can I come to see you, mister?'

'Who the hell is this?'

'We met on the beach in Nigeria. I remember you very well, Mr O'Rourke. I am in England now. Can I come to see you and Sarah? I do not have anywhere else to go.'

There was silence on the other end of the line. Then the man coughed, and started to laugh.

'This is a wind-up, right? Who is this? I'm warning you, I get nutters like you on my case all the time. Leave me alone, or you won't get away with it. My paper always prosecutes. They'll have this call traced and find out who you are and have you arrested. You wouldn't be the first.'

'You don't believe it is me?'

'Just leave me alone. Understand? I don't want to hear about it. All that stuff happened a long time ago and it wasn't my fault.'

'I will come to your house. That way you will believe it is me.'

'No.'

'I do not know anyone else in this country, Mr O'Rourke. I am sorry. I am just telling you, so that you can be ready.'

The man did not sound angry any more. He made a small sound, like a child when it is nervous about what will happen. I hung up the phone and turned round to the other girls. My heart was pounding so fast, I thought I would vomit right there on the linoleum floor. The other girls were staring at me, nervous and expectant.

'Well?' said the girl in the purple dress.

'Hmm?' I said.

'De *taxi*, darlin! What is happenin about de taxi?'

'Oh, yes, the taxi. The taxi man said a cab will pick us up in ten minutes. He said we are to wait outside.'

The girl in the purple dress, she smiled.

'Mi name is Yevette. From Jamaica, zeen. You *useful*, darlin. What dey call yu?'

'My name is Little Bee.'

'What kinda name yu call dat?'

'It is my name.'

'What kind of place yu come from, dey go roun callin little gals de names of insects?'

'Nigeria.'

Yevette laughed. It was a big laugh, like the way the chief baddy laughs in the pirate films. *WU-ha-ha-ha-ha!* It made the telephone receiver rattle in its cradle. *Nye-JIRRYA!* said Yevette. Then she turned round to the others, the girl in the sari and the girl with the documents. *Come wid us, gals,*

23

she said. *We de United Nations, see it, an today we is all followin Nye-JIRRYA. WU-ha-ha-ha-ha!*

Yevette was still laughing when the four of us girls walked out past the security desk, towards the door. The detention officer looked up from his newspaper when we went by. The topless girl was gone now – the officer had turned the page. I looked down at his newspaper. The headline on the new page said ASYLUM SEEKERS EATING OUR SWANS. I looked back at the detention officer, but he would not look up at me. While I looked, he moved his arm over the page to cover the headline. He made it look as if he needed to scratch his elbow. Or maybe he really *did* need to scratch his elbow. I realised I knew nothing about men apart from the fear. A uniform that is too big for you, a desk that is too small for you, an eight-hour shift that is too long for you, and suddenly here comes a girl with three kilos of documents and no motivation, another one with jelly-green eyes and a yellow sari who is so beautiful you cannot look at her for too long in case your eyeballs go *ploof*, a third girl from Nigeria who is named after a honeybee, and a noisy woman from Jamaica who laughs like the pirate Bluebeard. Perhaps this is exactly the type of circumstance that makes a man's elbow itch.

I turned to look back at the detention officer just before we went out through the double doors. He was watching us leave. He looked very small and lonely there, with his thin little wrists, under the fluorescent lights. The light made his skin look green, the colour of a baby caterpillar just out of the

24

egg. The early morning sunshine was shining in through the door glass. The officer screwed up his eyes against the daylight. I suppose we were just silhouettes to him. He opened his mouth, as if he was going to say something, but he stopped.

'What?' I said. I realised he was going to tell us there had been a mistake. I wondered if we should run. I did not want to go back in detention. I wondered how far we would get if we ran. I wondered if they would come after us with dogs.

The detention officer stood up. I heard his chair scrape on the linoleum floor. He stood there with his hands at his sides.

'Ladies?' he said.

'Yes?'

He looked down at the ground, and then up again.

'Best of luck,' he said.

And we girls turned round and walked towards the light.

I pushed open the double doors, and then I froze. It was the sunlight that stopped me. I felt so fragile from the detention centre, I was afraid those bright rays of sunshine would snap me in half. I couldn't take that first step outside.

'What is de hold-up, Lil Bee?'

Yevette was standing behind me. I was blocking the door for everyone.

'One moment, please.'

Outside, the fresh air smelled of wet grass. It blew in my face. The smell made me panic. For two years I had smelled only bleach, and my nail varnish, and the other detainees' cigarettes. Nothing natural. Nothing like this. I felt that if I took one step forward, the earth itself would rise up and reject me. There was nothing natural about me now. I stood there in my heavy boots with my breasts strapped down, neither a woman nor a girl, a creature who had forgotten her language and learned yours, whose past had crumbled to dust.

'What de hell yu waitin fo, darlin?'

'I am scared, Yevette.'

Yevette shook her head and she smiled.

'Maybe yu's right to be scared, Lil Bee, cos yu a smart girl. Maybe me jus too dumb to be fraid. But me spend eighteen month locked up in dat place, an if yu tink me dumb enough to wait one second longer on account of your tremblin an your quakin, yu better tink two times.'

I turned round to face her and I gripped on to the doorframe.

'I can't move,' I said.

That is when Yevette gave me a great push in the chest and I flew backwards. And that is how it was, the first time I touched the soil of England as a free woman, it was not with the soles of my boots but with the seat of my trousers.

'WU-ha-ha-ha-ha!' said Yevette. 'Welcome in de U-nited Kindom, int dat glorious?'

When I got my breath back, I started laughing too. I sat on the ground, with the warm sun shining on my back, and I realised that the earth had not rejected me and the sunlight had not snapped me in two.

26

I stood up and I smiled at Yevette. We all took a few steps away from the detention centre buildings. As we walked, when the other girls were not looking, I reached under my Hawaiian shirt and I undid the band of cotton that held my breasts down. I unwound it and threw it on the ground and ground it into the dirt with the heel of my boot. I breathed deeply in the fresh, clean air.

When we came to the main gate, the four of us girls stopped for a moment. We looked out through the high razor wire fence and down the slopes of Black Hill. The English country-side stretched away to the horizon. Soft mist was hanging in the valleys, and the tops of the low hills were gold in the morning sun, and I smiled because the whole world was fresh and new and bright.

2

From the spring of 2007 until the end of that long summer when Little Bee came to live with us, my son removed his Batman costume only at bathtimes. I ordered a twin costume that I substituted while he splashed in the suds, so that at least I could wash the boy-sweat and the grass stains out of the first. It was a dirty, green-kneed job, fighting master criminals. If it wasn't Mister Freeze with his dastardly ice ray, then it was the Penguin – Batman's deadly foe – or the even more sinister Puffin, whose absolute wickedness the original creators of the Batman franchise had inexplicably failed to chronicle. My son and I lived with the consequences – a houseful of acolytes, henchmen and stooges, ogling us from behind the sofa, cackling darkly in the thin gap beside the bookcase, and generally bursting out at us willy-nilly. It was one shock after another, in fact. At four years old, asleep and awake, my son lived at constant readiness. There was no question of separating him from the demonic bat mask, the Lycra suit, the glossy yellow utility belt and the jet-black cape. And there was no use addressing my son by his Christian name. He would only look behind him, cock his head, and shrug – as if to say, *My bat senses can detect no boy of that name here, madam.* The only name my son answered to, that summer, was 'Batman'. Nor was there any point explaining to him that his father had died. My son didn't believe in the physical possibility of death. Death was something that could only occur if the evil schemes of the baddies were not constantly foiled – and that, of course, was unthinkable.

That summer – the summer my husband died – we all had identities we were loath to let go of. My son had his Batman costume, I still used my husband's surname, and Little Bee, though she was relatively safe with us, still clung to the name she had taken in a time of terror. We were exiles from reality, that summer. We were refugees from ourselves.

To flee from cruelty is the most natural thing in the world, of course. And the timing that brought us together that summer was so very cruel. Little Bee telephoned us on the morning they released her from the detention centre. My husband picked up her call. I only found out much later that it was her – Andrew never told me. Apparently she let him know she was coming, but I don't suppose he felt up to seeing her face again. Five days later he killed himself by hanging.

They found my husband with his feet treading empty air, touching the soil of no country. Death, of course, is a refuge. It's where you go when a new name, or a mask and cape, can no longer hide you from yourself. It's where you run to when none of the principalities of your conscience will grant you asylum.

Little Bee knocked on my front door five days after my husband died, which was ten days after they released her from detention. After a journey of five thousand miles and two years, she arrived just too late to find Andrew alive, but just in time for his funeral. *Hello, Sarah*, she said.

Little Bee arrived at eight a.m. and the undertaker knocked at ten. Not one second to, or one second past. I imagine the undertaker had been silently standing outside our front door for several minutes, looking at his watch, waiting for our lives to converge onto the precise fault-line at which our past could be cleaved from our future with three soft strikes of the bright brass knocker.

My son opened the door, and took in the undertaker's height, his impeccable tailoring, and his sober demeanour. I suppose the undertaker looked for all the world like Batman's workaday alter ego. My son shouted along the hallway to me: *Mummy, it's Bruce Wayne!*

That morning I walked out onto the street and I stood there, looking at Andrew's coffin through the thick, slightly greenish glass of the hearse window. When Little Bee came out to join me, bringing Batman by the hand, the undertaker ushered us to a long, black limousine and nodded us in. I told him we'd rather walk.

We looked as if we'd been cobbled together in Photoshop, the three of us, walking to my husband's funeral. One white middle-class mother, one skinny black refugee girl, and one small dark knight from Gotham City. It seemed as if we'd been cut-and-pasted. My thoughts raced, nightmarish and disconnected.

It was only a few hundred yards to the church, and the three of us walked in the road ahead of the hearse while an angry queue of traffic built up behind. I felt awful about that.

I was wearing a dark grey skirt and jacket with gloves and charcoal stockings. Little Bee was wearing my smart black raincoat over the clothes they let her out of the detention centre in – a mortifyingly unfunereal Hawaiian shirt and blue jeans. My son was wearing an expression of absolute joy. He, Batman, had stopped the traffic. His cape swirled in his tiny slipstream as he strode proudly ahead, his grin stretching from bat ear to bat ear beneath the darkness of his mask. Occasionally his superior vision would detect an enemy that needed smiting, and when this occurred my son would simply stop, smite, and continue. He was worried that the Puffin's invisible hordes might attack me. I was worried that my son hadn't done a wee before we left the house, and might therefore do it in his bat pants. I was also worried about being a widow for the rest of my life.

31

At first I'd thought it was quite brave of me to insist on walking to the church, but now I felt dizzy and foolish. I thought I might faint. Little Bee held on to my elbow and whispered to me to take deep breaths. I remember thinking, How strange, that it should be *you* who is keeping *me* on my feet.

In the church I sat in the front pew, with Little Bee on my left and Batman on my right. The church was stuffed with mourners, of course. No one from work – I tried to keep my life and my magazine separate – but otherwise everybody Andrew and I knew was there. It was disorientating, like having the entire contents of one's address book dressed in black and exported into pews in non-alphabetical order. They had classified themselves according to some unwritten protocol of grief, blood relatives ghoulishly close to the coffin, old girlfriends in a reluctant cluster near the baptismal font. I couldn't bear to look behind me and see this new natural order of things. It was all very much too sudden. A week ago I had been a successful working mother. Now I was sitting at my husband's funeral, flanked by a superhero and a Nigerian refugee. It seemed like a dream that might be awoken from with relatively little effort. I stared at my husband's coffin, strewn with white lilies. Batman stared at the vicar. He cast an approving eye over the vicar's stole and surplice. He gave the vicar a solemn thumbs up, one caped crusader to another. The vicar returned the salute, then his thumb returned to the faded gilt edging of his Bible.

The church was falling quiet; expectant. My son looked all around, then back at me. *Where's Daddy?* he said.

I squeezed my son's hot, sweaty hand, and listened to the coughs and sniffles echoing round the church. I wondered how I could possibly explain my husband's death to his son. It was depression that killed Andrew, of course – depression and guilt. But my son didn't believe in death, let alone in the capacity of mere emotions to cause it. Mister Freeze's ice rays, perhaps. The Puffin's lethal wingspan, at a stretch. But an ordinary phone call, from a skinny African girl? It was impossible to explain.

I realised I would have to tell my son the whole story, some day. I wondered where I would begin. It was two years before, in the summer of 2005, that Andrew had begun his long, slow slide into the depression that finally claimed him. It started on the day we first met Little Bee, on a lonely beach in Nigeria. The only souvenir I have of that first meeting is an absence where the middle finger of my left hand used to be. The amputation is quite clean. In place of my finger is a stump, a phantom digit that used to be responsible for the E, D and C keys on my laptop. I can't rely on E, D, and C any more. They go missing when I need them most. 'Pleased' becomes 'please'. 'Ecstasies' becomes 'stasis'.

I miss my finger most on deadline days, when the copy-checkers have all gone home and I'm typing up the last-minute additions to my magazine. We published an editorial once where I said I was 'wary of sensitive men'. I meant to say

33

'weary', of course, and after a hundred outraged letters from the earnest boyfriends who'd happened to glance at my piece on their partner's coffee table (presumably in between giving a back rub and washing the dishes), I began to realise just how weary I was. It was a typographical accident, I told them. I didn't add, it was the kind of typographical accident that is caused by a steel machete on a Nigerian beach. I mean, what does one call the type of meeting where one gains an African girl and loses E, D and C? *I do not think you have a word for it in your language.* That's what Little Bee would say.

I sat in my pew, massaged the stump of my finger, and found myself acknowledging for the first time that my husband had been doomed since the day we met Little Bee. The intervening two years had brought a series of worsening premonitions, culminating in the horrible morning ten days earlier when I had woken up to the sound of the telephone ringing. My whole body had crawled with dread. It had been an ordinary weekday morning. The June issue of my magazine was almost ready to go to the printers, and Andrew's column for *The Times* was due in too. Just a normal morning, but the soft hairs on the backs of my arms were up.

I have never been one of those happy women who insist that disaster strikes from a clear blue sky. For me there were countless foretellings, innumerable small breaks with normalcy. Andrew's chin unshaved, a second bottle uncorked on a weekday night, the use of the passive voice on deadline Friday. *Certain attitudes which have been adopted by this society have left this commentator a little lost*. That was the very last sentence my husband wrote. In his *Times* column, he was always so precise with the written word. From a lay person, *lost* would be a synonym for *bewildered*. From my husband, it was a measured goodbye.

It was cold in the church. I listened to the vicar saying *Where, o death, is thy sting?* I stared at the lilies and smelled the sweet accusation of them. God, how I wish I had paid more attention to Andrew.

How to explain to my son that the warning signs were so slight? That disaster, when it is quite sure of its own strength, will announce itself by hardly moving its lips? They say that in the hour before an earthquake the clouds hang leaden in the sky, the wind slows to a hot breath, and the birds fall quiet in the trees of the town square. Yes, but these are the same portents that precede lunchtime, frankly. If we overreacted every time the wind eased up, we would forever be lying down under the dining-room table when we really should be laying the plates on top of it.

Would my son accept that this is how it was with his father? *The hairs on my arms went up, Batman, but I had a household to run. I never understood that he was actually going to do it.* All I would honestly be able to say is that I woke up with the phone ringing and my body predicting some event that had yet to happen, although I never imagined it would be so serious.

Charlie had still been asleep. Andrew picked up the phone

in his study, quickly, before the noise of the ringing could wake our son. Andrew's voice became agitated. I heard it quite clearly from the bedroom. *Just leave me alone*, he said. *All that stuff happened a long time ago and it wasn't my fault.*

The trouble was, my husband didn't really believe that.

I found him in tears. I asked him who it had been on the phone, but he wouldn't say. And then, since we were both awake and Charlie was still asleep, we made love. I used to do that with Andrew sometimes. More for him than for me, really. By that stage of our marriage it had become a maintenance thing, like bleeding the air out of the radiators – just another part of running a household. I didn't know – in fact I still don't know – what awful consequences are supposed to ensue if one fails to bleed the radiators. It's not something a cautious woman would ever allow herself to discover.

We didn't speak a word. I took Andrew into the bedroom and we lay on the bed beneath the tall Georgian windows with the yellow silk blinds. The blinds were embroidered with pale foliage. Silk birds hid there in a kind of silent apprehension. It was a bright May morning in Kingston-upon-Thames, but the sunlight through the blinds was a dark and florid saffron. It was feverish, almost malarial. The bedroom walls were yellow and ochre. Across the creaking landing, Andrew's study was white – the colour, I suppose, of blank pages. That's where I retrieved him, after the awful phone call. I read a few words of his column, over his shoulder. He'd been awake all night writing an opinion piece about the

Middle East, which was a region he had never visited and had no specialist knowledge of. It was the summer of 2007, and my son was fighting the Penguin and the Puffin, and my country was fighting Iraq and Iran, and my husband was forming public opinion. It was the kind of summer where no one took their costume off.

I pulled my husband away from the phone. I pulled him in to the bedroom by the tasselled cord of his dressing-gown, because I had read somewhere that this sort of behaviour would excite him. I pulled him down on to our bed.

I remember the way he moved inside me, like a clock with its mainspring running down. I pulled his face close to mine and I whispered, *Oh, God, Andrew, are you all right?* My husband didn't reply. He just closed his eyes against the tears and we began to move faster while small, involuntary moans came from our mouths and fled into the other's moaning in wordless desperation.

In on this small tragedy walked my son, who was more at home fighting evil on a larger, more knockabout scale. I opened my eyes and saw him standing in the bedroom door-way, watching us through the small, diamond-shaped eyeholes of his bat mask. From the expression on the part of his face that could be seen, he seemed to be wondering which (if any) of the gadgets on his utility belt might help in this situation.

When I saw my son, I pushed Andrew off me and scrabbled frantically for the duvet to cover us. I said, *Oh, God, Charlie, I'm so sorry.*

My son looked behind him, then back at me.

'Charlie isn't here. I'm Batman.'

I nodded, and bit my lip.

'Good morning, Batman.'

'What is you and Daddy doing, Mummy?'

'Er . . .'

'Is you getting baddies?'

'*Are* you getting baddies, Charlie. Not *is* you.'

'Are you?'

'Yes, Batman. Yes, that's exactly what we're doing.'

I smiled at my son, and waited. I wondered what Batman would say. What he said was, 'Someone done a poo in my costume, Mummy.'

'*Did* a poo, Charlie.'

'Yes. A big, big poo.'

'Oh, Batman. Have you really done a poo in your suit?'

Batman shook his head. His bat ears quivered. Beneath the mask an expression of great cunning settled upon the visible part of his face.

'I wasn't me that done the poo. It was the *Puffin*.'

(The italics were his.)

'Are you telling me that the Puffin came in the night and did a poo in your bat suit?'

Batman nodded, solemnly. I noticed he had kept his bat mask on but taken off his bat suit. He stood naked except for the mask and cape. He held up the bat suit for me to inspect. A lump of something fell from it and thumped on the carpet.

The smell was indescribable. I sat up in bed and saw a trail of lumps leading across the carpet from the bedroom door. Somewhere inside me the girl who had done science A levels noted, with empirical fascination, that faeces had also found their way into locations which included – but were not limited to – Batman's hands, the door-frame, the bedroom wall, my alarm clock radio and, of course, the bat suit. My son's shit was everywhere. There was shit on his hands. Shit on his face. Even on the black and yellow bat symbol of his bat suit there was shit. I tried, but I couldn't make myself believe that these were Puffin droppings. This was bat shit.

Distantly, I remembered something I'd read on the parenting page.

'It's all right, Batman. Mummy's not cross.'

'Mummy clean the poo up.'

'Um. Er. Jesus.'

Gravely, Batman shook his head.

'No, not Jesus. *Mummy.*'

Resentfulness was starting to overcome the embarrassment and guilt. I looked across to where Andrew lay with his eyes tight closed and his hands twisted at the exquisite awfulness of his clinical depression, our unhappy sex interrupted, and this very thick stink of shit.

'Batman, why don't you ask *Daddy* to clean you up?'

My son looked across at his father for a long time, then turned back to me. Patiently, as if explaining something to an imbecile, he shook his little head again.

39

'But why not?' (I was pleading now.) 'Why not ask Daddy?'

Batman looked solemn. 'Daddy is fighting baddies,' he said. The grammar was irreproachable. I looked across at his father with him, and I sighed. 'Yes,' I said, 'I suppose you're right.'

Five days later, on the last morning I saw my husband alive, I finished dressing my caped crusader, I breakfasted him, and I ran him down to his nursery's Early Birds club. Back at the house, I showered. Andrew watched me as I pulled on my tights. I always dressed up for deadline days. Heels, skirt, smart green jacket. Magazine publishing has its rhythms and if the editor won't dance to them, she can't expect her staff to. I don't float feature ideas in Fendi heels, and I don't close an issue in Pumas. So I dressed against the clock while Andrew lay naked on the bed and watched me. He didn't say a word. The last glimpse I had of him, before I closed the bedroom door, he was still watching. How to describe, to my son, his father's last-seen expression? I decided I would tell my son that his father had looked very peaceful. I decided I wouldn't tell him that my husband opened his mouth to say something, but that I was running late and turned away.

I arrived at the office around 9.30 a.m. The magazine was based in Spitalfields, on Commercial Street, ninety minutes by public transport from Kingston-upon-Thames. The worst moment comes when you leave the overland network and descend into the heat of the Underground. There were two hundred of us packed into each tube carriage. We listened to

40

the screech of the metal wheels on the track with our bodies pinned and immobile. For three stops I stood pressed against a thin man in a corduroy jacket who was quietly weeping. One would normally avert one's eyes, but my head was pinioned in such a position that I could only look. I should have liked to put an arm around the man – even a sympathetic touch on his shoulder would have been enough. But my arms were jammed by the commuters on each side of me. Perhaps a few of them wanted to reach out to the man too, but we were all squeezed in too tight to move. The sheer number of well-meaning people made compassion awkward. One of us would have had to push the others aside, and make an example of ourselves, which wouldn't have been terribly British. I wasn't sure I was up to administering tenderness like that, on a crowded train, under the silent gaze of others. It was awful of me not to help the man but I was torn between two kinds of shame. On the one hand, the disgrace of not discharging a human obligation. On the other hand, the madness of being the first in the crowd to move.

I smiled helplessly at the weeping man and I couldn't stop thinking about Andrew.

As soon as one emerges above ground, of course, one can quickly forget our human obligations. London is a beautiful machine for doing that. The city was bright, fresh and inviting that morning. I was excited about closing the June issue, and I practically ran the last two minutes to the office. On the outside of our building was the magazine's name, *NIXIE*, in three-foot-high pink neon letters. I stood outside for a moment, taking a few deep breaths. The air was still, and you could hear the neon crackling over the rumble of the traffic. I stood with my hand on the door and wondered what Andrew had been about to say, just before I left home.

My husband hadn't always been lost for words. The long silences only began on the day we met Little Bee. Before that, he wouldn't pipe down for a minute. On our honeymoon we talked and talked. We stayed in a beachfront villa, and we drank rum and lemonade and talked so much that I never even noticed what colour the sea was. Whenever I need to stop and remind myself how much I once loved Andrew, I only need to think about this. That the ocean covers seven tenths of the earth's surface, and yet my husband could make me not notice it. That is how big he was for me. When we got back to our new married house in Kingston, I asked Andrew about the colour of that honeymoon sea. He said, *Yeah, was it blue?* I said, *Come on, Andrew, you're a pro, you can do better than that.* And Andrew said, *Okay then, the awesome ocean fastness was a splendour of ultramarine crested with crimson and gold where the burnished sun blazed on the wave tops and sent them crashing into the gloomy troughs deepening to a dark malevolent indigo.*

He hung on the penultimate syllable, deepening his voice in comic pomposity even as he raised his eyebrows. INN-digo, he boomed.

42

Of course you know why I didn't notice the sea? It was because I spent two weeks with my head—

Well, where my husband's head was is between me and him.

We both giggled helplessly and rolled around on the bed and Charlie, dear Charlie, was conceived.

I pushed open the street door and stepped up into the lobby of the magazine. The black Italian marble floor was the only grace-note that had survived our tenancy of the offices. The rest of the lobby was pure us. Boxes of sample frocks from wannable fashion houses were stacked up along one wall. Some intern had triaged them with a chunky blue marker: YES KEEP FOR SHOOT, or OH I THINK NOT, or the triumphantly absolutist THIS IS NOT FASHION. A dead Japanese juniper tree stood in a cracked gold Otagiri vase. Three glittering Christmas baubles still hung from it. The walls were done up in fucshia and fairy lights, and even in the dim sunshine from the tinted windows that gave on to Commercial Street, the paintwork looked marked and tatty. I cultivated this unkempt look. *Nixie* wasn't supposed to be like the other women's magazines. Let them keep their spotless lobbies and their smug Eames chairs. When it comes right down to editorial choices, I would rather have a bright staff and a dim lobby.

Clarissa, my features editor, came through the doors just after me. We kissed once, twice, three times – we'd been friends since school – and she hooked her arm through mine

43

as we took the stairs together. The editorial floor was right at the top of the building. We were halfway up before I realised what was wrong with Clarissa.

'Clarissa, you're wearing yesterday's clothes.'

She smirked. 'So would you be, if you'd met yesterday's man.'

'Oh, Clarissa. What am I going to do with you?'

'Pay rise, strong coffee, paracetamol.'

She beamed as she ticked off the points on her fingers. I reminded myself that Clarissa did not have some of the wonderful things I had in my life, such as my beautiful son, Batman, and that she was therefore almost certainly less fulfilled than I was.

It was a 10.30 a.m. start for my junior staff, bless them, and none of them was in yet. Up on the editorial floor, the cleaners were still in. They were hoovering, and dusting desktops, and turning upside down all the framed photos of my staff's awful boyfriends, to prove they'd dusted under them. This was the grin-and-bear-it part of editing *Nixie*. At *Vogue* or *Marie Claire*, one's editorial staff would be at their desks by eight, dressed in Chloé and sipping green tea. On the other hand, they wouldn't still be there at midnight scrawling CECI N'EST PAS PRÊT-À-PORTER on a sample box they were returning to a venerable Paris fashion house.

Clarissa sat on the corner of my desk and I sat behind it, and we looked out over the open-plan at the gang of black faces spiriting away yesterday's fabric swatches and Starbucks cups.

We talked about the issue we were closing. The ad sales people had done unusually well that month – perhaps the spiralling cost of street drugs had forced them to spend more time in the office – and we realised we had more editorial material than space. I had a 'Real Life' feature I really thought should go in – a profile of a woman who was trying to get out of Baghdad – and Clarissa had a piece on a new kind of orgasm you could apparently only get with the boss. We talked about which of them we would run with. I was only half concentrating. I texted Andrew, to see how he was doing.

The flatscreen at our end of the floor was showing BBC News 24 with the sound down. They were running a segment on the war. Smoke was rising above one of the countries involved. Don't ask me which – I'd lost track by that stage. The war was four years old. It had started in the same month my son was born, and they'd grown up together. At first both of them were a huge shock and demanded constant attention, but as each year went by, they became more autonomous and one could start to take one's eye off them for extended periods. Sometimes a particular event would cause me momentarily to look at one or the other of them – my son, or the war – with my full attention, and at times like these I would always think, Gosh, haven't you grown?

I was interested in how this new kind of orgasm was meant to work. I looked up from texting.

'How come you can only have it with your boss?'

45

'It's a forbidden fruit thing, isn't it? You get an extra *frisson* from breaking the office taboo. From hormones and neuro-transmitters and so forth. You know. Science.'

'Um. Have scientists actually proved this?'

'Don't get empirical with me, Sarah. We're talking about a whole new realm of sexual pleasure. We're calling it the B-spot. B, as in boss. See what we did there?'

'Ingenious.'

'Thank you, darling. We do try.'

I wept inwardly at the thought of women up and down the country being pleasured by middle managers in shiny-bottomed suits. On the flatscreen, News 24 had panned from the Middle East to Africa. Different landscape, same column of thick black smoke. A pair of jaundiced eyes looking out with the same impassivity Andrew had shown, just before I turned away to leave for work. The hairs on my arms went up again. I looked away, and took the three steps to the window that gave out on to Commercial Street. I put my forehead against the glass, which is something I do when I'm trying to think.

'Are you all right, Sarah?'

'I'm fine. Listen, be a doll and go and grab us a couple of coffees, would you?'

Clarissa went off to our idiosyncratic coffee machine, the one that would have been an in-house *salon de thé* in Vogue's offices. Down on Commercial Street, a police patrol car pulled up and parked on the double yellow lines in front of our building. A uniformed officer got out on each side.

They looked at each other over the patrol car roof. One of them had blond, cropped hair and the other had a bald patch as round and neat as a monk's. I watched him tilt his head to listen to the radio on his lapel. I smiled, thinking absently about a project Charlie was doing at his nursery. 'The Police: People Who Help Us', it was called. My son – it goes without saying – was magnificently unconvinced. At constant high alert in his bat cape and mask, Charlie believed a proud citizenry should be ready to help itself.

Clarissa came back with two plasticky lattes. In one of them the coffee machine had deposited a clear acrylic stirrer. In the other, it had elected not to do so. Clarissa hesitated over which to give me.

'First big editorial decision of the day,' she said.

'Easy. I'm the boss. Give me the one with the stirrer.'

'What if I don't?'

'Then we may never get around to locating your B-spot, Clarissa. I'm warning you.'

Clarissa blanched, and passed me the coffee with the stirrer.

I said, 'I like the Baghdad piece.'

Clarissa sighed, and slumped her shoulders.

'So do I, Sarah, of course I do. It's a great article.'

'Five years ago, that's the one we'd have run with. No question.'

'Five years ago our circulation was so low we had to take those risks.'

'And that's how we got big – by being different. That's *us*.'

47

Clarissa shook her head. 'Getting big's different from staying big. You know as well as I do, we can't be serving up morality tales while the other majors are selling sex.'

'But why do you think our readers got dumber?'

'It's not that. I think our original readers aren't reading magazines any more, that's all. They moved on to greater things, the same way you could if you'd just play the bloody game. Maybe you don't realise just how big you are now, Sarah. Your next job could be editing a national newspaper.'

I sighed. 'How thrilling. I could put topless girls on every page.'

My missing finger itched. I looked back down at the police patrol car. The two officers were putting on their uniform caps. I tapped my mobile against my front teeth.

'Let's go for a drink after work, Clarissa. Bring your new man if you like. I'm bringing Andrew.'

'Seriously? Out in public? With your *husband*? Isn't that terribly last season?'

'It's terribly five years ago.'

Clarissa tilted her head at me.

'What are you telling me, Sarah?'

'I'm not telling you anything, Clar. I like you too much to *tell*. I'm just asking myself, really. I'm asking if maybe the kind of choices I made five years ago weren't so bad after all.'

Clarissa smiled resignedly. 'Fine. But don't expect me to

48

keep my hands off his hunky thighs under the table, just because he's your husband.'

'You do that, Clarissa, and I'll make you junior horoscopes editor for the rest of your natural life.'

My desk phone rang. I looked at the time on its screen. 10.25 a.m. It's funny how these details stay with you. I picked up the phone and it was reception, sounding bored to distraction. At *Nixie* we used reception as a sin bin – if a girl got too bitchy on the editorial floor, we sent her down to do a week on the shiniest desk.

'There are two policemen here.'

'Oh. They came in here? What do they want?'

'Okay, let's think about why I might have dialled your number.'

'They want to talk to me?'

'They did good when they made you the boss, Sarah.'

'Fuck off. Why do they want to talk to me?'

A pause.

'I could ask them, I suppose.'

'If it isn't too much trouble.'

A longer pause.

'They say they want to shoot a porny film in the office. They say they're not real policemen and their willies are simply enormous.'

'Oh, for God's sake. Tell them I'll be down.'

I hung up the phone and looked at Clarissa. The hairs on my arms were up again.

'The police,' I said.

'Relax,' said Clarissa. 'They can't bust you for conspiracy to run a serious feature piece.'

Behind her the flatscreen was showing Jon Stewart. He was laughing. His guest was laughing too. I felt better. You had to find something to laugh about, that summer, the number of places that were going up in smoke. You laughed, or you put on a superhero costume, or you tried for some kind of orgasm that science had somehow missed.

I took the stairs down to the lobby, speeding up as I went. The two police officers were standing rather too close together, with their caps in their hands and their big, sensible leather shoes on my black marble. The young one was blushing horribly.

'I'm so sorry,' I said.

I glared at the receptionist and she grinned back at me from beneath her perfect blond side parting.

'Sarah O'Rourke?'

'Summers.'

'Excuse me, madam?'

'Sarah Summers is my professional name.'

The older policeman looked at me with no expression.

'This is a personal matter, Mrs O'Rourke. Is there somewhere we can go?'

I walked them up to the boardroom on the first floor. Tones of pink and violet, long glass table, more neon.

'Can I get you a coffee? Or tea? I mean, I can't absolutely

guarantee it'll come out as coffee or tea. Our machine is a bit . . .'

'Perhaps you'd better sit down, Mrs O'Rourke.'

The officers' faces glowed unnaturally in the pinkish light. They looked like black and white movie men, coloured in by a computer. One older, the one with the bald patch. Maybe forty-five. The younger one, with the blond cropped hair, maybe twenty-two or twenty-four. Nice lips. Quite full, and rather juicy looking. He wasn't beautiful, but I was transfixed by the way he stood and cast his eyes down deferentially when he spoke. And of course there's always something about uniform. You wonder if the protocol will peel off with the jacket, I suppose.

The two of them placed their uniform caps on the purple smoked glass. They rotated the caps with their clean white fingers. Both of them stopped at exactly the same moment, as if some critical angle they had practised in basic training had precisely been attained.

They stared at me. My mobile chimed brashly on the glass desktop – a text message arriving. I smiled. That would be Andrew.

'I've got some bad news for you, Mrs O'Rourke,' said the older officer.

'What do you mean?'

It came out more aggressive than I intended. The policemen stared at their caps on the table. I needed to look at the text message that had just arrived. As I reached out my hand to pick up my phone, I saw the two of them staring at the stump of my missing finger.

'Oh. This? I lost it on holiday. On a beach, actually.'

The two policemen looked at each other. They turned back to me. The older one spoke. His voice was suddenly hoarse.

'We're very sorry, Mrs O'Rourke.'

'Oh, please, don't be. It's fine, really. I'm fine now. It's just a finger.'

'That's not what I meant, Mrs O'Rourke. I'm afraid we've been instructed to tell you that—'

'See, honestly, you get used to doing without the finger. At first you think it's a big deal and then you learn to use the other hand.'

I looked up and saw the two of them watching me, grey faced and serious. Neon crackled. On the wall clock, a fresh minute snapped over the old one.

'The really funny thing is, I still feel it, you know? My finger, I mean. This missing one. Sometimes it actually itches. And I go to scratch it and there's nothing there, of course. And in my dreams my finger grows back, and I'm so happy to have it back, even though I've learned to do without it. Isn't that silly? I miss it, do you see? It *itches*.'

The young officer took a deep breath and looked down at his notebook.

'Your husband was found unconscious at your property shortly after nine this morning, Mrs O'Rourke. Your neighbour heard cries and placed a 999 call to the effect that a male was apparently in distress. Police attended the address and forced entry to an upstairs room at nine fifteen, when Andrew O'Rourke was found unconscious. Our officers did everything they could and an ambulance attended and removed the casualty but I am very sorry to tell you, Mrs O'Rourke, that your husband was pronounced dead at the scene at . . . here we are, nine thirty-three am.'

The policeman closed his pad. 'We're very sorry, madam.'

I picked up my phone. The new text was indeed from Andrew. SO SORRY, it said.

He was sorry.

I switched the phone, and myself, on to silent mode. The silence lasted all week. It rumbled in the taxi home. It howled when I picked up Charlie from nursery. It crackled on the phone call with my parents. It roared in my ears while the undertaker explained the relative merits of oak and pine caskets. It cleared its throat apologetically when the obituaries editor of *The Times* telephoned to check some last details. Now the silence had followed me into the cold, echoing church.

How to explain death to a four-year-old superhero? How to announce the precipitous arrival of grief? I hadn't even accepted it myself. When the policemen told me that Andrew was dead, my mind refused to contain the information. I am a very ordinary woman, I think, and I am quite well equipped to deal with everyday evil. Interrupted sex, tough editorial decisions and malfunctioning coffee machines – these my mind could readily accept. But my Andrew, dead? It still seemed physically impossible. At one point he had covered more than seven tenths of the earth's surface.

And yet here I was, staring at Andrew's plain oak coffin (*A classic choice, madam*), and it seemed rather small in the wide nave of the church. A silent, sickening dream.

Mummy, where's Daddy?

I sat in the front pew of the church with my arms around my son, and realised I had begun to tremble. The vicar was delivering the eulogy. He was talking about my husband in the past tense. He made it sound very neat. It occurred to me that he had never had to deal with Andrew in the present tense, or proofread his columns, or feel him running down inside like a piece of broken clockwork.

Charlie squirmed in my arms and asked his question again, the same one he'd asked ten times a day since Andrew died. *Mummy, where's mine daddy exactly now?* I leaned down to his ear and whispered, *He's in a really nice bit of heaven this morning, Charlie. There's a lovely long room where they all go after breakfast, with lots of interesting books and things to do.*

– Oh. Is there painting-and-drawing?

– Yes, there's painting-and-drawing.

– Is mine Daddy doing drawing?

– No, Charlie, Daddy is opening the window and looking at the sky.

I shivered, and wondered how long I would have to go on narrating my husband's afterlife.

54

More words, then hymns. Hands took my elbows and led me outside. I observed myself standing in a graveyard beside a deep hole in the ground. Six suited undertakers were lowering a coffin on thick green silky ropes with tasselled ends. I recognised it as the coffin that had been standing on trestles at the front of the church. The coffin came to rest. The undertakers retrieved the ropes, each with a deft flick of his wrist. I remember thinking, I bet they do this all the time, as if it was some brilliant insight. Someone thrust a lump of clay into my hand. I realised I was being invited – urged, even – to throw it into the hole. I stepped up to the edge. Neat, clean greengrocer's grass had been laid around the border of the grave. I looked down and saw the coffin glowing palely in the depths. Batman held tight to my leg and peered down into the gloom with me.

'Mummy, why did the Bruce Wayne men putted that box down in the hole?'

'Let's not think about that now, darling.'

I'd spent so many hours explaining heaven to Charlie that week – every room and book shelf and sandpit of it – that I'd never really dealt with the issue of Andrew's physical body at all. I thought it would be too much to ask of my son, at four, to understand the separation between body and soul. Looking back on it now I think I underestimated a boy who could live simultaneously in Kingston-upon-Thames and Gotham City. I think if I'd managed to sit him down and explain it to him gently, he would have been perfectly happy with the duality.

I knelt and put my arm around my son's shoulders. I did it to be tender, but my head was swimming and I realised that perhaps it was only Charlie who was stopping me from falling down the hole. I held on tighter. Charlie put his mouth to my ear and whispered, 'Where's mine daddy right now?'

I whispered back, 'Your daddy is in the heaven hills, Charlie. Very popular at this time of year. I think he's very happy there.'

'Mmm. Is mine daddy coming back soon?'

'No, Charlie. People don't come back from heaven. We talked about that.'

Charlie pursed his lips. 'Mummy,' he said again, 'why did they put that box down there?'

'I suppose they want to keep it safe.'

'Oh. Is they going to come and get it later?'

'No, Charlie, I don't think so.'

Charlie blinked. Under his bat mask he screwed up his face with the effort of trying to understand.

'Where is heaven, Mummy?'

'Please, Charlie. Not now.'

'What's in that box?'

'Let's talk about this later, darling, all right? Mummy is feeling rather dizzy.'

Charlie stared at me. 'Is mine daddy in that box?'

'Your daddy is in heaven, Charlie.'

'IS THAT BOX HEAVEN?' said Charlie, loudly.

Everyone was watching us. I couldn't speak. My son stared into the hole. Then he looked up at me in absolute alarm.

'Mummy! Get him OUT! Get mine daddy out of heaven!'

I held tightly onto his shoulders. 'Oh, Charlie, please, you don't understand!'

'GET HIM OUT! GET HIM OUT!'

My son squirmed in my grip and broke free. It happened very quickly. He stood at the very edge of the hole. He looked back at me and then he turned and inched forward, but the greengrocer's grass overlapped the edge of the hole and it yielded under his feet and he fell, with his bat cape flying behind him, down into the grave. He landed with a thump on top of Andrew's coffin. There was a single, urgent scream from one of the other mourners. I think it was the first sound, since Andrew died, that really broke the silence.

The scream ran on and on in my mind. I felt nauseous, and the horizon lurched insanely. Still kneeling, I leaned out over the edge of the pit. Down below, in the dark shadow, my son was banging on the coffin and screaming, *Daddy, Daddy, get OUT!* He clung to the coffin lid, and planted his bat shoes against the side wall of the grave, and heaved against the screws that held the lid closed. I hung my arms down over the edge of the hole. I implored Charlie to take my hands so I could pull him back up. I don't think he heard me at all.

At first, my son moved with a breathless confidence. Batman was undefeated, after all, that spring. He had overcome the Penguin, the Puffin, and Mister Freeze. It was simply not a possibility in my son's mind that he might not overcome this new challenge. He screamed in rage and fury. He wouldn't give up, but if I am strict and force myself now to decide upon the precise moment in this whole story when my heart irreparably broke, it was the moment when I saw the weariness and the doubt creep into my son's small muscles as his fingers slipped, for the tenth time, from the pale oak lid.

The mourners clustered around the edge of the grave, paralysed by the horror of this thing, this first discovery of death that was worse than death itself. I tried to go forward but the hands on my elbows were holding me back. I strained against their grip and looked at all the horror-struck faces around the grave and I was thinking, Why doesn't someone do something?

But is hard, very hard, to be the first.

Finally it was Little Bee who went down into the grave and held up my son for other hands to haul out. Charlie was kicking and biting and struggling furiously in his muddied mask and cape. He wanted to go back down. And it was Little Bee, once she herself had been extricated, who hugged him and held him back as he screamed, NO, NO, NO, NO, NO, while each of the principal mourners stepped onto the thin strip of greengrocer's grass and dropped in their small handfuls of clay. My son's screaming seemed to go on for a cruelly long time. I remember wondering if my mind would shatter with the noise, like a wine glass broken by a soprano's voice. In fact, a former colleague of Andrew's, a war reporter who had been in Iraq and Darfur, did call me a few days later with the name of a combat fatigue counsellor he used. *That's kind of you*, I told him, *but I haven't been at war.*

At the graveside, when the screaming was over, I picked up Charlie and held him on my front, with his head resting on my shoulder. He was exhausted. Through the eyeholes of his bat mask, I could see his eyelids drooping. I watched the other mourners filing away in a slow line towards the car park. Brightly coloured umbrellas broke out above the sombre suits. It was starting to rain.

Little Bee stayed behind with me. We stood by the side of the grave and we stared at one another.

'Thank you,' I said.

'It is nothing,' said Little Bee. 'I just did what anyone would do.'

'Yes,' I said. 'Except that everyone else didn't.'

Little Bee shrugged. 'It is easier when you are from outside.'

I shivered. The rain came down harder.

'This is never going to end,' I said. 'Is it, Little Bee?'

'*However long the moon disappears, someday it must shine again.* That is what we used to say in my village.'

'*April showers bring May flowers.* That's what we used to say in mine.'

We tried to smile at one another.

I never did drop my own clay into the grave. I couldn't seem to put it down either. Two hours later, alone for a moment at the kitchen table of our house, I realised I was still gripping it.

I left it there on the tablecloth, a small beige lump on top of the clean blue cotton. When I came back a few minutes later, someone had been past and tidied it away.

A few days later the obituary in *The Times* noted that there had been poignant scenes at their former columnist's funeral. Andrew's editor sent me the cutting, in a heavy cream envelope, with a crisp white compliment slip.

3

One of the things I would have to explain to the girls from back home, if I was telling them this story, is the simple little word 'horror'. It means something different to the people from my village.

In your country, if you are not scared enough already, you can go to watch a horror film. Afterwards you can go out of the cinema into the night and for a little while there is horror in everything. Perhaps there are murderers lying in wait for you at home. You think this because there is a light on in your house that you are certain you did not leave on. And when you remove your make-up in the mirror last thing, you see a strange look in your own eyes. It is not you. For one hour you are haunted, and you do not trust anybody, and then the feeling fades away. Horror in your country is something you take a dose of to remind yourself that you are not suffering from it.

For me and the girls from my village, horror is a disease and we are sick with it. It is not an illness you can cure yourself of by standing up and letting the big red cinema seat fold itself up behind you. That would be a good trick. If I could do that, please believe me, I would already be standing in the foyer. I would be laughing with the kiosk boy, and exchanging British one-pound coins for hot buttered popcorn, and saying, *Phew, thank the good Lord all that is over, that is the most frightening film I ever saw and I think next time I will go to see a comedy, or maybe a romantic film with kissing*. But the film in your memory, you cannot walk out of it so easily. Wherever you go it is always playing. So when I say that I am a refugee, you must understand that there is no refuge.

Some days I wonder how many there are just like me. Thousands, I think, just floating on the oceans right now. In between our world and yours. If we cannot pay smugglers to transport us, we stow away on cargo ships. In the dark, in freight containers. Breathing quietly in the darkness, hungry, hearing the strange clanking sounds of ships, smelling the diesel oil and the paint, listening to the bom-bom-bom of the engines. Wide awake at night, hearing the singing of whales rising up from the deep sea and vibrating through the ship. All of us whispering, praying, thinking. And what are we thinking of? Of physical safety, of peace of mind. Of all these imaginary countries that are now being served in the foyer.

I stowed away in a great steel boat, but the horror stowed away inside me. When I left my homeland I thought I had escaped, but out on the open sea, I started to have nightmares. I was naïve to suppose I had left my country with nothing. It was a heavy cargo that I carried.

They unloaded my cargo in a port on the estuary of the Thames river. I did not walk across the gangplank, I was carried off the ship by your immigration officials and they put me into detention. It was no joke inside the detention centre. What will I say about this? Your system is cruel, but many of you were kind to me. You sent charity boxes. You dressed my horror in boots and a colourful shirt. You sent it something to paint its nails with. You posted it books and newspapers. Now the horror can speak the Queen's English. This is how we can speak now of sanctuary and refuge. This is how I can tell you – *soon-soon* as we say in my country – a little about the thing I was running from.

There are things the men can do to you in this life, I promise you, it would be much better to kill yourself first. Once you have this knowledge, your eyes are always flickering from this place to that, watching for the moment when the men will come.

In the immigration detention centre, they told us we must be disciplined to overcome our fears. This is the discipline I learned: whenever I go into a new place, I work out how I would kill myself there. In case the men come suddenly, I make sure I am ready. The first time I went into Sarah's

63

bathroom I was thinking, Yes, Little Bee, in here you would break the mirror of that medicine cabinet and cut your wrists with the splinters. When Sarah took me for a ride in her car I was thinking, Here, Little Bee, you would roll down the window and unbuckle your seat belt and tip yourself out of the window, no fuss, in front of the very next lorry that comes the other way. And when Sarah took me for a day in Richmond Park, she was looking at the scenery but I was looking for a hollow in the ground where I could hide and lie very still until all that you would find of me was a small white skull that the foxes and the rabbits would fuss over with their soft, wet noses.

If the men come suddenly, I will be ready to kill myself. Do you feel sorry for me, for thinking always in this way? If the men come and they find you not ready, then it will be me who is feeling sorry for you.

For the first six months in the detention centre, I screamed every night and in the day I imagined a thousand ways to kill myself. I worked out how to kill myself in every single one of the situations a girl like me might get into in the detention centre. In the medical wing, morphine. In the cleaners' room, bleach. In the kitchens, boiling fat. You think I am exaggerating? Some of the others that were detained with me, they really did these things. The detention officers sent the bodies away in the night, because it was not good for the local people to see the slow ambulances leaving that place.

Or what if they released me? And I went to a movie and I had to kill myself there? I would throw myself down from the projection gallery. Or a restaurant? I would hide in the biggest refrigerator and go into a long, cool sleep. Or the seaside? Ah, at the seaside, I would steal an ice-cream van and drive it into the sea. You would never see me again. The only thing to show that a frightened African girl had ever existed would be two thousand melting ice-creams, bobbing in their packets on the cool blue waves.

After a hundred sleepless nights I had finished working out how to kill myself in every single corner of the detention centre and the country outside, but I still carried on imagining. I was weak from horror and they put me in the medical wing. Away from the other prisoners I lay between the scratchy sheets and I spent each day all alone in my mind. I knew they planned to deport me so I started to imagine killing myself back home in Nigeria. It was just like killing myself in the detention centre but the scenery was nicer. This was a small and unexpected happiness. In forests, in quiet villages, on the sides of mountains I took my own life again and again.

In the most beautiful places I secretly lingered over the act. Once, in a deep and hot jungle that smelled of wet moss and the excrement of monkeys, I took nearly one whole day to chop down trees and build a tall tower to hang myself from by the neck. I had a machete. I imagined the sticky sap on my hands and the sweet honey smell of it, the good tired feeling in

65

my arms from the chopping, and the screeches of the monkeys who were angry when I cut their trees down. I worked hard in my imagination and I tied the tree trunks together with vines and creepers and I used a special knot that my sister Nkiruka showed me. It was a big day's work for a small girl. I was proud. At the end of that whole day alone in my sick bed working on my suicide tower, I realised I could just have climbed a jungle tree and jumped with my silly head first onto a rock.

This was the first time that I smiled.

I began to eat the meals they brought me. I thought to myself, you must keep up your strength, Little Bee, or you will be too weak to kill your foolish self when the time arrives, and then you will be sorry. I started to walk from the medical wing to the canteen at mealtimes, so that I could choose my food instead of having it brought to me. I started asking myself questions like: Which will make me stronger for the act of suicide? The carrots or the peas?

In the canteen there was a television that was always on. I began to learn more about life in your country. I watched programmes called *Love Island* and *Hell's Kitchen* and *Who Wants To Be A Millionaire?* and I worked out how I would kill myself on all of those shows. Drowning, knives, and ask the audience.

One day the detention officers gave all of us a copy of a book called *Life in the United Kingdom*. It explains the history of your country and how to fit in. I planned how I

66

would kill myself in the time of Churchill (stand under bombs), Victoria (throw myself under a horse), and Henry the Eighth (marry Henry the Eighth). I worked out how to kill myself under Labour and Conservative governments, and why it was not important to have a plan for suicide under the Liberal Democrats. I began to understand how your country worked.

They moved me out of the medical wing. I still screamed in the night, but not every night. I realised that I was carrying two cargoes. Yes, one of them was horror, but the other one was hope. I realised I had killed myself back to life.

I read your novels. I read the newspapers you sent. In the opinion columns I underlined the grand sentences and I looked up every word in my Collins Gem. I practised for hours in front of the mirror until I could make the big words look natural in my mouth.

I read a lot about your Royal Family. I like your Queen more than I like her English. Do you know how you would kill yourself during a garden party with Queen Elizabeth the Second on the great lawn of Buckingham Palace in London, just in case you were invited? I do. Me, I would kill myself with a broken champagne glass, or maybe a sharp lobster claw, or even a small piece of cucumber that I could suck down into my windpipe, if the men suddenly came.

I often wonder what the Queen would do, if the men suddenly came. You cannot tell me she does not think about it a lot. When I read in *Life in the United Kingdom* about some of the things that have happened to the women in the Queen's job, I understood that she must think about it all of the time. I think that if the Queen and I met then we would have many things in common.

The Queen smiles sometimes but if you look at her eyes in her portrait on the back of the five-pound note, you will see she is carrying a heavy cargo too. The Queen and me, we are ready for the worst. In public you will see both of us smiling and sometimes even laughing, but if you were a man who looked at us in a certain way we would both of us make sure we were dead before you could lay a single finger on our bodies. Me and the Queen of England, we would not give you the satisfaction.

It is good to live like this. Once you are ready to die, you do not suffer so badly from the horror. So I was nervous but I was smiling, because I was ready to die, that morning they let us girls out of detention.

I will tell you what happened when the taxi-driver came. The four of us girls, we were waiting outside the immigration detention centre. We were keeping our backs to it, because this is what you do to a big grey monster who has kept you in his belly for two years, when he suddenly spits you out. You keep your back to him and you talk in whispers, in case he remembers you and the clever idea comes into his mind to swallow you all up again.

I looked across to Yevette, the tall pretty girl from Jamaica. Every time I looked at her before, she was laughing and smiling. But now her smile looked as nervous as mine.

68

'What is wrong?' I whispered.

Yevette moved her mouth close to my ear. 'It ain't safe out ere.'

'But they have released us, haven't they? We are free to go. What is the problem?'

Yevette shook her head and whispered again, 'Ain't dat simple, darlin. Dere's freedom as in, *yu girls is free to go*, and den dere's freedom as in, *yu girls is free to go till we catches yu*. Sorry, but it's dat second kind of freedom we got right now, Lil Bee. Truth. Dey call it bein a *illegal immigrant*.'

'I don't understand, Yevette.'

'Yeh, an I can't explain it to yu here.'

Yevette looked across at the other two girls, and behind her at the detention centre. When she turned back to me, she leaned close in to my ear again. 'I played a trick to get us let out of dere.'

'What sort of trick?'

'Shh, darlin. Dey is too many lisseners in dis place, Bee. Trus me, we got to find someplace we can hide up. Den I can explain de situation to yu at *leisure*.'

Now the other two girls were staring at us. I smiled at them and I tried not to think about what Yevette had said. We were sitting on our heels at the main gate of the detention centre. The fences stretched away from us on both sides. The fences were as high as four men and they had razor wire on the tops, in nasty black rolls. I looked at the other three girls and I started giggling. Yevette stood up and she put her hands on her hips and made big eyes at me.

'Why de hell yu laughin, Little Bug?'

'My name is Little Bee, Yevette, and I am laughing because of this fence.'

Yevette looked up at it.

'My god, darlin, yu Nye-jirryans is worse dan yu look. Yu tink dis fence is funny, me hope me never see de fence yu considda to be *sirius*.'

'It is the razor wire, Yevette. I mean, look at us girls. Me with my underwear in a see-through plastic bag and you in your flip-flops, and this girl in her nice yellow sari, and this one with her documents. Do we look like we could climb that fence? I am telling you, girls, they could take away that razor wire and they could put pound coins and fresh mangoes on the top of the fence and we still could not climb out.'

Now Yevette started to laugh, *WU-ha-ha-ha-ha*, and she scolded me with her finger.

'Yu foolish girl! Yu tink dey build dis fence for to keep us girls *in*? Yu crazy? Dey build dis fence for to keep all de boys *out*. Dem boys know de quality of de oomans dey keep lock up in dis place, dey be brekkin down de doors!'

I was laughing, but then the girl with the documents spoke. She was sitting on her heels and looking down at her Dunlop Green Flash trainers.

'Where all of us going to go?'

'Wherever de taxi take us, yu nah see it? An den we take it on from dere. Brighten up dat gloomy face, darlin! We going *dere*, in *England*.'

Yevette pointed her finger out through the open gate. The girl with the documents looked up at where she was pointing, and so did the sari girl, and so did I.

It was a bright morning, I told you this already. It was the month of May and there was warm sunshine dripping through the holes between the clouds, like the sky was a broken blue bowl and a child was trying to keep honey in it. We were at the top of the hill. There was a long tarmac road winding from our gate all the way to the horizon. There was no traffic on it. At our end, the road finished where we sat – it did not go anywhere else. On both sides of the road there were fields. And these were beautiful fields, with bright green grass so fresh it made you hungry. I looked at those fields and I thought, I could get down on my hands and my knees and put my face into that grass and eat and eat and *eat*. And that is what a very great number of cows were doing to the left of the road, and an even greater number of sheep to the right.

In the nearest field, a white man in a small blue tractor was pulling some implement across the ground, but do not ask me what was its function. Another white man in blue clothes that I think you call overalls, he was tying a gate closed with bright orange rope. The fields were very neat and square, and the hedgerows between them were straight and low.

'It is big,' said the girl with the documents.

71

'Nah, it ain't *nuthin*,' said Yevette. 'We jus got to get to London. Me know pipple dere.'

'I do not know people,' said the girl with the documents. 'I do not know anyone.'

'Well, yu jus gonna do yore best, darlin.'

The girl with the documents frowned. 'How come there no one here to help us? How come my caseworker she not here to fetch me? How come they give us no release papers?'

Yevette shook her head.

'Ain't yu got nuff papers in dat bag of yours already, darlin? Some people, yu give em de inch, dey want de whole mile.'

Yevette laughed, but her eyes looked desperate. 'Now where is dat dam taxi?' she said.

'The man on the phone said ten minutes.'

'Feel like ten years already, truth.'

Yevette fell quiet. We looked out over the countryside again. The landscape was deep and wide. A breeze blew across it. We sat there on our heels and we watched the cows and the sheep and the white man tying the gates closed around them.

After some time, our taxi came into sight. We watched it from the moment it was a small white speck at the distant end of the road. Yevette turned to me and she smiled.

'Dis taxi-driver, he soun cute on de phone?'

'I did not talk to the driver. I only talked to the taxi controller.'

'Eighteen month I gone without a man, Bug. Dis taxi-driver better be a rill Mister Mention, yu know what I'm sayin? Me like

72

em tall, wid a bit o fat on 'em. Me no like no skinny boys. An me like em dress fine. Got no time fo loosers, ain't dat right?'

I shrugged. I watched the taxi getting nearer. Yevette looked at me.

'What sorta man yu like, Lil Bug?'

I looked at the ground. There was grass there, pushing out through the tarmac, and I twisted it in my hands. When I thought about men, I felt a fear in my belly so sharp it was like knives piercing me. I did not want to speak, but Yevette nudged me with her elbow.

'Come on, Bug, what sorta boy be madam's type?'

'Oh, you know, the usual sort.'

'What? What yu mean, de *yoo*-sual sort? Tall, short, skinny, fat?'

I looked down at my hands. 'I think my ideal man would speak many languages. He would speak Ibo and Yoruba and English and French and all of the others. He could speak with any person, even the soldiers, and if there was violence in their heart he could change it. He would not have to fight, do you see? Maybe he would not be very handsome, but he would be beautiful when he spoke. He would be very kind, even if you burned his food because you were laughing and talking with your girlfriends instead of watching the cooking. He would just say, *Ah, never mind.*'

Yevette looked at me.

'Forgive me, Bug, but yore ideal man, he don't sound very rill-*istic*.'

73

The girl with the documents, she looked up from her Dunlop Green Flash trainers. 'Leave her alone. Can't you see she is a virgin?'

I looked at the ground. Yevette, she stared at me for a long time and then she put her hand on the back of my neck. I ground the toe of my boot into the ground and Yevette looked at the girl with the documents.

'How yu know dis, darlin?'

The girl shrugged and she pointed at the documents in her see-through plastic bag. 'I have seen things. I know about people.'

'So how come yu so quiet, if yu know so damn much?'

The girl shrugged again. Yevette stared at her.

'What dey call yu anyway, darlin?'

'I do not tell people my name. This way it is safer.'

Yevette rolled her eyes. 'Bet you don't give de boys your phone number, neither.'

The girl with the documents, she stared at Yevette. Then she spat on the ground. She was trembling.

'You don't know anything,' she said. 'If you knew one thing about this life you would not think it was so funny.'

Yevette put her hands on her hips. She shook her head slowly.

'Darlin,' she said. 'Life did take its gifts back from yu and me in de diffren order, dat's all. Truth to tell, funny is all me got lef wid. An yu, darlin, all yu got left is paperwork.'

They stopped then, because the taxi was pulling up. It stopped just in front of us. The side window was open and there was music blasting out. I will tell you what that music was. It was a song called 'We Are The Champions' by a British music band called Queen. This is why I knew the song: it is because one of the officers in the immigration detention centre, he liked the band very much. He used to bring his stereo and play the music to us when we were locked in our cells. If you danced and swayed to show you liked the music, he would bring you extra food. One time he showed me a picture of the band. It was the picture from the CD box. One of the musicians in the picture, he had a lot of hair. It was black with tight curls and it sat on the top of his head like a heavy weight and it went right down the back of his neck to his shoulders. I understand *fashion* in your language, but this hair did not look like fashion, I am telling you – it looked like a punishment.

One of the other detention officers came past while we were looking at the picture on the CD box, and he pointed to the musician with all that hair and he said, *What a cock.* I remember that I was very pleased, because I was still learning to really speak your language back then, and I was just beginning to understand that one word can have two meanings. I understood this word straight away. I could see that *cock* referred to the musician's hair. It was like a cockerel's comb, you see. So a *cock* was a cockerel, and it was also a man with that kind of hair.

I am telling you this because the taxi-driver had exactly that kind of hair.

When the taxi stopped outside the main gate of the detention centre, the driver did not get out of his seat. He looked at us through the open window. He was a thin white man and he was wearing sunglasses with dark green lenses and shiny gold frames. The girl in the yellow sari, she was amazed by the taxi car. I think she was like me and she had never seen such a big and new and shining white car. She walked all around it and stroked her hands across its surfaces and she said, *Mmmm*. She was still holding the empty see-through bag. She took one hand off the bag and traced the letters on the back of the car with her finger. She spoke their names very slowly and carefully, the way she had learned them in the detention centre. She said, *F. . . O. . . R. . . D. . . hmm! Fod!* When she got to the front of the car, she looked at the headlights, and she blinked. She put her head on one side, and then she put it straight again, and she looked the car in the eyes and giggled. The taxi-driver watched her all this time. Then he turned back to the rest of us girls and the expression on his face was like a man who has just realised he has swallowed a hand grenade because he thought it was a plum.

'Your friend's not right in the head,' he said.

Yevette poked me in the stomach with her elbow. 'Yu better do de talkin, Lil Bug,' she whispered.

I looked at the taxi-driver. 'We Are The Champions' was still playing on his stereo, very loud. I realised I needed to tell the taxi-driver something that showed him we were not refugees. I wanted to show that we were British and we spoke your language and understood all the subtle things about your culture. Also, I wanted to make him happy. This is why I smiled and walked up to the open window and said to the taxi-driver, 'Hello, I see that you are a cock.'

I do not think the driver understood me. The sour expression on his face became even worse. He shook his head from side to side, very slowly. He said, 'Don't they teach you monkeys any manners in the jungle?'

And then he drove away, very quickly, so that the tyres of his taxi squealed like a baby when you take its milk away. The four of us girls, we stood and watched the taxi disappearing back down the hill. The sheep to the right of the road and the cows to the left of the road, they watched it too. Then they went back to eating the grass, and we girls went back to sitting on our heels. The wind blew, and the rolls of razor wire rattled on the top of the fence. The shadows of small high clouds drifted across the countryside.

It was a long time before any of us spoke.

'Mebbe we shoulda let Sari Girl do de talkin.'

'I'm sorry.'

'Damn Africans. You always tink you so smart but yu *ignorant*.'

I stood and walked up to the fence. I held on to the chain link and stared through it, down the hill and over the fields.

Down there the two farmers were still working, the one driving the tractor and the other tying up the gates.

Yevette came and stood beside me. 'What we gonna do now, Bug? No way we can stay here. Let's jus walk, okay?'

I shook my head. 'What about those men down there?'

'You tink dey gonna stop us?'

I gripped on tighter to the wire. 'I don't know, Yevette. I am scared.'

'What yu scared of, Bug? Maybe dey jus leave us be. Unless yu plannin on callin dem names too, like you done dat taxi man?'

I smiled and shook my head.

'Well all right den. Don be fraid. Me come wid yu, any road. Keep a check on dem monkey manners you got.'

Yevette turned to the girl with the documents. 'What bout you, lil miss no-name? You commin wid?'

The girl looked back at the detention centre. 'Why they didn't give us more help? Why they didn't send our caseworkers to meet us?'

'Well, cos dey did not elect to *do* dat, darlin. So what yu gonna do? Yu gonna go back in dere, ask em fo a car, an a boyfren, an mebbe some nice *jool*-rie?'

The girl shook her head. Yevette smiled.

'Bless yu, darlin. An now fo yu, Sari Girl. Me gonna make dis easy fo yu. Yu comin wid us, darlin. If yu agree, say nuthin.'

The girl with the sari blinked at her, and tilted her head to one side.

78

'Good. We all in, Lil Bug. We all walking out of dis place.'

Yevette turned towards me but I was still watching the girl. The wind blew at her yellow sari and I saw there was a scar across her throat, right across it, thick like your little finger. It was white as a bone against her dark skin. It was knotted and curled around her windpipe, like it did not want to let go. Like it thought it still had a chance of finishing her off. She saw me looking and she hid the scar with her hand, so I looked at her hand. There were scars on that too. We have our agreement about scars, I know, but this time I looked away because sometimes you can see too much beauty.

We walked through the gates and down the tarmac road to the bottom of the hill. Yevette went first and I was second and the other two went behind me. I looked down at Yevette's heels all the way. I did not look left or right. My heart was pounding when we reached the bottom of the hill. The rumbling noise of the tractor grew louder until it drowned out the sound of Yevette's flip-flops. When the tractor noise grew quieter behind us I breathed more easily again. It is okay, I thought. We have passed them, and of course there wasn't any trouble. How foolish I was to be scared. Then the tractor noise stopped. Somewhere near by a bird sang, in the sudden silence.

'Wait,' said a man's voice.

I whispered to Yevette, 'Keep walking.'

'WAIT!'

Yevette stopped. I tried to go past her but she held on to my arm.

79

'Be *sirius*, darlin. Where yu gonna run to?'

I stopped. I was so scared, I was struggling to breathe. The other girls looked the same. The girl with no name, she whispered in my ear, 'Please. Let us turn around and go back up the hill. These people do not like us, can't you see?'

The tractor man got down from his cab. The other man, the one who was tying up the gates, he came and joined the first man. They stood in the road, between us and the detention centre. The tractor driver was wearing a green jacket and a cap. He stood with his hands in his pockets. The man who had been tying the gates – the man in the blue overalls – he was very big. The tractor driver only came up to his chest. He was so tall that the trousers of his overalls ended higher than his socks, and he was very fat too. There was a wide pink roll of fat under his neck, and the fat bulged out in the gaps between the bottom of his overalls and the top of his socks. He was wearing a woollen hat pulled down tight. He took a packet of tobacco out of his pocket, and he made a cigarette without taking his eyes off us girls. He had not shaved, and his nose was swollen and red. His eyes were red too. He lit his cigarette, and blew out the smoke, and spat on the ground. When he spoke, his fat wobbled.

'You escaped, 'ave you, my children?'

The tractor driver laughed. 'Don't mind Small Albert,' he said.

We girls looked at the ground. Me and Yevette, we were in front, and the girl with the yellow sari and the girl with no name stood behind us. The girl with no name, she whispered in my ear again. 'Please. Let us turn around and go. These people will not help us, can't you see?'

'They cannot hurt us. We are in England now. It is not like it was where we came from.'

'Please, let's just *go*.'

I watched her hopping from one foot to the other foot in her Dunlop Green Flash trainers. I did not know whether to run or to stay.

'But 'ave you?' said the tall fat man. 'Escaped?'

I shook my head. 'No, mister. We have been released. We are official refugees.'

'You got proof of that, I suppose?'

'Our papers are held by our caseworkers,' said the girl with no name.

The tall fat man looked all around us. He looked up and down the road. He stretched up to look over the hedge into the next field.

'I don't see no caseworkers,' he said.

'Call them if you do not believe us,' said the girl with no name. 'Call the Border and Immigration Agency. Tell them to check their files. They will tell you we are legal.'

She looked in her plastic bag full of documents until she found the paper she wanted.

'Here,' she said. 'The number is here. Call it, and you will see.'

'No. Please. Don't do dat.' said Yevette.

The girl with no name stared at her. 'What is the problem?' she said. 'They released us, didn't they?'

Yevette gripped her hands together. 'It ain't dat simple,' she whispered.

The girl with no name stared at Yevette. There was fury in her eyes. '*What have you done?*' she said.

'What me had to do,' said Yevette.

At first the girl with no name looked angry and then she was confused and then, slowly, I could see the terror come into her eyes. Yevette reached out her hands to her. 'Sorry, darlin. I wish it weren't dis way.'

The girl pushed Yevette's hands away.

The tractor driver took a step forward, and looked at us, and sighed.

'I reckon it's bloody typical, Small Albert, I really do.'

He looked at me with sadness and I felt my stomach twisting.

'You ladies are in a very vulnerable situation without papers, aren't you? Certain people might take advantage of that.'

The wind blew through the fields. My throat was closed so tight I could not speak. The tractor driver coughed.

'It's bloody typical of this government,' he said. 'I don't give a damn if you're legal or illegal. But how can they release you without papers? Left hand doesn't know what the right hand is up to. Is that everything you've got?'

I held up my see-through plastic bag, and when the other girls saw me they held up theirs too. The tractor driver shook his head.

'Bloody typical, isn't it, Albert?'

'Wouldn't know, Mr Ayres.'

'This government doesn't care about anyone. You're not the first people we've seen, wandering through these fields like Martians. You don't even know what planet you're on, do you? Bloody government. Doesn't care about you refugees, doesn't care about the countryside, doesn't care about farmers. All this bloody government cares about is foxes and townspeople.'

He looked up at the razor wire of the detention centre behind us, then he looked at each of us girls in turn.

'You shouldn't even be in this situation in the first place. It's a disgrace, that's what it is, keeping girls like you locked up in a place like that. Isn't that right, Albert?'

Small Albert took off his woollen hat and scratched his head, and looked up at the detention centre. He blew cigarette smoke out of his nose. He did not say anything.

Mr Ayres looked at the four of us girls.

'So. What are we going to do with you? You want me to go back up there with you and tell them they've got to hold on to you till your caseworkers can be contacted?'

Yevette's eyes went very wide when Mr Ayres said this.

'No way, mister. Me ain't nivver goin back in that hell place no more. Not fo one minnit, kill me dead. Uh-uh.'

My Ayres looked at me then.

'I'm thinking they might have let you out by mistake,' he said. 'Yes, that's what I'm thinking. Am I right?'

I shrugged. The sari girl and the girl with no name, they just looked at the rest of us to see what was going to happen.

'Have you girls got anywhere to go? Any relatives? People expecting you somewhere?'

I looked at the other girls, and then I looked back at him and shook my head no.

'Is there any way you can prove that you're legal? I could be in trouble if I let you onto my land and then it turns out I'm harbouring illegal immigrants. I have a wife and three children. This is a serious question I'm asking you.'

'I am sorry, Mr Ayres. We will not go on your land. We will just go.'

Mr Ayres nodded, and took off his flat cap, and looked at the inside of it, and turned it around and around in his hands. I watched his fingers twisting in the green cloth. His nails were thick and yellow. His fingers were dirty with earth.

A large black bird flapped over our heads and flew away in the direction where our taxi had disappeared. Mr Ayres, he took a deep breath and he held up the inside of his cap for me to see. There was a name sewn in the lining of the hat. The name was written in handwriting on a white cloth label. The label was yellow from sweat.

'You read English? You see what that name label says?'

'It says AYRES, mister.'

84

'That's right. Yes, that's it. I am Ayres, and this is my hat, and this land you girls are standing on is Ayres Farm. I work this land but I don't make the law for it, I just plough it spring and autumn and parallel with the contours. Do you suppose that gives me the right to say if these women can stay on it, Small Albert?'

The wind was the only sound for a while. Small Albert spat on the ground. 'Well, Mr Ayres, I ain't a lawyer. I'm a cow-and-pig man at the end of the day, ain't I?'

Mr Ayres laughed. 'You ladies can stay,' he said.

Then there was sobbing from behind me. It was the girl with no name. She held on to her bag of documents and she cried, and the girl with the yellow sari put her arms around her. She sang to her in a quiet voice, the way we would sing to a baby who was woken in the night by the sound of distant guns and who must be soothed without being further excited. I do not know if you have a word for this kind of singing.

Albert took the cigarette from his mouth. He pinched it out between his thumb and forefinger. He rolled it into a little ball and dropped it into the pocket of his overalls. He spat on the ground again, and he put his woollen hat back on.

'What's she blubbin' for?'

Yevette shrugged. 'Mebbe de girl jus ain't used to kind-ness.'

Albert thought about this. Then he nodded, slowly. 'I could put em in the pickers' barn, Mr Ayres?'

'Thanks, Albert. Yes, take them there and get them settled

in. I'll get my wife to dig out what they need.' He turned to us girls. 'We have a dormitory where our seasonal labourers sleep. It's empty at the moment. It's only needed around harvest and lambing. You can stay there a week, no longer. After that, you're not my problem.'

I smiled at Mr Ayres, but Mr Ayres waved away my smile with his hand. Maybe this is the way you would wave away a bee before it came too close. The four of us girls, we followed Albert across the fields. We walked in a single line. Albert walked in front in his wool hat and blue overalls. He was carrying a large ball of bright orange plastic rope. Then it was Yevette in her purple A-line dress and flip-flops, then me, and I was wearing the blue jeans and the Hawaiian shirt. Behind me there was the girl with no name, and she was still weeping, and then there was the girl in the yellow sari, who was still singing to her. The cows and the sheep moved aside to watch us as we walked across their fields. You could see them thinking, Here are some strange new creatures that Small Albert is leading.

He took us to a long building beside a stream. The building had low brick walls, as high as my shoulder, but it had a high metal roof that rose in an arch from the walls, so that the building was like a tunnel. The metal roof was not painted. There were no windows in the walls but there were plastic skylights in the roof. The building stood in a dirt field where pigs and hens were scratching at the ground. When we appeared, the pigs stayed where they were and stared at us. The hens moved away with a nervous walk, looking behind them to make sure we were not following.

The hens were ready to run if they needed to. They picked up each foot with a jerky movement and when they put the foot back down you could see the claws trembling. They moved closer to each other and made a muttering sound. The pitch of the noise rose each time one of us girls took a step closer, and it fell each time the hens put the distance back between them and us. It made me very unhappy to watch those hens. The way they moved and the noise they made, this is exactly how it was when Nkiruka and me finally left our village back home.

We joined a group of women and girls and we ran off into the jungle one morning and we walked until it was dark and then we lay down to sleep beside the path. We did not dare to make a fire. In the night we heard gun shots. We heard men screaming like pigs when they are waiting in the cage to have their throats cut. There was a full moon that night and if the moon had opened its mouth and started screaming I would not have been more terrified. Nkiruka held me tight. There were babies in our group and some of them woke up and had to have songs sung to them before they would settle. In the morning there was a tall, evil line of smoke rising over the fields where our village was. It was black smoke and it curled and boiled as it rose up into the blue sky. Some of the very young children in our group asked what the smoke was from, and the women smiled and told them, *It is just the smoke from a volcano, little ones. It is nothing to worry about.* And I watched the way the smiles left their faces when they turned away from their children's eyes and stared back into the blue sky filling with black.

'You all right?'

Albert was staring at me. I blinked. 'Yes. Thank you, mister.'

'Daydreaming, were you?'

'Yes, sir.'

Albert shook his head and laughed. 'Honestly, you young people. Heads in the clouds.'

He unlocked the long building and let us in. Inside there were two rows of beds, one row on each long wall. The beds were made of metal and they were painted dark green. There were clean white mattresses on the beds, and pillows without pillowcases. The floor was concrete painted grey, and it was shining and swept. The sunlight came down in thick stripes from the skylights. There were long loops of chain hanging down. They stretched right up into the roof, which was the height of five men at the centre of the building. Albert showed us how to pull on one side of each chain loop to open the skylight, and on the other side of the chain to close it. He showed us the cubicles at the end of the building where we could take a shower or use the toilet. Then he winked at us.

'There you go, ladies. The accommodation ain't up to 'otel standard, I'll grant you, but then show me the 'otel where you can get twenty Polish girls sharing your room and the management don't even bat an eyelid. You should see some of the things our harvesters get up to after lights out. I'm telling you, I should chuck in the livestock work and make a film.'

Albert was laughing but the four of us girls, we stood there just looking back at him. I did not understand why he was talking about films. In my village, each year when the rains stopped, the men went to the town and they brought back a projector and a diesel generator, and they tied a rope between two trees, and we watched a film on a white sheet that they hung from the rope. There was no sound with the film, only the rumble of the generator and the shrieking of the creatures in the jungle. This is how we learned about your world. The only film we had was called *Top Gun* and we watched it five times. I remember the first time we saw it, the boys in my village were excited because they thought it was going to be a film about a gun, but it was not a film about a gun. It was a film about a man who had to travel everywhere very fast, sometimes on a motorbike and sometimes in an aeroplane that he flew himself, and sometimes upside down. We discussed this, the children in my village, and we decided two things: one, that the film should really be called *The Man Who Was In A Great Hurry* and two, that the moral of the film was that he should get up earlier so that he would not have to rush to fit everything into his day, instead of lying in bed with the woman with blond hair that we called 'The Stay-in-Bed Woman'. That was the only film I had ever seen, so I did not understand when Albert said he should make a film.

He did not look like he could fly an aeroplane upside down. In fact I had noticed how Mr Ayres did not even let him drive his blue tractor. Albert saw us girls staring back at him, and he shook his head.

'Oh, never mind,' he said. 'Look, there's blankets and towels and what 'ave you in them cupboards over there. I dare say Mrs Ayres will be down later with some food for you. I'll see you ladies around the farm, I shouldn't wonder.'

The four of us girls, we stood in the centre of the building and we watched Albert as he walked out between the two lines of beds. He was still laughing to himself when he walked out into the daylight. Yevette looked at the rest of us and she tapped her finger on the side of her head.

'Nivver mind im. De white mens is all crazy.'

She sat down on the edge of the nearest bed and she took a dried pineapple slice out of her see-through plastic bag and she started to chew on it. I sat down next to her, while the sari girl took the girl with no name down the room a little way to lie down because she was still crying.

Albert had left the door open, and a few hens came in and began to look for food under the beds. The girl with no name screamed when she saw the hens coming in to the building, and she pulled her knees close to her chest and held a pillow in front of her. She sat there with her wide eyes poking out over the top of the pillow, and her Dunlop Green Flash trainers sticking out underneath it.

'*Re-LAX*, darlin. Dey int gonna hurt yu, dey is only chickens, yu nah see it?'

Yevette sighed. 'Here we go again, huh, Lil Bug?'

'Yes. Here we go again.'

'Dat girl in a bad way, huh?'

I looked over at the girl with no name. She was staring at Yevette and making the sign of the cross.

'Yes,' I said.

'Mebbe dis is de hardest part, now dey is lettin us out. In dat detention centre dey was always tellin yu, *do dis, do dat*. No time to tink. But now dey all ovva sudden gone quiet, no? Dat dangerous, me tellin yu. Let all de bad memory come back.'

'You think that is why she is crying?'

'Me know it, darlin. We all gotta mind our heads now, truth.'

I shrugged and pulled my knees up to my chin. 'What do we do now, Yevette?'

'No idea, darlin. Yu ask me, dis gonna be our nummer one problem in dis country. Where me come from, we ain't got no peace but we got a thousand rumours. Yu always got a whisper where yu can go for dis or dat. But here we got de opposite problem, Bug. We got peace but we ain't go no in-fo-may-shun, you know what I'm sayin?'

I looked Yevette in the eyes. 'What is going on, Yevette? What is this trick you have done? How come they let us out of that place without papers?'

Yevette sighed. 'Me did a *favour* for one of dem immigration men, all right? He make a few changes on de computer, jus put a tick in de right box, you know, an – POW! – up come de names for release. Yu, me an dem two other girls. Dem detention officers don't be askin no questions. Dey jus see de names come up on dere computer screen dis morning and – BAM! – dey take yu from your room and dey show you de door. Dey don't care if yore caseworker be dere to pick yu up or not. Dey too busy peekin at de titty-swingers in de newspaper, truth. So here we is. Free and ee-zee.'

'Except we don't have papers.'

'Yeah. But I ain't afraid.'

'I am afraid.'

'Don be.'

Yevette squeezed my hand and I smiled.

'Dat's me girl.'

I looked around the room. The sari girl and the girl with no name, they were six beds further along. I leaned in close to Yevette and I whispered to her. 'Do you know anyone in this country?'

'Sure, darlin. Williyam Shakespeare, Lady Diana, Battle of Britten. Me know dem all. Learned de names for me Citizenship Exam. Yu can test me.'

'No. I mean, do you know where you will go if we can get out of here?'

'Sure, darlin. I got pipple in London. Got de half of Jamaica livin down on Cole Harbour Lane. Prob'ly bitchin on how

92

much dey vexed by all de Nye-*jirryans* livin nex door. How bout yu? Yu got famly dere?'

I showed her the United Kingdom driver's licence from my see-through plastic bag. It was a small plastic card with Andrew O'Rourke's photo on it. Yevette held it up to look at it.

'What ting is dis?'

'It is a driving licence. It has the man's address on it. I am going to visit him.'

Yevette held the photocard close and stared at it. Then she held it far from her eyes and squinted down her nose at it. Then she looked up close again. She blinked.

'Dis is a *white man*, Lil Bug.'

'I know that.'

'Okay, okay, jus checkin. Jus establishin whether yu blind or stupid.'

I smiled but Yevette did not.

'We should stick together, darlin. Why yu no come to London wid me? For sure we gonna find some of your pipple down dere.'

'But I will not know them, Yevette. I will not know I can trust them.'

'What, and yu trust dis man?'

'I met him once.'

'Scuse me, Bug, but dis man don't look like yo *type*.'

'I met him in my country.'

'What de hell was dis man's business in Nye-*jirrya*?'

'I met him on a beach.'

Yevette threw her head back and slapped her thighs. 'WU-ha-ha-ha-ha! Now me see. An dey tole me yu was a *virgin*!'

I shook my head. 'It was not like that.'

'Don tell me it wasn't like dat, Lil miss Sexy-Bug. Yu mus of done *someting* to de man, make him want to give yu dis *vall-able dockerment*.'

'His *wife* was there too, Yevette. She is a beautiful lady. She is called Sarah.'

'So why he give yu his driver licence? His wife be so beautiful, he be tinking, Damn, me won't be needin dis again, me lady so pretty I ain't nivver gonna drive nowhere no more, me jus gonna sit home an stare at de wife?'

I looked away.

'What, den? Yu stole dis dockerment?'

'No.'

'What, den? What happen?'

'I cannot talk about it. It happened in another lifetime.'

'Mebbe yu bin spending too much time learnin yore fancy English, Lil Bug, cos dat is crazy talk. Yu only be livin one life, darlin. Don't matter yu don't uh-*preshie*-ate part of it, cos it don't stop bein part of yu.'

I shrugged and I lay back on the bed and I watched the nearest chain dangling from the roof. Every link was joined to the one before and the one after. It was too strong for a girl like me to break. The whole chain swayed back and fro and it shone in the sun from the skylights. Like you could pull on the grown-up end and sooner or later you would get to the child, just like pulling a bucket out of a well. Like you would never be left holding a broken end, with nothing attached to it at all.

'It is hard for me to think about the day I met Andrew and Sarah, Yevette. Now I cannot decide if I should go to visit them or not.'

'So tell me all about it, Bug. Me tell yu if dey sound good fo yu.'

'I do not want to talk about it with you, Yevette.'

Yevette put her fists on her hips and made her big eyes at me.

'Well get *yu*, lil miss Africa!'

I smiled. 'I am sure there are parts of your life you do not like to talk about, Yevette.'

'Only so *yu* no get *jealous*, Bug. Me tell yu some of de tings me done in me life of ease an luxury, yu be gettin yu self so jealous you gonna explode, and den Sari Girl over dere gonna have to mop up de mess, an she looks tired enough, yu ask me.'

'No, I am serious, Yevette. Do you talk about what happened to you, to make you come to the United Kingdom?'

Yevette stopped smiling. 'Nah. Me tell pipple what happen to me, dey ain't nivver gonna believe it. Pipple tink Jamaica be all sunshine an ganja an Jah Rastafari. But it ain't. Yu get on de wrong side of de politics, Bug, dey gonna make yu suffah. An dey gonna make yore family suffah. An me don't mean suffah, like no ice-cream fo a week. Me mean suffah, like you

95

wake up in you chillen's blood, an suddenly yo house is very very quiet, fo ivver an ivver, amen.'

Yevette sat completely still and she looked down at her flip-flops. I put my hand on her hand. Above our heads the chains swung to and fro, and then Yevette sighed.

'But pipple nivver believe dat about me country.'

'So what did you tell the man from the Home Office?'

'For me asylum interview? You wanna know what I tole him?'

'Yes.'

Yevette shrugged. 'I tole him if he arrange to get me release from dat place, he can do what he want wid me.'

'I don't understand.'

Yevette rolled her eyes. 'Well tank de lord de Home Office man was a lil bit smarter dan yu, Bug. Yu nivver notice dey interview rooms didn't have no windows? Me swear to yu, dat man's ooman mus of kept her legs cross for de las ten year, de way he took me up on me offer. An it wasn't jus on de one day, mind. It took de man *four interviews* fore he was certain me papers was in order, yu know what I'm sayin?'

I stroked her hand. 'Oh, Yevette.'

'It was nuthin, Bug. Compare to what dey do to me, if I be sent back to Jamaica? *Nuthin.*'

Yevette smiled at me. The tears flowed from the corners of her eyes and around the curve of her cheek. I started to wipe her tears away and then I started crying as well, so Yevette had to wipe my tears too. It was funny, because we could not stop crying. Yevette started laughing, and then I was laughing too, and the more we laughed the more we could not stop crying, until we made so much noise that the sari girl hissed at us to shush so we would not disturb the woman with no name, who was making crazy talk to herself in some language.

'Oh, look at de state of us, Bug. What we gonna do wid our selves?'

'I do not know. You really think you were released because of what you did with the Home Office man?'

'Me know it, Bug. De man even tole me de date.'

'But he didn't give you your papers?'

'Uh-uh. No papers. Him say dere a limit to his powah, yu see what I'm sayin? He be tickin one little box on de computer to tell dem officers to let us free, him can jus say, *Me hand slipped*. But approvin de asylum application? Dat's a diffren story.'

'So you're illegal now?'

Yevette nodded. 'Yu an me both, Bug. You an me an dem other two also. All four of us gettin let out cos of what I done fo de Home Office man.'

'Why all four of us, Yevette?'

'Him say it look suspicious on im, if it just be me gettin let go.'

'How did he choose the rest of us?'

Yevette shrugged. 'Close is eyes and stick a pin in de list, I dunno.'

I shook my head and looked down.

'What?' said Yevette. 'Yu no like it, Bug? Yu girls should uh-*preshie*-ate what I done fo yu.'

'But we can't do anything without papers, Yevette. Don't you see? If we had stayed, if we had gone through the proper procedure, maybe they would have released us with papers.'

'Uh-uh, Bug, uh-uh. It don't work like dat. Not for pipple from Jamaica, an not for pipple from Nye-*jirrya* neither. Get dis into yore head, darlin: dere is only one place where de proper procedure ends, an dat is de-por-tay-shun.'

She tapped the syllables out on my forehead with the palm of her hand, and then she smiled at me.

'If dey deport us, we gonna be killed when we get back home. Right? Dis way at leas we got a chance, darlin, yu better believe it.'

'But we can't work if we are illegal, Yevette. We can't earn money. We can't live.'

Yevette shrugged. 'Yu can't live if yu dead, neither. Yu probly too smart to get dat.'

I sighed and I shook my head. Yevette grinned.

'Dat's what I like to see,' she said. 'A young ting like yu being rill-*istic*. Now, lissen. Yu tink dese English people yu know could help us?'

I looked down at the driver's licence.

'I do not know.'

'But yu don't know no one else, huh?'

'No.'

'An what we gonna do when we get dere, if I come wid yu?'

98

'I don't know. Maybe we could find work, somewhere where they do not ask us for papers.'

'Easy fo yu. Yu smart, yu talk nice. Plenty work fo a girl like yu.'

'You talk nice too, Yevette.'

'Me talk like a ooman who *swallowed* a ooman who talk nice. Me *dumb*, yu nuh see it?'

'You are not dumb, Yevette. All of us who have got this far, all of us who have survived – how can we be dumb? Dumb could not come this far, I am telling you.'

Yevette leaned in towards me and whispered, 'Are you *sirius*? Yu no see de way Sari Girl start gigglin at dat taxi back dere?'

'Okay. Maybe Sari Girl is not very clever. But she is prettier than all of us.'

Yevette made her big eyes and snatched her see-though bag closer to her body. 'Dat hurts, Bug. How dare yu say she de prettiest? Me was gonna share me pineapple slice wid yu, but now yu on ya *own*, darlin.'

I giggled, and Yevette smiled and rubbed the top of my head.

Then we turned round very fast because there was a scream from the girl with no name. She was standing on her bed and she held her bag of documents against her chest with both hands, and she started to scream again.

'Make them stop coming! They will kill us all, you girls do not understand!'

Yevette stood up and walked over to her. She looked up at the girl with no name. The hens pecked and clucked around Yevette's flip-flops.

'Lissen, darlin. Dese ain't mens commin to kill yu, I tole yu before. Dese is *chickens*. Dey is more scared of us dan we is of dem. Look yu!'

Yevette put her head down and ran into a group of hens. There was a great explosion of flapping wings and flying feathers, and the hens were jumping up onto the mattresses, and the girl with no name was screaming and screaming and kicking at the hens with her Dunlop Green Flash trainers. Suddenly she stopped screaming and pointed. I could not see where she was pointing because there were hen feathers everywhere, falling down in the bright beams of sunshine from the skylights. Her pointing finger was trembling and she was whispering, 'Look! Look! My child!'

All of us girls were looking, but when the feathers finished falling there was nothing there. The girl with no name, she was just smiling at a bright beam of sunlight on the clean grey painted floor. There were tears falling from her eyes. 'My child,' she said, and she held her arms outstretched towards the beam of light. I watched her fingers trembling.

I looked at Yevette and the sari girl. The sari girl looked down at the floor. Yevette shrugged at me. I looked back at the girl with no name and I spoke to her. 'What is your child's name?'

The girl with no name smiled. Her face shone. 'This is Aabirah. She is my youngest. Isn't she beautiful?'

I looked at the place she was looking. 'Yes. She is lovely.' I looked at Yevette and made my eyes wide at her. 'Isn't she lovely, Yevette?'

'Oh. Yeah. Sure. She a rill heartbrekka. What yu say yu callin her?'

'Aabirah.'

'Dat's nice. Lissen, Aa-BI-rah, why don't yu come wid me, an help me chase de fowls outta dis barn?'

And so Yevette and the sari girl and the youngest daughter of the girl with no name, they started chasing the hens out of the building. Me, I sat and held the hand of the girl with no name. I said, 'Your daughter is very helpful. Look how she chases those hens.' The girl with no name, she was smiling. I was smiling too. I think it was nice for both of us that she had her daughter back.

If I was telling this story to the girls from back home, then one of the new words I would have to explain to them is 'efficiency'. We refugees are very efficient. We do not have the things we need – our children, for example – and so we are clever at making things stretch a little further. Just see what that girl with no name could make out of one little patch of sunlight. Or look how the sari girl could fit the entire colour of yellow into one empty see-through plastic bag.

I lay back on the bed and looked up at the chains. I was thinking, That sunshine, that colour yellow, maybe I will not see very much of these now. Maybe the new colour of my life was grey. Two years in the grey detention centre, and now I was an illegal immigrant. That means, you are free until they catch you. That means, you live in a grey area. I thought about how I was going to live. I thought about the years, living as quiet as could be. Hiding my colours and living in the twilight and the shadows. I sighed, and I tried to breathe deeply. I wanted to cry when I looked up at those chains and thought about the colour grey.

I was thinking, if the head of the United Nations telephoned one morning and said, *Greetings, Little Bee, to you falls the great honour of designing a national flag for all the world's refugees*, then the flag I would make would be grey. You would not need any particular fabric to make it. I would say that the flag could be any shape and it could be made with anything you had. A worn-out old brassiere, for example, that has been washed so many times it has become grey. You could fly it on the end of a broom handle, if you did not have a flag-pole. Although if you did have a spare flag-pole, for example, in that line of tall white flag-poles outside the United Nations building in New York City, then I think that old grey brassiere would make a fine spectacle, flying in the long colourful line of flags. I would fly it between the Stars and Stripes and the big red Chinese flag. That would be a good trick. Thinking about this, I made myself laugh.

'What de hell you laughin at, Bug?'

'I was thinking about the colour grey.'

Yevette frowned. 'Don't you go crazy too please, Bug,' she said.

I lay back on the bed again and I looked up to the ceiling, but all that was there were those long chains dangling down. I thought, I could hang myself by the neck from those, no problem.

In the afternoon the farmer's wife came. She brought food. There was bread and cheese in a basket, and a sharp knife to cut the bread with. I thought, I can cut open my veins with that knife, if the men come. The farmer's wife was a kind woman. I asked her why was she doing this good thing for us. She said it was because we were all human beings. I said, *Excuse me, miss, but I do not think Yevette is a human being. I think she is another species with a louder mouth.* Yevette and the farmer's wife started laughing then, and we talked for a little while about where we had all come from and where we were going to. She told me the direction to go to Kingston-upon-Thames, but she also told me that I shouldn't. *You don't want to go to the suburbs, dear,* she said. *Neither fish nor flesh, the suburbs. Unnatural places, full of unnatural people.* I laughed. I told her, *Maybe I will fit right in.*

The farmer's wife was surprised when we asked for five plates instead of four, but she brought them anyway. We divided the food into five portions, and we gave the biggest helping to the daughter of the woman with no name, because she was still growing.

That night I dreamed about my village before the men came. There was a swing that the boys had made. It was the old tyre of a car, and the boys had tied ropes around it and suspended it from the high branch of a tree. This was a big old limba tree and it grew a little way apart from our homes, near to the schoolhouse. Even before I was big enough to go on the swing, my mother would sit me down in the dark red dust by the trunk of the limba, so I could watch the big children swinging. I loved to listen to them laughing and singing. Two, three, four children at once, all ways up, with legs and arms and heads all tangled up and dragging in the red scrape of dust at the lowest point of the swing. *Aie! Ouch! Get off me in the name of God! Do not push!* There was always a lot of chatter and joking around the swing, and up above my head in the branches of the limba tree there were grumpy hornbills that shouted back at us. Nkiruka would get down from the swing sometimes and pick me up in her arms and give me little pieces of soft uncooked dough to squeeze between my chubby fingers.

Everything was happiness and singing when I was a little girl. There was plenty of time for it. We did not have to hurry. We did not have electricity or fresh water or sadness either, because none of these had been connected to our village yet. I sat in between the roots of my limba tree and I laughed while I watched Nkiruka swinging back and fro, back and fro. The tether of the swing was very long, so it took a long time for her to travel from one end of its swing to the other. It never looked as though it was in a rush, that swing. I used to watch it all day long and I never realised I was watching a pendulum counting down the last seasons of peace in my village.

In my dream I watched that tyre swinging back and fro, back and fro, in that village we did not yet know was built on an oilfield and would soon be fought over by men in a crazy hurry to drill down into the oil. This is the trouble with happiness – all of it is built on top of something that men want.

I dreamed of watching Nkiruka swinging back and fro, back and fro, and when I woke up there were tears in my eyes and in the light of the moon I was watching something else swinging back and fro, back and fro. I could not tell what it was. I wiped the tears from my eyes and I opened them fully, and then I saw what it was that was swinging through the air at the end of my bed.

It was a single Dunlop Green Flash trainer. The other one had fallen off the foot of the woman with no name. She had hanged herself from one of the long chains that reached up to the roof. Her body was naked apart from that one shoe. She was very thin. Her ribs and her hip-bones were sharp. Her eyes bulged open and pointed up into thin blue light. They glittered. The chain had crushed her neck as thin as her ankle. I watched the Dunlop Green Flash trainer and the bare dark brown foot with its grey sole swinging back and fro past the end of my bed. The Green Flash trainer glowed in the moonlight, like a slow and shining silver fish, and the bare foot chased it like a shark. They swum circles around one another. The chain squeaked quietly.

I went and touched the bare leg of the girl with no name. It was cold. I looked over at Yevette and the sari girl. They were sleeping. Yevette was muttering in her sleep. I started to walk over to Yevette's bed to wake her, but my foot slipped on something wet. I knelt down and touched it. It was urine. It was as cold as the painted concrete floor. A puddle of it had collected underneath the girl with no name. I looked up and I saw a single drop of urine hang from the big toe of her bare foot, then sparkle as it fell to the floor. I stood up quickly. I felt so depressed about the urine. I did not want to wake up the other girls because then they would see it too, and then we would all be seeing it, and then none of us could deny it. I do not know why the small puddle of urine made me start to cry. I do not know why the mind chooses these small things to break itself on.

I went over to the bed that the girl with no name had been sleeping on, and I picked up her T-shirt. I was going to go back and use the T-shirt to wipe up the urine, but then I saw the see-through plastic bag of documents on the end of the bed. I opened it and I started to read the story of the girl with no name.

The-men-came-and-they . . . I was still crying, and it was difficult to read in the dim light from the moon. I put the girl's documents back down on the bed and I closed the bag carefully. I held it tightly in my hands. I was thinking, I could take this girl's story for my own. I could take these documents and I could take this story with its official red stamp at the end of it that tells everyone it is TRUE. Maybe I can win my asylum case with these papers. I thought about it for one minute, but while I held the girl's story in my hands the squeaking of her chain seemed to get louder, and I had to drop her story back down on the bed because I knew how it ended. A story is a powerful thing in my country, and God help the girl who takes one that is not her own. So I left it on the girl's bed, every word of it, including the paper-clips and all the photographs of the scar tissue and the names of the missing daughters, and all of the red ink that said this was CONFIRMED.

Me, I put one small kiss on the cheek of Yevette, who was still sleeping, and I walked off quietly across the fields.

Leaving Yevette, that was the hardest thing I had to do since I left my village. But if you are a refugee, when death comes you do not stay for one minute in the place it has visited. Many things arrive after death – sadness, questions, and policemen – and none of these can be answered when your papers are not in order.

Truly, there is no flag for us floating people. We are millions, but we are not a nation. We cannot stay together. Maybe we get together in ones and twos, for a day or a month or even a year, but then the wind changes and carries the hope away. Death came and I left in fear. Now all I have is my shame and the memory of bright colours and the echo of

Yevette's laugh. Sometimes I feel as lonely as the Queen of England.

It was not difficult to know which way to go. London lit up the sky. The clouds glowed orange, as if the city that awaited me was burning. I walked uphill, through fields with some kind of grain and into a high wood of some kind of trees, and when I looked back down towards the farm for the last time I saw a floodlight come on outside the barn they put us in. I think it was an automatic light, and standing in the middle of the beam there was the single bright lemon yellow dot of the sari girl. It was too far away to see her face, but I imagined her blinking in surprise when the light came on. Like an actress who has walked onto the stage by mistake. Like a girl who does not have a speaking part, who is thinking, Why have they turned this great light upon me now?

I was very scared but I did not feel alone. All through that night it seemed to me as if my big sister Nkiruka walked beside me. I could almost see her face, glowing in the pale orange light. We walked all night, across fields and through woods. We steered around the lights of villages. Whenever we saw a farmhouse we went around that too. Once, the farm dogs heard us and barked, but there was no trouble. We kept on walking. My legs were tired. Two years I had been in that detention centre, going nowhere, and I was weak. But although my ankles hurt and the backs of my legs ached, it felt very good to be moving, and to be free, and to feel the night air on my face and the grass on my legs, wet from the dew. I know my sister was happy too. She was whistling under her breath. Once when we stopped to rest, she dug her toes into the earth at the edge of a field and smiled. When I saw her smile, I felt strong enough to carry on.

The orange glow of the night faded, and I started to see the fields and the hedges around us. Everything was grey at first, but then the colours began to come into the land – blue and green, but very soft, as if the colours did not have any happiness in them. Then the sun rose, and the whole world turned to gold. The gold was all around me and I was walking through clouds of it. The sun was blazing on the white mist that hung over the fields, and the mist swirled around my legs. I looked over at my sister, but she had disappeared with the night. I smiled though, because I realised that she had left me with her strength. I looked around me at the beautiful sunrise and I was thinking, Yes, yes, everything will be beautiful like this now. I will never be afraid again. I will never spend another day trapped in the colour grey.

There was a low roaring, rumbling sound ahead of me. The noise rose and fell in the mist. It is a waterfall, I thought. I must be careful not to fall into the river in this mist.

I walked on, more carefully now, and the noise got louder. Now it did not sound like a river any more. There were individual sounds in the middle of the roaring. Each sound got louder, rumbling and shaking and then fading away. There was a dirty, sharp smell in the air. Now I could hear the sound of cars and trucks. I went closer. I came to the top of a green grass slope and there it was in front of me. The road was incredible. On my side of it there were three lines of traffic going from right to left. Then there was a low metal barrier, and another three lines of traffic going from left to right. The cars and the trucks were moving very fast. I walked down to the edge of the road and put out my hand to stop the traffic, so I could cross, but the traffic did not stop. A truck blew its horn at me, and I had to step back.

I waited for a gap in the traffic and then I ran across to the centre of the road. I climbed over the metal barrier. This time a great many car horns were blown at me. I ran across, and up the green grass bank at the other side of the road. I sat down. I was out of breath. I watched the traffic racing past below me, three lines in one direction and three lines in the other. If I was telling this story to the girls from back home they would be saying, *Okay, it was the morning so the people were travelling to work in the fields. But why do the people who are driving from right to left not exchange their fields with the people who are driving from left to right? That way everyone could work in the fields near to their homes.* And then I would just shrug because there are no answers that would not lead to more foolish questions, like: *What is an office and what crops can you grow in it?*

I just fixed the motorway in my mind as a place I could run back to and kill myself very easily if the men suddenly came, and then I stood up and carried on going. I walked for another hour across fields. Then I came to some small roads, and these roads had houses on them. I was amazed when I saw them. They were two storeys high and made out of strong red bricks. They had sloping roofs with neat rows of tiles on them. They had white windows, and there was glass in all of them. Nothing was broken. All the houses were very smart, and each one looked like the next. In front of nearly every house there was a car. I walked along the street and I stared at the shining rows of them. These were beautiful cars, sleek and shining, not the kind of vehicles we saw where I came from. In my village there were two cars, one Peugeot and one Mercedes. The Peugeot came before I was born. I know this because the driver was my father, and my village was the place where his Peugeot coughed twice and died in the red dust. He went into the first house in the village to ask if they had a mechanic. They did not have a mechanic but what they did have was my mother, and my father realised he needed her more than he needed a mechanic in any case, and so he stayed. The Mercedes arrived when I was five years old. The driver was drunk, and he crashed into my father's Peugeot, which was still standing exactly how my father had left it except that the boys had taken one of its tyres away to use as the seat of the swing on the limba tree. The driver of the Mercedes got out and he walked over to the first house and met my father there and he said, *Sorry*. And my father smiled at him and said, *We should be thanking you, sir, you have really put our village on the map – this is our very first road traffic accident.* And the driver of that Mercedes, he laughed, and he stayed too, and he became great friends with my father, so much that I called him my uncle. And my father and my uncle lived very happily in that place until the afternoon when the men came and shot them.

So it was astonishing to see all these new, beautiful shining cars parked outside these big, perfect houses. I walked through many streets like this.

I walked all morning. The buildings got bigger and heavier. The streets got wider and busier. I stared at everything, and I did not mind the hunger in my stomach or the aching in my legs because I was amazed by each new wonder. Each time I saw something for the first time – a nearly naked girl on an advertising billboard, or a red double-decker bus, or a glittering building so tall it made you dizzy – the excitement in my stomach was so fierce it hurt. The noise was too much – the roar of the traffic and the shouting. Soon there were such crowds on the streets that it seemed I was nothing. I was pushed and bumped all over the pavements, and no one took any notice of me. I kept on walking as straight as I could, following one street and then another, and just as the buildings got so big it seemed they could not possibly stand up, and the noise got so loud it seemed as if my body would be shaken to pieces, I turned a corner and I gasped and ran across one last busy road, with car horns blasting and the drivers screaming, and I leaned over a low white stone wall and stared and stared, because there in front of me was the River Thames. Boats were pushing along through the muddy brown water, honking their horns under the bridges. All along the river to the left and the right, there were huge towers that rose high into the blue sky. Some were still being built, with huge yellow cranes moving above them. *They even trained the birds of the air to help them build? Weh!*

I stayed there on the bank of the river and I stared and stared at these marvels. The sun shone out of the bright blue sky. It was warm, and a soft breeze blew along the bank of the river. I whispered to my sister Nkiruka, because it seemed to me that she was there in the flowing of the river and the blowing of the breeze.

'Look at this place, sister. We are going to be all right here. There will be room for two girls like us in a country as fine as this. We are not going to suffer any more.'

I smiled, and I walked away down the embankment of the river, in the direction of the west. I knew that if I followed along the bank, I would get to Kingston – that is why they call it Kingston-upon-Thames. I wanted to get there as quick as I could, because now the crowds in London were starting to frighten me. In my village we never saw more than fifty people in one place. If you ever saw more than that, it meant that you had died and gone to the city of the spirits. That is where the dead go, to a city, to live together in their thousands because they do not need the space to grow their fields of cassava. When you are dead you are not hungry for cassava, only for company.

A million people were all around me. Their faces hurried past. I looked and looked. I never saw the faces of my family but when you have lost everyone, you never lose the habit of looking. My sister, my mother, my father and my uncle. Every face I see, I am looking for them in it. If I did meet you then the first thing you would have noticed would have been my eyes staring at your face, as if they were trying to see someone else in you, as if they were desperate to make you into a ghost. If we did meet, I hope you did not take this personally.

I hurried along the river embankment, through the crowds, through my memories, through this city of the dead. Once, beside a tall stone needle engraved with strange symbols, my legs burned and I needed to rest, so I stood still for a moment and the dead flowed around me, like the muddy brown Thames flowing around the pillar of a bridge.

If I was telling this story to the girls from back home, I would have to explain to them how it was possible to be drowning in a river of people and also to feel so very, very alone. But truly, I do not think I would have the words.

4

Early on the morning of Andrew's funeral, before Little Bee arrived, I remember looking down from the bedroom window of our house in Kingston-upon-Thames. Out by the pond, Batman was poking at baddies with a plastic junior golf club, looking skinny and forlorn. I wondered if I should warm up some milk and make him a cup of something. I remember wondering if there was anything that could be put into a cup that would actually be of practical help. My mind was set in that crystalline, self-conscious state that comes with lack of sleep.

Beyond our garden I could see the whole street's back gardens, curving away like a bent green spine, with barbecues and faded plastic swings for vertebrae. Through the double glazing came the braying of a car alarm and the drone of planes climbing out of Heathrow. I pressed my nose against the glass and I thought: these bloody suburbs are purgatory. How did we all wash up here? How did so many of us end up so very far downwind?

In the garden next door, on that morning of the funeral, my neighbour was hanging out his blue Y-fronts to dry. His cat was curling around his legs. In my bedroom the *Today Programme* was on the radio. John Humphrys said the FTSE was rather badly down.

Yes, but I have lost my husband. I said it out loud, while a trapped fly flew feebly at the window-pane. I said: *My husband is dead, I'm afraid. My husband Andrew O'Rourke, the celebrated columnist, has taken his own life. And I feel . . .*

Actually I didn't know how I felt. We don't have a grown-up language for grief. Daytime shows do it much better. I knew I ought to feel *devastated*, of course. My life had *fallen apart*. Isn't that the phrase? But Andrew had been dead nearly a whole week now and here I still was, dry eyed, with the whole house reeking of gin and lilies. Still trying to feel appropriately sad. Still drilling down through the memories of my short, mixed life with poor Andrew. Searching for the capstone, the memory which when cracked would release some symptom of anguish. Tears, perhaps, under unbelievable pressure. *My life entered a vicious downhill spiral, Trisha. I couldn't imagine getting through the day without him.*

It was exhausting, prospecting for grief like this, unsure if grief was even there to be found. Perhaps it was just too soon.

For the moment I felt more pity for a trapped fly that buzzed against the window. I opened the latch and out it flew, vulnerable and weak, back in the game.

On the other side of the glass, the day smelled of summer. My neighbour had shuffled along his washing line, three feet to the left. He'd finished pegging Y-fronts. Now he was on to socks. His washing hung like prayer flags, petitioning daytime gods: *I seem to have moved to the suburbs, I'm afraid. Can anything be done?*

A thought of escape presented itself, rascalish and unannounced. I could simply leave, right now, couldn't I? I could take Charlie, my credit card and my favourite pink shoes and we could all get on a plane together. The house and the job and the grief would all shrink to a point behind me. I remember realising, with a guilty thrill, that there was no longer one single reason for me to be here – far from the centre of my heart, cast away here in its suburbs.

But life is not inclined to let any of us escape. That was the moment I heard a knock at the door. I opened the door to Little Bee, and for the longest time I simply stared at her. Neither of us spoke. After a few moments I let her in and I sat her down on the sofa. Black girl in a red and white Hawaiian shirt, stained by the Surrey clay. Sofa from Habitat. Memories from hell.

'I don't know what to say. I thought you must be dead.'

'I am not dead, Sarah. Maybe it would be better if I was.'

'Don't say that. You look very tired. You need some rest, I should think.'

There was a silence that went on too long.

'Yes. You are right. I need some rest.'

'How on earth did you . . . I mean, how did you survive? How did you get here?'

'I walked.'

'From Nigeria?'

'Please. I am very tired.'

'Oh. Yes. Of course. Yes. Would you like a cup of, you know . . .'

I didn't wait for the answer. I fled. I left Little Bee sitting on the sofa, propped up on the John Lewis cushions, and I ran upstairs. I closed my eyes and rolled my forehead against the cool glass of the bedroom window. I dialled someone. A friend. More than a friend, actually. That's what Lawrence was.

'What is it?' said Lawrence.

'You sound cross.'

'Oh. Sarah. It's you. God, I'm sorry. I thought you were the nanny. She's late. And the baby's just been sick on my tie. *Shit.*'

'Something's happened, Lawrence.'

'What?'

'Someone's turned up I really wasn't expecting.'

'Funerals are always like that. All the old skeletons come theatrically out of their closets. You can't keep the bastards away.'

'Yes, of course, but this is more than that. It's, it's . . .' I stammered away and fell silent.

'Sorry, Sarah, I know this sounds awful, but I'm in a terrible rush here. Is it something I can actually help with?'

I pressed my flushed face against the cold glass. 'Sorry. I'm a bit confused.'

'It's the funeral. You're *going* to feel a bit scatty, aren't you? I'm sorry, but there's no way around that. I wish you'd let me come. How are you feeling about it all?'

'About the funeral?'

'About the whole situation.'

I sighed.

'I don't feel anything. I feel numb.'

'Oh, Sarah.'

'I'm just waiting for the undertaker now. I'm slightly nervous, maybe. That's all. Like waiting at the dentist's.'

'Right,' said Lawrence, carefully.

A pause. In the background, the sound of Lawrence's children squabbling at the breakfast table. I realised I couldn't tell Lawrence about Little Bee turning up. Not now. It suddenly didn't seem fair, to add it to his list of problems. Late for work, baby sick on tie, tardy nanny . . . oh, and now a presumed-dead Nigerian girl, resurrected on his mistress's sofa. I didn't think I could do that to him. Because this is the thing, with being lovers. It isn't like being married. To remain in the game, one has to be considerate. One has to acknowledge a certain right-to-life of the other. So I stayed silent. I listened to Lawrence taking a deep breath, on the edge of exasperation.

'So what's confusing you? Is it that you're not feeling anything much and you think you should be?'

'It's my husband's funeral. I should be sad, at least.'

'You're in control of yourself. You're not a gusher. Celebrate that.'

'I can't cry for Andrew. I keep thinking about that day in Africa. On the beach.'

'Sarah?'

'Yes?'

'I thought we agreed it was best that you forget all that. What happened, happened. We agreed that you were just going to move on, didn't we. Hmm?'

I pressed my left hand flat against the window-pane and stared at the stump of my lost finger.

'I don't think "moving on" is going to work any more, Lawrence. I don't think I can just continue to deny what happened. I don't think I'll be able to. I . . .' My voice trailed off.

'Sarah? Deep breaths.'

I opened my eyes. Outside, Batman was still poking fiercely at the pond. The *Today Programme* scolded away on the radio. Next door the neighbour had finished pegging his washing and now he simply stood there, eyes half closed. Soon he would move on to a new task: the percolation of coffee, perhaps, or the application of replacement twine to the spool of a strimmer. Small problems. Neat problems.

'Now that Andrew's, well, *gone*, Lawrence. Do you think you and I will be . . .'

A pause on the other end of the phone. Then Lawrence – careful Lawrence – non-committal.

'Andrew didn't stop us while he was alive,' he said. 'Do you see any reason to change things now?'

I sighed again.

'Sarah?'

'Yes?'

'Just focus on today for now, will you? Focus on the funeral, hold it together, get through today. Stop smearing that fucking toast on the *computer*!'

'Lawrence?'

'Sorry. That was the baby. He's got a piece of buttered toast and he's wiping it all over . . . sorry, have to go.'

Lawrence hung up. I turned from the window and sat on the bed. I waited. I was putting off having to go downstairs and deal with Little Bee. Instead of moving I watched myself, in the mirror, as a widow. I tried to find some physical sign of Andrew's passing. No extra line on the forehead? No darkening of the skin under the eyes? Really? Nothing?

How calm my eyes were, since that day on the beach in Africa. When there has been a loss so fundamental, I suppose that to lose just one more thing – a finger, perhaps, or a husband – is of absolutely no consequence at all. In the mirror my green eyes were placid – as still as a body of water that is either very deep, or very shallow.

Why couldn't I cry? Soon I would have to go and face a church full of mourners. I rubbed my eyes, harder than our beauty experts advise. I needed to show red eyes to the mourners, at least. I needed to show them that I *had* cared for Andrew, truly cared for him. Even if, since Africa, I hadn't really bought the idea of love as a permanent thing, measurable in self-administered surveys, present if you answered mostly B. So I gouged my thumbs into the skin beneath my lashes. If I couldn't show the world grief, at least I would show the world what it did to your eyes.

Finally I went downstairs and stared at Little Bee. She was still sitting there on the sofa, her eyes closed, her head propped on the cushions. I coughed, and she snapped awake. Brown eyes, orange patterned silk cushions. She blinked at me and I stared at her, with the mud still caking her boots. I felt nothing.

'Why did you come here?' I said.

'I did not have any other place to go. The only people I know in this country are you and Andrew.'

'You hardly know us. We met, that's all.'

Little Bee shrugged. 'You and Andrew are the only ones I met,' she said.

'Andrew is dead. We are going to bury him this morning.'

Little Bee just blinked at me, glazedly.

'Do you understand?' I said. 'My husband *died*. We are going to have a *funeral*. It's a kind of ceremony. In a church. It's what we do in this country.'

Little Bee nodded. 'I know what you do in this country,' she said.

There was something in her voice – so old, so tired – that terrified me. That was when the door-knocker sounded again and Charlie answered the door to the undertaker and called down the hallway, *Mummy, it's Bruce Wayne!*

'Run out and play in the garden, darling,' I said.

'But Mummy, I want to see Bruce Wayne!'

'*Please*, darling. Just go.'

When I came to the door, the undertaker glanced at the stump of my finger. People generally do, but rarely with that professional gaze that notes: *Left hand, second finger, first and second phalanx, yes, we could fix that with a wax* prosthetic, a slender one, with a light Caucasian flesh tone, and we could use Kryolan foundation to cover the join, and we could fold the right hand over the left in the coffin, and Bob would be your mother's brother, madam.

I was thinking, Clever undertaker. If only I was dead, you could make a whole woman out of me.

'My deepest condolences, madam. We are ready for you whenever you feel ready to come.'

'Thank you. I'll just get my son and my . . . well. My friend.'

I watched the undertaker ignoring the smell of gin on my breath. He looked back at me. There was a small scar on his forehead. His nose was flattened and skewed. His face registered nothing. It was as blank as my mind.

'Take all the time you need, madam.'

I went out into the back garden. Batman was digging away at something under the roses. I went over to him. He had a trowel and he was lifting a dandelion, pulling its root to the tip. Our resident robin was hungry and he watched from six yards away. Batman raised the dandelion from the soil and brought it close to examine its root. Kneeling, he looked up at me.

'Is this a weed, Mummy?' he said.

'Yes, darling. Next time, if you're not sure, ask before you dig it up.'

Batman shrugged. 'Shall I put it in the wild patch?' he said.

I nodded, and Batman carried the dandelion over to a small part of the garden where Andrew had given a home to such rascals, in the hope that they would attract butterflies and bees. *In our small garden, I have made a wild place to remind me of chaos*, Andrew once wrote in his column. *Our modern lives are too ordered, too antiseptic.*

That had been before Africa.

Batman bedded in the dandelion amongst the nettles.

'Mummy, is weeds baddies?'

I said that it depended if you were a boy or a butterfly. Batman rolled his eyes, like a newsman interviewing an equivocating politician. I couldn't help smiling.

'Who is that woman on the sofa, Mummy?'

'Her name is Little Bee.'

'That's a funny name.'

'Not if you're a bee.'

'But she isn't a bee.'

'No. She's a person. She's from a country called Nigeria.'

'Mmm. Is she a goody?'

I stood up straight. 'We have to go now, darling,' I said. 'The undertaker is here to collect us.'

'Bruce Wayne?'

'Yes.'

'Is we going to the bat cave?'

'*Are we* going to the bat cave.'

'Are we?'

'Sort of.'

'Hmm. I is coming in a minute.'

I felt the perspiration starting on my back. I had on a grey woollen suit and a hat that was not black but a late evening nod to it. It didn't scorn tradition, but nor had it entirely submitted to darkness. Folded up over the hat was a black veil, ready to bring down when the right moment came. I hoped someone would tell me when that was.

I wore navy blue gloves, which were borderline dark enough for a funeral. The middle finger of the left-hand glove was truncated and stitched. I'd done it two nights earlier, as soon as I was drunk enough to bear it, in a merciful hour between insobriety and incapacity. The glove's severed finger was still lying on my sewing table. It was hard to throw away.

In my suit pocket was my phone, set to quiet mode in case I forgot to do it later. I also had a ten-pound note ready for the collection, in case there was a collection. It seemed unlikely at a funeral, but I wasn't sure. (And if there was a collection, was ten pounds about right? Five seemed ridiculously mean; twenty obscenely flashy.)

There was nobody left to ask about ordinary things. Little Bee was no use. I couldn't ask her: *Are these blue gloves okay?* She'd only stare at them, as if they were the first pair of gloves she had ever seen, which was quite possibly the case. (*Yes, but are they dark enough, Little Bee? Between you and me—you as the refugee from horror and me as the editor of an edgy monthly magazine— would we call that shade blue, courageous, or blue, irreverent?*)

Ordinary things were going to be the hardest, I realised. This was something undeniable, now that Andrew was gone: there was nobody left with a strong opinion about life in a civilised country.

Our robin hopped out from the foxgloves with a worm in its beak. The wormskin was puce, the colour of bruising.

'Come on, Batman, we have to go.'

'In a *minute*, Mummy.'

In the quiet of the garden then the robin shook his worm, and swallowed its life from the light into darkness with the quick indifference of a god. I felt nothing at all. I looked at my son, pale and bemused in the neatly planted garden, and I looked past him at Little Bee, tired and mudstained, waiting for us to go through into the house.

So, I realised – life had finally broken through. How silly it looked now, my careful set of defences against nature: my brazen magazine, my handsome husband, my Maginot line of motherhood and affairs. The world, the real world, had found a way through. It had sat down on my sofa and it would not be denied any longer.

I went through the house to the front door to tell the undertaker we would be with him in a minute. He nodded. I looked behind the undertaker at his men, pale and hung-over in their coat-tails. I have drunk gin myself in my time and I recognised that solemn expression they wore. One part pity, three parts I'll-*never*-drink-again. The men nodded at me. It is a peculiar sensation, as a woman with a very good job, to be pitied by men with tattoos and headaches. It's the way people will always look at me now, I suppose, as a foreigner in this country of my heart I should never have come to.

On the street in front of our house, the hearse and the limo stood waiting. I went out into the driveway to look through the green glass of the hearse. Andrew's coffin was there, lying on bright chrome rollers. Andrew, my husband of eight years. I thought: I should feel something now. I thought: Rollers. How practical.

On our street, the semi-detached houses stretched to infinity in both directions. The clouds scrolled across the sky, blandly oppressive, each one resembling the next, all threatening rain. I looked back at Andrew's coffin and I thought about his face. I thought about it dead. How slowly he had died, over those last two years. How imperceptible it had been, that transition in his facial expression, from deadly serious to seriously dead. Already those two faces were blurring together for me. My husband alive and my husband dead – they now seemed only semi-detached, as if under the coffin lid I would find the two of them fused like Siamese twins, eyes agape, looking to infinity in both directions.

And now this thought came into my head with the full clarity of horror: *Andrew was once a passionate, loving, brilliant man.*

Staring at my husband's coffin, I clung to this thought. I held it up before my own memory like a tentative flag of truce. I remembered Andrew at the newspaper we both worked for when we met, having a shouting match with his editor over some lofty point of principle that got him gloriously fired, on the spot, and sent him striding fierce and beautiful into the corridor. The first time that I thought, This is a man to be proud of. And then Andrew practically tripping over me eavesdropping in the corridor, open mouthed, pretending I was walking past on my way to the newsroom. Andrew grinning at me, unhesitatingly, and saying, *Fancy buying a former colleague a spot of dinner?* It was one in a billion. It was like catching lightning in a bottle.

The marriage cooled when Charlie was born. As if that one lightning strike was all we got, and most of the heat from it had to go into our child. Nigeria had accelerated the decline and now death had finished it, but my disaffection and my affair with Lawrence had come first. That was what my mind was stuck on, I realised. There was no quick grief for Andrew because he had been so slowly lost. First from my heart, then from my mind, and only finally from my life.

This, then, was when real sorrow arrived. This was the shock that set me trembling, as if something seismic had been released deep inside me and was blindly inching towards the surface. I trembled, but there was no release of tears.

I went back inside the house, and collected my son and Little Bee. Mismatched, dazed, semi-detached, we walked to my husband's funeral. Still shaking, in the pew, I understood that it isn't the dead we cry for. We cry for ourselves, and I didn't deserve my own pity.

After it was all over, someone or other drove us home. I clung on to Charlie in the back seat of a car. I remember the car smelled of stale cigarettes. I stroked Charlie's head and pointed out the everyday things that we passed, invoking the comfort of houses and shops and cars by the hopeful magic of whispering their names. Ordinary nouns were what we needed, I decided. Everyday things would get us through. Never mind that Charlie's Batman costume was covered in grave mud. When we got home I put it in the wash and I gave him the clean one. When it hurt too much to prise open the box of washing powder, I used the other hand.

I remember sitting with Charlie while we watched the water flood into the machine, rising behind the round glass door. The machine lurched into its familiar grinding preamble, and Charlie and I had a perfectly ordinary conversation. That was the worst moment for me. We talked about what he wanted for lunch. Charlie said he wanted crisps. I demurred. He insisted. I acquiesced. I was a pushover at that moment and my son knew it. I conceded on tomato ketchup and ice-cream too, and there was triumph in Charlie's face and horror in his eyes. I realised that for Charlie, and for me, there was extraordinary pain behind the ordinary nouns.

We ate, and then Little Bee took Charlie out into the garden to play. I had been so focused on my son that I had forgotten all about her and it actually surprised me that she was still there.

I sat very still at my kitchen table. My mother and my sister had come back with us from the church and they orbited me in a blur of fussing and tidying, so that if a photograph had been taken of us all with a very long exposure it would have shown only me, in sharp focus, surrounded by a ghostly halo that took its azure colour from my sister's cardigan and its eccentricity from my mother's tendency to close in on me at one end of her orbit, and ask if I was all right. I hardly heard her, I think. They carried on around me for an hour, respectful of my silence, washing the teacups without unnecessary clink, alphabetising condolence cards whilst minimising rustle, until I begged them, if they loved me, to go home.

After they left, with tender, drawn-out hugs that made me regret banishing them, I sat back down at the kitchen table and watched Little Bee playing in the garden with Batman. I suppose it had been reckless of us to abandon our home and spend the whole morning at a funeral. In our absence some baddies of the worst stripe had occupied the laurel bush, and now had to be flushed out with water pistols and bamboo canes. It seemed to be dangerous and painstaking work. First Little Bee would creep up to the laurel on her hands and knees, with the hem of her oversized Hawaiian shirt dragging in the dirt. When she spotted a lurking baddy she would jab at him with a yell, causing him to break out into the open. There my son was ready with the water pistol to deliver the *coup de grâce*. I marvelled at how quickly they had become a team. I wasn't sure I wanted them to be. But what was I to do? To stride out into the garden and say, *Little Bee, could you please stop making friends with my son?* My son would loudly demand an explanation and it would be no use telling him that Little Bee wasn't on our side. Not now that she and he had killed so many of those baddies together.

No, it wasn't going to work any more, denying her, or denying what had happened in Africa. A memory can be banished, even indefinitely, deported from consciousness by the relentless everydayness of running a successful magazine, mothering a son, and burying a husband. A human being, though, is a different thing entirely. The existence of a Nigerian girl, alive and standing in one's own garden – governments may deny such things, or brush them off as statistical anomalies, but human beings cannot.

131

I sat at the kitchen table and stared through suddenly wet eyes at the stump where my finger used to be. I realised that it was finally time to face up to what had happened on the beach.

It should never have happened, of course, in the ordinary run of things. There are countries of the world, and regions of one's own mind, where it is unwise to travel. I have always thought so, and I have always struck myself as a sensible woman. Independent of mind, but not recklessly so. I would love to have the same arm's-length relationship with foreign places that other sensible women seem to have.

Clever me, I went on holiday somewhere different. That season in Nigeria, there was an oil war. Andrew and I hadn't known. The struggle was brief, confused, and scarcely reported. The British and Nigerian governments both deny to this day that it even took place. God knows, they aren't the only ones who tried denial.

I still wonder why it came into my head to accept a holiday in Nigeria. I wish I could claim it was the only tourist board freebie that arrived at the magazine that spring, but we had boxes full of them – crates of unopened envelopes haemorrhaging Piz Buin from ruptured sample sachets. I could have chosen Tuscany, or Belize. The former Soviet states were big that season. But no. The cussed streak in me – the one that made me launch *Nixie* instead of joining some tamer glossy; the one that made me start an affair with Lawrence instead of mending my fences with Andrew – that enduring outward-bound streak gave me an adolescent thrill when a package landed on my desk emblazoned with the question FOR YOUR HOLIDAY THIS YEAR, WHY NOT TRY NIGERIA? Some wag on my editorial staff had scrawled under this, in chunky black marker, the obvious response. But I was intrigued, and I opened the package. Out fell two open-ended airline tickets and a hotel reservation. It was as simple as turning up at the airport with a bikini.

Andrew came with me, against his better judgement. The Foreign Office were advising against travel to some parts of Nigeria, but we didn't think that included ours. He took some convincing, but I reminded him that we'd taken our honeymoon in Cuba, and parts of that place were horrific. Andrew gave in. Looking back on it now I suppose he thought he had no choice if he wanted to keep me.

The tourist board that sent the freebies noted that Ibeno Beach was an 'adventurous destination'. Actually, at the time we went, it was a cataclysm with borders. To the north, there was a malarial jungle and to the west, a wide brown river delta. The river was iridescent with oil. It was, I now know, bloated with the corpses of oil workers. To the south was the Atlantic Ocean. On that southern edge I met a girl who was not my magazine's target reader. Little Bee had fled south-east on bleeding feet from what had once been her village and was shortly to become an oilfield. She fled from the men who would kill her because they were paid to, and the children who would kill her because they were told to. I sat at my kitchen table and I imagined her fleeing through the fields and the jungle, as fast as she could, until she arrived at the beach where Andrew and I were being unconventional. That beach was as far as she got.

My missing finger itched, just thinking about it.

When they came in from the garden, I sent Batman to play in his bat cave and I showed Little Bee where the shower was. I found some clothes for her. Later, when Batman was in bed, I made two G&Ts. Little Bee sat and held hers in her hands, rattling the ice-cubes. I drank mine down like medicine.

'All right,' I said. 'I'm ready. I'm ready for you to tell me what happened.'

'You want to know how I survived?'

'Start from the beginning, will you? Tell me how it was when you first reached the sea.'

So she told me how she hid, on the day she arrived at the beach. She had been running for six days, travelling through the fields by night and hiding in jungles and swamps when daybreak came. I turned off the radio in the kitchen, and I sat very quietly while she told me how she holed up in a salient of jungle that grew right down to the sand. She lay there all through the hottest part of the day, watching the waves. She told me she hadn't seen the sea before, and she didn't quite believe in it.

In the late afternoon, Little Bee's sister, Nkiruka, came down out of the jungle and found her hiding place. She sat down next to her. They hugged for a long time. They were happy that Nkiruka had managed to follow Little Bee's trail, but they were scared because it meant that others could do it too. Nkiruka looked into her sister's eyes and said that they must make-up new names for themselves. It was not safe to use their true names, which spoke so loudly of their tribe and of their region. Nkiruka said her name was 'Kindness' now. Her younger sister wanted to reply to Kindness, but she could not think of a name for herself.

The two sisters waited. The shadows were deepening. A pair of hornbills came to crack seeds in the trees above their heads. And then – sitting at my kitchen table she said she remembered this so clearly that she could almost reach out and stroke the fuzzy black back of the thing – a bee blew in on the sea breeze and it landed between the two sisters. The bee was small and it touched down on a pale flower – frangipani, she told me, although she said she wasn't sure about the European name – and then the bee flew off again, without any fuss. She hadn't noticed the flower before the bee came, but now she saw that the flower was beautiful. She turned to Kindness.

'My name is Little Bee,' she said.

When she heard this name, Kindness smiled. Little Bee told me that her big sister was a very pretty girl. She was the kind of girl the men said could make them forget their troubles. She was the kind of girl the women said *was* trouble. Little Bee wondered which it was going to be.

The two sisters lay still and quiet till sunset. Then they crept down the sand to wash their feet in the surf. The salt stung in their cuts but they did not cry out. It was sensible of them to keep quiet. The men chasing them might have given up, or they might not. The trouble was, the sisters had seen what had been done to their village. There weren't supposed to be any survivors to tell the story. The men were hunting down the fleeing women and children and burying their bodies under branches and rocks.

Back under cover, the girls bound each other's feet in fresh green leaves and they waited for the dawn. It was not cold, but they hadn't eaten for two days. They shivered. Monkeys screamed under the moon.

I still think about the two sisters there, shivering through the night. While I watch them in my mind, again and again, small pink crabs follow the thin smell of blood to the place where their feet recently stood in the shorebreak, but they do not find anything dead there yet. The soft pink crabs make hard little clicking noises under the bright white stars. One by one, they dig themselves back into the sand to wait.

I wish my brain did not fill in the frightful details like this. I wish I was a woman who cared deeply about shoes and concealer. I wish I was not the sort of woman who ended up sitting at her kitchen table listening to a refugee girl talking about her awful fear of the dawn.

The way Little Bee told it, at sunrise there was a white mist hanging thick in the jungle and spilling out over the sand. The sisters watched a white couple walking up the beach. The language they spoke was the official language of Little Bee's country, but these were the first whites she had seen. She and Kindness watched them from behind a stand of palms. They drew back when the couple came level with their hiding place. The whites stopped to look out at the sea.

'Listen to that surf, Andrew,' the white woman said. 'It's so unbelievably peaceful here.'

'I'm still a bit scared, frankly. We should go back inside the hotel compound.'

The white woman smiled. 'Compounds are made for stepping outside. I was scared of you, the first time I met you.'

'Course you were. Big Irish hunk of love like me. We're savages, don't you know.'

'Barbarians.'

'Vagabonds.'

'Cunts.'

'Oh, come on now, dear, that's just your mother talking.'

The white woman laughed, and pulled herself close to the man's body. She kissed him on the cheek.

'I love you, Andrew. I'm pleased we came away. I'm so sorry I let you down. It won't happen again.'

'Really?'

'Really. I don't love Lawrence. How could I? Let's make a fresh start, hmm?'

On the beach, the white man smiled. In the shadows, Little Bee cupped her hand over Kindness's ear. She whispered: *What is a cunt?* Kindness looked back at her, and rolled her

eyes. *Right down there, girl, right close to your vagabond.*
Little Bee bit her hand so she wouldn't giggle.

But then the sisters heard dogs. They could hear everything,
because there was a cool morning breeze, a land breeze that
carried all sounds. The dogs were still a long way off, but the
sisters heard them barking. Kindness grabbed Little Bee's
arm. Down on the beach, the white woman looked up at the
jungle.

'Oh, listen, Andrew,' she said. 'Dogs!'

'Probably the local lads are hunting. Must be plenty to
catch in this jungle.'

'Still, I wouldn't have thought they'd use dogs.'

'So what in the hell did you think they'd use?'

The white woman shrugged. 'I don't know,' she said.
'Elephants?'

The white man laughed. 'You insufferable English,' he
said. 'The empire's still alive for you, isn't it? You only need
to close your eyes.'

Now a soldier came running up the beach from the direction the white couple had come. He was panting. He wore
olive-green trousers and a light grey vest dark with sweat. He
had military boots on, and they were heavy with damp sand.
He had a rifle slung on his back, and the barrel was swinging
at the sky.

'Oh, for fuck's sake,' the white man said, 'here comes that
doofus of a guard again.'

'He's only doing his job.'

'Yeah, but can't they let us do our own thing even for one minute?'

'Oh, relax. The holiday was free, remember? We were never going to have it all our own way.'

The guard came level with the white couple and he stopped. He was coughing. He had his hands on his knees.

'Please, mister, missus,' he said. 'Sorry please to come back to hotel compound.'

'But why?' the white woman said. 'We were just going for a walk along the beach.'

'It is not safe, missus,' the guard said. 'Not safe for you and mister. Sorry, boss.'

'But why?' said the white man. 'What is actually the problem?'

'No problem,' said the guard. 'Here is very good place. Very good. But all tourist must stay please in hotel compound.'

Unseen in the jungle, the dogs were barking louder now. The sisters could hear the shouts of the men running with them. Kindness was trembling. The two sisters held each other. Now one of the dogs howled and the others joined in. In the hiding place there was a splashing on the dry leaves and a smell of urine – the reality of Kindness's fear. Little Bee looked into her eyes. It didn't look as if her sister was even seeing her.

Down on the beach the white man was saying, 'Is this about money?'

And the guard was saying, 'No, mister.'

The guard stood up straight and looked into the jungle where the noise of the dogs was. He unslung his rifle. Little Bee saw the way he held it. He took the safety catch off and he reached down to check the magazine. Two magazines – I remember that myself – bound back-to-back with blue insulation tape.

The white man said, 'Oh, don't give us the big performance. Just tell us how much you want. Come on. My wife is sick to the gills of being cooped up in that fuckin' compound. What will you take to let us go for a walk on our own? One dollar?'

The guard shook his head. He wasn't looking at the white man. He was watching a flock of red birds flying up from the jungle, two hundred yards away.

'No dollar,' the guard said.

'Ten dollars, then,' the white woman said.

'Oh, for the love of God, Sarah,' the white man said. 'That is *way* too much. That's a week's wages here.'

'Don't be such a tight-arse,' the white woman said. 'What's ten dollars to us? It's nice to be able to do something for these people. God knows they have little enough.'

'Well, look then, five dollars,' the white man said.

The guard was watching the treetops. One hundred and fifty yards away, up a shallow gully, the tips of the palm ferns were twitching.

'You come back with me now,' the guard said. 'Hotel compound is best for you.'

'Listen,' the white man said. 'I'm sorry if we offended you by offering money and I respect you for not taking it. But I have my editor telling me what's best for me fifty-one weeks of the year. I didn't come here to have anyone edit my holiday.'

The guard lifted the muzzle of his gun. He fired three shots in the air, just above the white man's head. The barking of the dogs and the yelling of the men stopped for a moment. Then they started up again, louder. The white couple stood very still. Their mouths were open. They were struck, perhaps, by the bullets that had missed them.

'Please, mister and missus,' the guard said. 'Trouble is come here. You do not know my country.'

The sisters heard the thwack of machetes clearing a path. Kindness grabbed Little Bee's hand and pulled her to her feet. The two sisters walked out of the cover of the jungle and onto the sand. Holding hands, they stood there looking up at the white man and the white woman – Andrew, and me – in hope and expectation. I suppose there was nothing else in the developing world they could do.

They stood on the sand, clutching one another, keeping themselves upright on their failing legs, Kindness straining her head to watch for the approaching dogs, but Little Bee looking steadily at me, ignoring Andrew, ignoring the guard.

'Please, missus,' she said, 'take us to the hotel compound with you.'

The guard looked at her, then he looked back up at the jungle. He shook his head.

'Hotel compound is for tourist,' he said. 'Not for you girls.'

'Please,' said Little Bee, looking directly at me. 'Bad men are hunting us. They will kill us.'

She spoke to me as a woman, knowing I would understand. But I didn't understand. Three days earlier, just before we left for Heathrow, I had been standing on a bare concrete slab in our garden, asking Andrew exactly when the hell he planned to build his bloody glasshouse there. That was the biggest issue in my life – that glasshouse, or the lack of it. That absent glasshouse, and all other structures past and future that might helpfully be erected in the larger emotional absence between me and my husband. I was a modern woman and disappointment was something I understood better than fear. The hunters would *kill* her? My stomach lurched, but my mind still asserted it was just a figure of speech.

'Oh, for goodness' sake,' I said. 'You're a child. Why would anyone want to kill you?'

Little Bee looked back at me and she said, 'Because we saw them killing everyone else.'

I opened my mouth but Andrew spoke first. I think he was suffering the same intellectual jetlag. As if our hearts had now arrived on the beach but our minds were still hours behind. Andrew's eyes were terrified but his voice said, 'This is fuckin' bullshit. This is a classic Nigeria scam. Come on, we're going back to the hotel.'

Andrew started to pull me back along the beach. I went with him, twisting my head to look back at the sisters. The guard followed behind us. He walked backwards and aimed his gun at the jungle. Little Bee followed with Kindness, ten yards behind.

The guard said, 'You girls stop following us.'

He pointed his gun at the sisters. They looked right back at him. The guard was slightly older than the girls, maybe sixteen or seventeen, and he had a thin moustache. I suppose he was proud he could grow one. He had a green beret and there was sweat trickling from under it. I could see the veins in his temples. The whites of his eyes were yellow.

Little Bee said, 'What is your name, soldier?'

And he said, 'My name is "I will shoot if you don't stop following".'

Little Bee shrugged and tapped her chest. 'My name is Little Bee,' she said. 'Here is my heart. Shoot here if you want.'

And Kindness said, 'Bullets is okay. Bullets is quick.'

They kept on following us along the beach. The guard's eyes went wide. 'Who is chasing you girls?'

'The same men who burned our village. The oil company's men.'

The rifle began to shake in the guard's hand. '*Christjesus*,' he said.

There were men's shouts and dogs' barking, very loud now. I couldn't hear the surf any more.

143

Five brown dogs came out of the jungle, running. They were mad from howling. Their sides and their paws were bleeding from the jungle thorns. The sisters screamed and ran past the guard. The guard stopped and he lifted his gun and he fired. The lead dog somersaulted over in the sand. His ear was shot off and a piece of his head too, I think. The pack of dogs skidded and stopped and they tore into the fallen dog. They were biting out chunks of the neck flesh while the back legs were still thrashing and twitching. I screamed. The guard was shaking.

From out of the jungle, six men came running. They wore tracksuit trousers, all torn, and vests and running shoes, gold chains. They moved quickly up on us. They ignored the dogs. One was holding a bow, holding it drawn. The others were waving their machetes, daring the guard to shoot. They came right up to us.

There was a leader. He had a wound in his neck. It was rotting – I could smell it. I knew he was going to die soon. Another of the men wore a wire necklace and it was strung with dried brown things that looked like mushrooms. When he saw Kindness, this man pointed at her, then he made circles on his nipples with his fingers and he grinned. I am trying to report this as matter-of-factly as I know how.

The guard said, 'Keep walking, mister and missus.'

But the man with the neck wound – the leader – said, 'No, you stop.'

'I will shoot,' the guard said.

But the man said, 'Maybe you will get one of us, maybe two.'

The man with the bow was aiming at the guard's neck, and he said, 'Maybe you get none of us. Maybe you should of shoot us when we was far away.'

The guard stopped walking backwards, and we stopped too. Little Bee and Kindness went round behind us. They put me and my husband between themselves and the hunters.

The hunters were passing round a bottle of something I thought was wine. They were taking turns to drink. The man with the bow and arrows was getting an erection. I could see it under his tracksuit trousers. But his expression didn't change and his eyes never moved from our guard's neck. He was wearing a black bandanna. The bandanna said EMPORIO ARMANI. I looked at Andrew. I tried to speak calmly, but the words were crushed in my throat.

'Andrew,' I said. 'Please give them anything they want.'

Andrew looked at the man with the neck wound and he said, 'What do you want?'

The hunters looked at each other. The man with the neck wound stepped up to me. His eyes flickered, rolled up inside his head, then snapped back down and stared madly at me, the pupils tiny and the irises bullet-hard and gleaming like copper. His mouth twitched from a smile, to a grimace, to a cruel thin line, to a bitter and amused disdain. The emotions played across his face like a television flipped impatiently between channels. I smelled his sweat and his rot. He made a sound, an involuntary moan which seemed to surprise him – his eyes went wide – and he tore off my beach wrap. He looked down at the pale lilac material in his hands, curiously, and seemed to be wondering how it had got there. I screamed and clasped my arms over my breasts. I cringed away from the man, from the way he looked at me – now patiently, as if encouraging a slow learner; now furiously; now with a pregnant, vespertine calm.

I was wearing a very small green bikini. I will say that again, and maybe I will begin to understand it myself. In the contested delta area of an African country in the middle of a three-way oil war, because there was a beach next to the war, because the state tourist board had mail merged tickets for that beach to every magazine listed in the *Writers' and Artists' Yearbook*, because it was that year's cut, and because as editor I was first in the queue when distributors sent their own freebies to my magazine's office, I was wearing a very small green bandeau bikini from Hermès. It occurred to me, as I stood there with my arms crossed over my tits, that I had freeloaded myself to annihilation.

The wounded man stepped so close to me that I felt the sand sink under my feet from his weight. He ran his finger over my shoulder, over my bare skin, and he said, 'What do we *want*? We want . . . to practise . . . our English.'

The hunters exploded into laughter. They passed round the bottle again. For a moment, when one of them raised the bottle, I saw something with a pupil staring out of it. It was pressed up against the glass. Then the man put the bottle down, and the thing disappeared back into the liquid. I say liquid because I didn't think it was wine any more.

Andrew said, 'We have money, and we can get more later.'

The wounded man giggled and made a noise like a pig, which made him giggle more. Then his face set suddenly into an expression of complete seriousness. He said, 'You give me what you got now. There is no later.'

Andrew took his wallet from his pocket. He passed it to the wounded man. The man took it – his hand was shaking – and he pulled out the banknotes and threw the wallet down on the sand. He passed the money behind him to the men, without looking or counting. He was breathing very heavily and there was sweat running down his face. His neck wound was wide open. It was green-blue. It was obscene.

I said, 'You need medical attention. We could get help for you at the hotel.'

The man said, 'Medicine not fix what these girls have seen. These girls got to pay for what they seen. Give me the girls.'

I said, 'No.'

The wounded man looked at me, astonished. 'What you say?'

'I said no. These girls are coming with us to the compound. If you try to stop them, our guard will shoot you.'

The wounded man widened his eyes in an indulgent simulacrum of fear. He put both his hands on the top of his head and turned himself through two shuffling circles on the sand. When he faced me again he grinned and said, 'Where are you from, missus?'

'We live in Kingston,' I said.

The man cocked his head and looked interestedly at me.

'Kingston-upon-Thames,' I said. 'It's in London.'

The man nodded. 'I know where Kingston is,' he said. 'I studied mechanical engineering there.'

He looked down at the sand. He stood in silence for a moment. Then he moved, and it was very quick. I saw his machete go up, I saw the blade flash in the rising sun, I saw a tiny flinch – that was all the guard had time for. The blade went into the guard's throat and it rang. It rang when it struck the bones of the neck. The metal was still ringing when the man yanked it out and the guard dropped into the sand. The blade rang, I remember, as if the machete was a bell and the guard's life was the clapper.

The killer said, 'You ever hear a noise like that in Kingston-upon-Thames?'

There seemed to be more blood than one skinny African boy could possibly have had inside him. It went on and on. That guard lying there with sand covering his eyeballs and his neck gaping, as if it was hanging on a hinge, wide open. It looked like a mouth. This very calm, middle-class voice in my head said: *Pac-Man. Pac-Man. Oh gosh, he looks just like Pac-Man.* We all stood in silence as we watched the guard bleed to death. It took the longest time. I remember thinking, *Thank God we left Charlie with my parents.*

When I lifted my head, the killer was watching me. It wasn't a mean expression. I have seen checkout girls look at me like that when I forget my reward card. I have seen Lawrence look at me that way when I tell him I have my period. The killer was watching me with an expression, really, of mild annoyance.

'This guard died because of you,' he said.

I must have felt things, back in those days, because tears were running down my face.

'You're crazy,' I said.

The killer shook his head. He made a steeple of his fingers around the handle of the machete, held it up so that the point aligned with my throat, and eyed me sorrowfully along the trembling axis of the blade.

'I live here,' he said. 'You were crazy to come.'

I began to cry then, out of fear. Andrew was shaking. Kindness began to pray in her tribal language.

'Ekenem-i Maria,' she said, 'gratia ju-i obi Dinweni nonyel-i, I nwe ngozi kali ikporo nine na ngozi dili nwa afo-i bu Jesu.'

The killer looked up at Kindness and he said, 'You will die next.'

Kindness looked back at him. 'Nso Maria Nne Ciuku,' she said, 'yo nyel'anyi bu ndi njo, kita, n'ubosi nke onwu anyi. Amen.'

The killer nodded. He breathed. I heard the cold surf in ebb and resurgent. The brown dogs left off the carcass of the killed dog and they came closer. They stood with their legs trembling and their hackles up, the blood stiff on their fur. The killer took one step towards Kindness but I did not think my mind could survive seeing the machete cut into her.

I said, 'No. Please . . . please, leave her alone.'

The killer stopped and he turned to me and he said, 'You again?'

He was smiling.

Andrew said, 'Sarah, please, I think the best thing we can do here is to . . .'

'To *what*, Andrew? To shut up and hope they won't get round to killing us too?'

'I just think this is not our affair and so . . .'

'Ah,' the killer said. 'Not your affair.'

He turned to the other hunters and spread his arms.

'Not his affair, him say. Him say, this is black man business. Ha ha ha ha!'

The hunters laughed. They slapped each other on the back and the dogs started to circle us. When the killer turned back, his face was serious.

'First time I hear white man say my business not his business. You got our gold. You got our oil. What is wrong with our girls?'

'Nothing,' said poor Andrew. 'I didn't mean that.'

'Are you a racist?'

Rassist, was how he pronounced the word.

'No, of course not.'

The killer stared at Andrew. 'Well?' he said. 'You want to save these girls, mister?'

Andrew coughed. I watched him. My husband's hands twitched – his strong, fine hands I had often watched, gripping coffees, clicking across keyboards, making deadlines. My husband, who had filed his Sunday column from the departure lounge of the airport the previous day, down to the wire as usual. I'd been scanning it for typos when they called our flight. The last paragraph went: *We are a self-interested society. How will our children learn to put others before themselves, if we do not?*

'Well?' said the killer. 'You want to save them?'

Andrew looked down at his hands. He stood like that for a long time. Above us, seabirds circled and called to each other in that agonised way they have. I tried to stop my legs from shaking.

'Please,' I said. 'If you will let us take the girls with us, then we will do whatever you want. Let us all go back to the compound, please, and we will give you anything. Money, medicine, anything.'

The killer made a high, shrill yelp and a shiver shook his whole body. He giggled, and a dribble of blood escaped through his neat white teeth to splash down onto the dirty green nylon of his tracksuit top.

'You think I care bout that stuff?' he said. 'You don't see this hole in my neck? I am dead in two days. You think I care bout money and medicine?'

'So what do you want?' Andrew said.

The killer moved his machete from his right hand to his left. He raised his right hand with the middle finger extended. He held it, shaking, one inch from Andrew's face and he said, 'White man been giving me this finger all my life. Today you can give it me to keep. Now cut off your middle finger, mister, and give it me.'

Andrew flinched and he shook his head and he curled his hands into balls. He folded the thumbs over the fingers. The killer took his machete by the blade and he held the handle out to my husband.

'Do it,' he said. 'Chop chop. Give me your finger and I will give you the girls.'

A long pause.

'What if I don't?'

'Then you are free to go. But first you will hear the noises these children make dying. You ever hear a girl dying slow?'

'No.'

The killer closed his eyes and shook his head, unhurriedly.

'It is nasty music,' he said. 'You will not forget. Maybe one day you will wake up in Kingston-upon-Thames and you will understand you lost more than your finger.'

Little Bee was crying now. Kindness held her hand.

'Do not be afraid,' she said. 'If they kill us today we will eat bread tonight with Jesus.'

The killer snapped open his eyes and he stared at Andrew and he said, 'Please, mister. I am not a savage. I do not want to kill these girls.'

Andrew reached out his hand and he took the killer's machete. There was blood on the handle, the guard's blood. Andrew looked across at me. I stepped over to him and I put my hand on his chest, gently. I was crying.

'Oh, Andrew. I think you have to do it.'

'I can't.'

'It's just a finger.'

'We didn't do anything wrong. We were just walking down the beach.'

'Just a finger, Andrew, and then we'll walk back again.'

Andrew sank to his knees in the sand. He said, 'I can't believe this is happening.' He looked at the machete blade and he scraped it on the sand to clean it. He put his left hand on the sand, palm up, and he folded all the fingers except the middle one. Then he held up the machete in his right hand, but he didn't bring it down. He said, 'How do we know he won't kill the girls anyway, Sarah, after I've done it?'

'You'll know you did what you could.'

'I could get Aids from this blade. I could die.'

'I'll be with you. I'm so proud of you.'

It was quiet on the beach. Seabirds hung low in the hot blue sky, without flapping their wings, upheld on the sea breeze. The rhythm of the surf was unchanged, although the interval between one wave and the next seemed infinite. I watched with the girls and the men and the bloodied dogs to see what my husband would do, and it seemed in that moment that we were all the same, just creatures in nature hanging without

153

any great effort upon the vast warm wind of events that were greater than us.

Andrew screamed, then, and he chopped down with the machete. The blade made a whipping sound in the hot air. Then it sliced down into the sand. It was really quite far from his hand.

'I won't do it,' he said. 'This is just fuckin' bullshit. I don't believe he'll let the girls go. Look at him. He's just going to kill them whatever.'

Andrew stood, and he left the machete in the sand. I looked at him, and that is when I stopped feeling. I realised I was no longer scared. And I wasn't angry with Andrew. When I looked at him I hardly saw a man any more. I thought we would all be killed now, and it worried me much less than I would have expected. It troubled me that we had never got around to building the glasshouse at the end of our garden. A sensible thought occurred to me: *How lucky I am to have two healthy parents who will take good care of Charlie.*

The killer sighed and he shrugged and he said, 'Okay, Mister made his choice. Now, Mister, run back home to England. You can tell them you came to Africa and you met a real savage.'

When the killer turned away, I dropped to my knees. I looked straight at Little Bee. She saw what the killer did not see. She saw the white woman put her own left hand down on the hard sand, and she saw her pick up the machete, and she saw her chop off her middle finger with one simple chop, like a girl topping a carrot, neatly, on a quiet Surrey Saturday, between gymkhana and lunch. She saw her drop the machete and rock back on her heels, holding her hand. I suppose the white woman looked just amazed.

'Oh,' I think I said. 'Oh, oh, oh.'

The killer span round and he saw me with the blood welling through my closed fist. On the sand in front of me, there was my finger lying. The finger looked silly and naked. I was embarrassed for it. The killer's eyes went wide.

'Oh fuck, oh fuck,' Andrew said. 'Oh, what the fuck have you done, Sarah? What the fuck have you done?'

He knelt down and he hugged me to him but I pushed him away with my good hand. There was mucus streaming from my mouth and nose.

'It hurts, Andrew. It hurts, you *shit*.'

The killer nodded. He reached down and he picked up my dead finger. He pointed it at Little Bee.

'You will live,' he said. 'The missus has paid for your life.'

Then he pointed my finger at Kindness.

'But you will die, little one,' he said. 'The mister would not pay for you. And my boys, you know, they must have their taste of blood.'

Kindness gripped Little Bee's hand. She held her head up.

'I am not afraid,' she said. 'The Lord is my shepherd.'

The killer sighed.

'Then he is a vain and careless shepherd,' he said.

Then – and it was louder than the surf – there was the sound of my husband sobbing.

Two years later, sitting at my table in Kingston-upon-Thames, I found I could still hear it. I stared down at my damaged hand, spread palm-down on the blue tablecloth.

Little Bee had fallen asleep on the sofa, with her G&T untouched by her side. I realised I couldn't remember the point at which she had stopped telling the story and I had picked up remembering it. I stood up from the kitchen table to fix myself another drink. There were no lemons, so I made do with a little squirt of plasticky juice from the Jif lemon in the fridge. When I picked up my glass, the ice-cubes rattled uncontrollably. The G&T tasted vile but it gave me courage. I picked up the phone and dialled the number of the man I suppose I must call my 'lover', although that word rather makes me squirm.

I realised it was the second time I'd phoned Lawrence that day. I'd been trying not to. I'd lasted almost a whole week, since Andrew died. It was the longest I'd been faithful to my husband in years.

'Sarah? Is that you?'

Lawrence's voice was a whisper. My throat tightened. I found that I couldn't reply straight away.

'Sarah? I've been thinking about you all day. Was it horrible? You should have let me come to the funeral.'

I swallowed. 'It would have been inappropriate.'

'Oh, Sarah, who would have known?'

'I would have known, Lawrence. My conscience is about all I've got left.'

Silence. His slow breath over the phone. 'It's okay to still love Andrew, you know. It's okay with me, anyway.'

'You think I still love him?'

'I'm suggesting it. In case it helps.'

I laughed – an almost inaudible exhalation of air.

'Everybody's trying to help me today. Even Charlie went to bed without the slightest fuss.'

'It's normal that people want to help. You're suffering.'

'Insufferable, is what I am. It amazes me that people like you still care about me.'

'You're being hard on yourself.'

'Am I? I saw my husband's coffin today, being shunted about on rollers. When are you going to take a look at yourself, if not on a day like this?'

'Mmm,' said Lawrence.

'Not many men would cut off a finger, would they, Lawrence?'

'What? No. I definitely don't think I would.'

My throat burned. 'I expected too much of Andrew, didn't I? Not just on the beach. I expected too much of life.'

A long silence.

'What did you expect of me?' said Lawrence.

The question caught me unprepared and there was anger in his voice. My phone hand trembled.

'You're using the past tense,' I said. 'I wish you wouldn't.'

157

'No?'

'No. Please, no.'

'Oh. I thought that's what this call was about. I was thinking, That's why she didn't ask me to the funeral. Because this is the way you'd do, isn't it, if you broke up with me? There'd be preamble where you reminded me what a difficult person you are, and then you'd prove it.'

'Please, Lawrence. That's horrible.'

'Oh, God, I know. I'm sorry.'

'Please don't be angry with me. I'm phoning to ask your advice.'

A pause. Then a laugh down the phone. Not bitter, but bleak.

'You don't ask for advice, Sarah.'

'No?'

'No. Not ever. Not about things that matter, anyway. You ask whether your tights look right with your shoes. You ask which bracelet suits your wrist. You're not asking for input. You're asking your admirers to prove they're paying attention.'

'Am I really that bad?'

'Actually you're worse. Because if I do ever tell you gold looks nice with your skin, you make a special point of wearing silver.'

'Do I? I never even noticed. I'm sorry.'

'Don't be. I love that you don't even notice. There are plenty of women who care what one thinks of their jewellery.'

I swirled my G&T and took a careful sip.

'You're trying to make me feel better about myself, aren't you?'

'I'm just saying you're not the kind of woman you meet every day.'

'And that's praise, is it?'

'It's relative praise, yes. Now stop fishing.'

I smiled, for the first time in a week, I think.

'We've never talked like this before, have we?' I said. 'Talked honestly, I mean.'

'You want the honest answer?'

'Apparently not.'

'I have talked honestly and you haven't listened.'

Around me the house was dark and silent. The only sound was the rattle of the ice-cubes in my drink. When I spoke, my voice had a break in it.

'I'm listening now, Lawrence. God knows, I'm listening now.'

A brief silence. Then another voice carried over the line. It was Lawrence's wife Linda, shouting in the background: *Who's on the phone?* And Lawrence shouted back: *Just someone from work.*

Oh, Lawrence. As if one would throw in that 'just', if it really was someone from work. You would simply say, *It's work*, wouldn't you? I thought about Linda then, and how it must feel to have to share Lawrence with me. Her cold fury – not at the necessity of sharing, but at Lawrence's naïvety in imagining that Linda didn't absolutely *know*. I thought about how the deceit must have acquired a certain uneven symmetry in their couple. I imagined the drab and ordinary lover that Linda would have taken in revenge – in spite and in haste. Oh, it was too awful. Out of respect for Linda, I hung up.

I steadied the hand that gripped my G&T and I looked over at Little Bee, sleeping. The memories from the beach swirled in my mind, inchoate, senseless, awful. I called Lawrence again.

'Can you come over?'

'I'd love to but I can't tonight. Linda's going out with a friend and I've got the kids.'

'Can you get a babysitter?'

I realised I sounded plaintive, and I cursed myself for it. Lawrence had picked up my tone too.

'Darling?' he said. 'You know I'd come if I could, don't you?'

'Sure.'

'Will you cope okay without me?'

'Of course.'

'How?'

'Oh, I dare say I'll cope the way British women always used to cope, before the invention of weakness.'

Lawrence laughed. 'Fine. Look, you said you wanted advice. Can we talk about it on the phone?'

'Yes. Of course. I. Look. I need to tell you something. It's all got a little bit complicated. Little Bee turned up here this morning.'

'Who?'

'One of the Nigerian girls. From that day on the beach.'

'Jesus! I thought you said the men killed her.'

'I was sure they had. I saw the men drag her off. Her and the other one. I watched them being dragged kicking and screaming up the beach. I watched them till they were tiny dots and something in me just died.'

'But now, what? She just turned up on your doorstep?'

'This morning. Two hours before the funeral.'

'And you let her *in*?'

'Wouldn't anyone?'

'No, Sarah. Most people would not.'

'It was as if she'd returned from the dead, Lawrence. I could hardly just slam the door on her.'

'But where was she, then, if she wasn't dead?'

'On a boat, apparently. She got out of the country and came here. Then she was two years in an immigration detention centre in Essex.'

'A detention centre? Christ, what did she do?'

'Nothing. Asylum seekers, apparently they just lock them up when they arrive here.'

'For two *years*?'

'You don't believe me?'

'I don't believe *her*. Two *years* in detention? She must have done something.'

'She was African and she didn't have any money. I suppose they gave her a year for each.'

'Don't be facetious. How did she find you?'

'Apparently she had Andrew's driving licence. He dropped his wallet in the sand.'

'Oh my God. And she's still *there*?'

'She's asleep on my sofa.'

'You must be completely freaked out.'

'This morning I thought I was losing my mind. It didn't seem real.'

'Why didn't you call me?'

'I did, remember? Your nanny was late. You were in a rush.'

'Is she threatening you? Tell me you've called the police.'

'No, it's not like that. She played really nicely with Charlie, all afternoon. He was Batman, she was Robin. They made quite a team.'

'And that doesn't freak you out?'

'If I start freaking out now, I won't ever know how to stop.'

'But what's she *doing* there? What does she want?'

'I suppose she wants to stay here for a while. She says she doesn't know anyone else.'

'Are you serious? *Can* she stay? Legally, I mean?'

'I'm not sure. I haven't asked. She's exhausted. I think she walked here all the way from the detention centre.'

'She's insane.'

'She didn't have any money. She could hardly take a bus.'

'Look, I don't like it. I'm worried about you being all alone with her.'

'So what do you think I should do?'

'I think you should wake her up and ask her to leave. I'm serious.'

'Leave for where? What if she refuses?'

'Then I want you to call the police and have her removed.'

I said nothing.

'Do you hear me, Sarah? I want you to call the police.'

'I heard you. I wish you wouldn't say "*I want*".'

'It's you I'm thinking about. What if she turns nasty?'

'Little Bee? I don't think she's got a nasty bone in her.'

'How do you know? You know nothing about the woman. What if she comes into your room in the night with a kitchen knife? What if she's crazy?'

I shook my head. 'My son would know, Lawrence. His bat senses would tell him.'

'*Fuck*, Sarah! This isn't funny! Call the police.'

I looked at Little Bee, fast asleep on my sofa with her mouth slightly open and her knees drawn up to her chest. I fell silent.

'Sarah?'

'I'm not going to call the police. I'm going to let her stay.'

'But why? What possible good can come of this?'

'I couldn't help her last time. Maybe now I can.'

'And that would prove what, exactly?'

I sighed. 'I suppose it would prove your point, Lawrence, about me not being good at taking advice.'

'You know that's not what I meant.'

'Yes. Which brings us back to my original point.'

'Which was what?'

'That I'm difficult sometimes.'

Lawrence laughed, but I think he was forcing himself.

I put down the phone and stared for a long time at the long, smooth white planks of the kitchen floor. Then I went upstairs to sleep on the floor of my son's room. I wanted to be there with him. I admitted to myself that Lawrence had a point: I didn't know what Little Bee might do in the night.

Sitting with my back against the cold radiator of Charlie's bedroom, with my knees bunched up under a duvet, I tried to remember what I saw in Lawrence. I finished my G&T and winced at the taste of the ersatz lemon. It was a small problem to have: a lack of real lemons. It was almost a comfort. I come from a family whose problems were always small and surmountable.

We didn't have extra-marital affairs in my family. Mummy and Daddy loved each other very much, or else they had hired failed actors to play the role of affable lovebirds in our family home, for twenty-five years, and then kept those actors on a retainer so that they could be summoned back at the drop of a hat whenever one of their clients' offspring threatened a weekend visit home from university, or a Sunday-lunch-with-parents-and-boyfriend. In my family we took our holidays in Devon and our partners for life. I wondered how it was that I had broken the mould.

I looked over at my son, asleep under his duvet, motionless and pale in his Batman costume. I listened to the sound of his breathing, regular and solid and utterly asleep. I couldn't remember sleeping like that, not since I married Andrew. Within the first month, I'd known he wasn't the right man. After that, it's the growing sense of dissatisfaction that keeps one awake at night. The brain refusing to let go of those alternative lives that might have been. It isn't the strong sleepers who sleep around.

But I was a happy child, at least, and my name was Sarah Summers. I still use Summers as my professional name, but personally it is lost. As a girl I liked what all girls like: pink plastic bracelets and later silver ones; a few practice boy-friends and then, in no particular hurry, men. England was made of dawn mists that rose to the horse's shoulder, of cakes cooled on wire trays for the cutting, of soft awakenings. My first real choice was what to take at university. My teachers all said I should study law, so naturally I chose journalism. I met Andrew O'Rourke when we were both working on a London evening paper. Ours seemed to perfectly express the spirit of the city. Thirty-one pages of celebrity goings-on about town, and one page of news from the world which existed beyond London's orbital motorway – the paper offered it up as a sort of *memento mori*.

London was fun. Men blew through like tall ships, some of them already wrecked. I liked Andrew because he wasn't like the rest. Maybe it was his Irish blood, but he wouldn't let himself be carried along. Andrew was the foreign news editor at the paper, which was a bit like being the wheels on a boat.

He was fired for sheer obstinacy and I took him home to meet my parents. Then I took his name so that no one else could have it.

O'Rourke is a sharp name and I imagined my happiness would soften it. But as Sarah O'Rourke I lost the habit of happiness. In its place came a sense of amazed separation. The marriage was all so sudden. I suppose if I'd stopped to think about it, I would have realised that Andrew was too like me – that we were as stubborn as each other; that our admiration would inevitably become attrition. The only reason we were married in such haste was that my mother begged me not to marry Andrew at all. One of you in a marriage has to be *soft*, she said. One of you has to know how to say, 'Have it your way.' That's not going to be you, dear, so it might as well be the man.

Taking Andrew O'Rourke's name was the second real decision of my life, and it was wrong. I suppose Little Bee would understand me. As soon as we let go of our real names, she and I, we were lost.

Ask her to leave, Lawrence had said. But no, no, I couldn't. We were joined by what had happened on the beach. Getting rid of her would be like losing a part of me. It would be like shedding a finger, or a name. I wasn't going to let that happen again. I sat on the floor and watched my son sleeping peacefully. I did envy him for being able to sleep like that.

I didn't sleep at all, not for an entire week, after Africa. The killers just walked away down the beach, and Andrew and I walked back to the hotel compound, in silence, and set about packing up our things after an agonising half-hour with the compound doctor, who packed the stump of my finger with gauze and wrapped it up tightly. I was in a daze. I remember on the flight home to London that I was vaguely surprised, just as I had been at the end of my childhood, that such a big story could simply continue without me. But that is the way it is with killers, I suppose. What is the end of all innocence for you is just another Tuesday morning for them, and they walk off back to their planet of death giving no more thought to the world of the living than we would give to any other tourist destination: a place to be visited briefly and returned from with souvenirs and a haunting sensation that we could have paid less for them.

On the plane home I held my injured hand high, where it throbbed less painfully. Through the fog of painkillers, its approach unseen and unexpected, the thought presented itself to me that it would be sensible not to let Andrew touch my injury, then or ever again. In my mind I watched the killers taking Little Bee and Kindness along the beach. I watched them disappear. I watched them pass over the horizon of my world into that dangerous country in my mind where I lay awake at night, thinking of the things those men might have done to them.

It never faded. But I went back to the magazine. Starting *Nixie* had been the third real decision of my life, and I refused ever to regret it. Nor was I going to give up on decision four –

Charlie, my best decision of all – or decision five, Lawrence, who I had truly meant to renounce until the horror of Nigeria made me realise that was unnecessary. I threw myself into making my life work, and I forced myself to let the beach seem distant and impersonal. There was trouble in Africa, of course there was. But there was no sense getting hung up about one particular incident and missing the big picture. Lawrence insisted on that, and for once I took his advice. I set up direct debits from my bank account to a couple of African charities. When people asked what had happened to my finger, I said that Andrew and I had hired a scooter out there and been involved in a minor accident. My soul entered a kind of suspended animation. At home I was calm. At work I was the boss. At night I did not sleep, but I thought I could probably make the days work indefinitely.

But now I stood up from the floor of Charlie's room. I went to look at myself again in the mirror. There were bags under my eyes now, and sharp new lines across my forehead. The mask was finally cracking. I thought, This isn't about the decisions you made any more. Because the biggest thing in your life, the thing that killed Andrew and the thing that means you can't sleep, is something that happened without you.

I realised, more than anything, that I needed to know now. I needed to know what had happened after the killers took those girls away down the beach. I needed to know what had happened next.

5

I woke up on Sarah's sofa. At first I did not know where I was. I had to open my eyes and look all around me. There were cushions on the sofa and they were made of orange silk. The cushions had birds and flowers embroidered on them. The sun was coming in through the windows, and these windows had curtains that reached all the way down to the floor. They were made of orange velvet. There was a coffee table with a glass top, so thick that it looked green from the side. On the shelf underneath the tabletop there were magazines. One was about fashion and one was concerned with how to make the home more beautiful. I sat up and put my feet on the floor. The floor was covered with wood.

If I was telling this story to the girls back home they would be asking me, *How can a table be made of coffee and what is this thing called velvet and how come that woman you were staying with did not keep her wood in a pile at the side of the house like everybody else? How come she left it lying all over her floor, was she very lazy?* And I would have to tell them: a coffee table is not made out of coffee, and velvet is a fabric as soft as the underside of infant clouds, and the wood on Sarah's floor was not firewood, it was a SWEDISH ENGINEERED FLOOR WITH THREE-STRIP ANTIQUE LACQUER AND MINIMUM 3MM REAL WOOD VENEER CERTIFIED BY THE FOREST STEWARDSHIP COUNCIL (FSC) AS BEING MANUFACTURED USING ETHICAL FORESTRY PRACTICES, and I know this because I saw a floor just like it advertised in the magazine that was underneath the coffee table and which concerned beautiful homes. And the girls from back home, their eyes would go wide and they would say, *Weh*, because now they would understand that I had finally arrived in a place beyond the end of the world – a place where wood was made by machines – and they would be wondering what sorcery I survived next.

Imagine how tired I would become, telling my story to the girls from back home. This is the real reason why no one tells us Africans anything. It is not because anyone wants to keep my continent in ignorance. It is because nobody has the time to sit down and explain the First World from first principles. Or maybe you would like to, but you can't. Your culture has become sophisticated, like a computer, or a drug that you take for a headache. You can use it, but you cannot explain how it works. Certainly not to girls who stack up their firewood against the side of the house.

If I mention to you, casually, that Sarah's house was close to a large park full of deer that were very tame, you do not jump up out of your seat and shout, *My God! Fetch me my gun and I will go to hunt one of those foolish animals!* No, instead you stay seated and you rub your chin wisely and you say to yourself, *Hmm, I suppose that must be Richmond Park, just outside London.*

This is a story for sophisticated people, like you.

I do not have to describe to you the taste of the tea that Sarah made for me when she came down into the living room of her house that morning. We never tasted tea in my village, even though they grow it in the east of my country, where the land rises up into the clouds and the trees grow long soft beards of moss from the wet air. There in the east, the plantations stretch up the green hillsides and vanish into the mist. The tea they grow, that vanishes too. I think all of it is exported. Myself I never tasted tea until I was exported with it. The boat I travelled in to your country, it was loaded with tea. It was piled up in the cargo hold in thick brown paper sacks. I dug into the sacks to hide. After two days I was too weak to hide any more, so I came up out of the hold. The captain of the ship, he locked me in a cabin. He said it would not be safe to put me with the crew. So for three weeks and five thousand miles I looked at the ocean through a small round window of glass and I read a book that the captain gave me. The book was called *Great Expectations* and it was about a boy called Pip but I do not know how it ended because the boat arrived in the UK and the captain handed me over to the immigration authorities.

Three weeks and five thousand miles on a tea ship – maybe if you scratched me you would still find that my skin smells of it. When they put me in the immigration detention centre, they gave me a brown blanket and a white plastic cup of tea. And when I tasted it, all I wanted to do was to get back into the boat and go home again, to my country. Tea is the taste of my land: it is bitter and warm, strong, and sharp with memory. It tastes of longing. It tastes of the distance between where you are and where you come from. Also, it vanishes – the taste of it vanishes from your tongue while your lips are still hot from the cup. It disappears, like plantations stretching up into the mist. I have heard that your country drinks more tea than any other. How sad that must make you – like children who long for absent mothers. I am sorry.

So, we drank tea in Sarah's kitchen. Charlie was still asleep in his bedroom at the top of the stairs. Sarah put her hand on mine.

'We need to talk about what happened,' she said. 'Are you ready to talk about that? About what happened after the men took you away down the beach?'

I did not reply straight away. I sat at the table, with my eyes looking all around the kitchen, taking in all the new and wonderful sights. For example, there was a refrigerator in Sarah's kitchen, a huge silver box with an icemaker machine built into it. The front of the icemaker machine was clear glass and you could see what it was doing inside there. It was making a small, bright cube of ice. It was nearly ready. You will laugh at me – silly village girl – for staring at an ice-cube like this. You will laugh, but this was the first time I had seen water made solid. It was beautiful – because if this could be done, then perhaps it could be done to everything else that was always escaping and running away and vanishing into sand or mist. Everything could be made solid again, yes, even the time when I played with Nkiruka in the red dust under the rope swing. In those days I believed such things were possible in your country. I knew there were large miracles just waiting for me to discover them, if only I could find the centre, the source of all these small wonders.

Behind the cold glass, the ice-cube trembled on its little metal arm. It glistened, like a human soul. Sarah looked at me. Her eyes were shining.

'Bee?' she said. 'I really need to know. Are you ready to talk about it?'

The ice-cube was finished. THUNK, it went, down into the collecting tray. Sarah blinked. The icemaker started making a new cube.

'Sarah,' I said, 'you do not need to know what happened. It was not your fault.'

Sarah held my hands between hers. 'Please, Bee,' she said. 'I need to know.'

I sighed. I was angry. I did not want to talk about it, but if this woman was going to make me do it then I would do it quickly and I would not spare her.

'Okay, Sarah,' I said. 'After you left, the men took us away down the beach. We walked for a short time, maybe one hour. We came to a boat on the sand. It was upside down. Some of its planks were broken. It looked like it had been broken by a storm and thrown up onto the beach and left there. The underside of the boat was white from the sun. All the paint had cracked and peeled off it. Even the barnacles on the boat were crumbling off it. The hunters pushed me under the boat and they told me to listen. They said they would let me go, once it was over. It was dark under the boat, and there were crabs moving around under there. They raped my sister. They pushed her up against the side of the boat and they raped her. I heard her moaning. I could not hear everything, through the planks of the boat. It was muffled, the sound. I heard my sister choking, like she was being strangled. I heard the sound of her body beating against the planks. It went on for a very long time. It went on into the hot part of the day, but it was dark and cool under the boat. At first my sister shouted out verses from the scriptures but later her mind began to go, and then she started to shout out the songs we sang when we were children. In the end there were just screams. At first they were screams of pain but finally they changed and they were like the screams of a newborn baby. There was no grief in them. They were automatic. They went on and on. Each scream was exactly the same, like a machine was making them.'

I looked up and I saw Sarah staring at me. Her face was completely white and her eyes were red and her hands were up to cover her mouth. She was shaking and I was shaking too, because I had never told this to anyone before.

'I could not see what they did to my sister. It was on the other side of the boat that the planks were broken. That is the side I could see through. The killer, the one with the wound in his neck, I could see him. He was far off from his men. He was walking in the shorebreak. He was smoking cigarettes from a packet he had taken out of the pocket of the guard he killed. He was looking out over the ocean. It looked as if he was waiting for something to come from there. Sometimes he put his hand up to touch the wound in his neck. His shoulders were down. It was as if he was carrying a weight.'

Sarah's whole body was shaking, so hard that the kitchen table was trembling. She was crying.

'Your sister,' she was saying. 'Your beautiful sister, oh my God, oh Jesus, I . . .'

I did not want to hurt Sarah any more. I did not want to tell her what happened, but I had to now. I could not stop talking because now I had started my story, it wanted to be finished. We cannot choose where to start and stop. Our stories are the tellers of us.

'Near the end, I heard Nkiruka begging to die. I heard the hunters laughing. Then I listened to my sister's bones being broken one by one. That is how my sister died. Yes, she was a beautiful girl, you are right. In my village they said she was the kind of girl that could make a man forget his troubles. But sometimes it does not work out like people say. When the men and the dogs were finished with my sister, the only parts of her that they threw into the sea were the parts that could not be eaten.'

Sarah stopped crying and shaking then. She was very still. She was holding on to her tea, as though she would be blown away if she did not grip on to it.

'And you,' she whispered. 'What happened to you?'

I nodded.

'In the afternoon it got very hot, even under the boat. A breeze started blowing from the sea. It blew sand up against the side of the boat. The sand hissed against the planks. I looked out through the gaps to see what was happening. Out past the surf there were seagulls gliding on the wind. They were very calm. Sometimes they dropped into the sea and swam back up with silver fish in their beaks. I looked at them very hard, because I thought that what had happened to my sister was going to happen to me now, and I wanted to fix my thoughts on something beautiful. But the men did not come for me. After they finished with my sister, the hunters and the dogs went up into the jungle to sleep. But the leader, he did not return to his men. He stood in the surf. The waves were breaking around his knees. He was leaning into the wind. Later it got so hot that the seagulls stopped their fishing. They were just floating on the waves with their heads tucked into their breasts, like this. Then the leader, he stepped forward into the waves. When the water came up to his chest he began to swim. He went straight out into the sea. The seagulls flew up out of his way and then they flapped back down. They only wanted to sleep. The man, he swam out, straight out, and soon I could not see him any more. He disappeared and all I could see was this line, the line between the sea and the sky, and then it got so hot that even the line disappeared. That is when I came out from under the boat, because I knew the men would be sleeping. I looked all around. There was nobody on the beach and there was no shade. It was so hot I thought I might die just from the heat. I went down into the shorebreak and I made my clothes wet and I ran towards the hotel compound. I ran through the shallow water so that I would not leave marks on the sand for the men to follow. I came to the place where they murdered the guard. There were more seagulls there. They were fighting over the guard's body. They flew up when I walked up the beach. I could not look at the guard's face. There were these little crabs crawling in and out of his trouser leg. There was a wallet on the ground and I picked it up. It was Andrew's wallet, Sarah. I am sorry. I looked inside. There were many plastic cards inside it. There was one that said DRIVING LICENCE and it had a photo of your husband. That is the one that had your address on it. That is the one that I took. There was another card too, his business card, the one with the telephone number, and I took that too. It blew out of my hand into the waves, but I got it back. Then I went to hide in the jungle, but I stayed where I could still see the beach. Then it began to get cooler and a truck drove up from the direction of the hotel compound. It was a canvas-top truck, a military one. Six soldiers jumped down from the back and they stood looking at the guard. They were poking at his body with the toes of their boots. There was a radio in the cab of the truck and it was playing 'One' by U2. I knew this song. It was always playing in our home. This is because the men came from the city one day and they gave us clockwork radios, one to each family in the village. We were supposed to wind them up and listen to the World Service from the BBC, but my sister Nkiruka tuned ours in to the Port Harcourt music station instead. We used to fight over the little wind-up box because I liked to listen to the news and the current affairs. But now that I was hiding in the jungle behind the beach I wished I had never fought with my sister. Nkiruka loved music and now I saw that she was right because life is extremely short and you cannot dance to current affairs. That is when I started to cry. I did not cry when they killed my sister but I did cry when I heard the music coming out of the soldiers' truck because I was thinking, That is my sister's favourite song and she will never hear it again. Do you think I am crazy, Sarah?'

Sarah shook her head. She was biting her nails.

'Everyone in my village liked U2,' I said. 'Everyone in my country, maybe. Wouldn't that be funny, if the oil rebels were playing U2 in their jungle camps, and the government soldiers were playing U2 in their trucks. I think everyone was killing everyone else and listening to the same music. Do you know what? The first week I was in the detention centre, U2 were

178

number one here too. That is a good trick about this world, Sarah. No one likes each other, but everyone likes U2.'

Sarah twisted her hands together on the table. She looked at me. 'Are you all right to go on?' she said. 'Can you tell me how you got away?'

I sighed. 'Okay,' I said. 'The guards were tapping their boots to the music. They rolled the body onto a sheet. They picked up the sheet by the corners and they lifted it into the truck. I thought I should run out to them and ask them to help me. But I was scared, so I stayed where I was. The soldiers drove back down the beach, and then it was very quiet again. When it was sunset I decided I did not want to go to the hotel compound. I was too scared of the soldiers, so I walked the other way. There were fruit bats flying all around. I waited till it was dark before I went past the place where they killed my sister. There was no moonlight, there was only a blue glow from the small creatures in the sea. Sometimes there was a freshwater stream that ran down the beach where I could drink. I walked all night and when it got light I went back into the jungle. I found a red fruit to eat. I did not know its name but I was hungry. It was bitter and I was very sick. I was very scared the men would come and find me again. When I had to go to the toilet I buried my excrement so that I would not leave any traces. Every noise I heard, I thought it was the men coming back. I said to myself, *Little Bee, the men are coming to tear your wings off.* It was like this for two more nights and on the last night I came to a port. There were red and green

179

lights flashing out in the sea, and there was a long concrete sea wall. I walked all along the top of the wall. There were waves crashing all over me, but there were no guards. Near the end of the sea wall, on the land side, there were two ships tied up next to each other. The near one had an Italian flag. The other one was British, so I climbed over the Italian ship to get to it. I went down into the cargo hold. It was easy to find it because there were signs written in English. And English, you know, it is the official language of my country.'

I stopped talking then, and I looked down at the table-cloth. Sarah came around to my side of the table and she sat on the chair beside me and she hugged me for a long time. Then we sat there holding our cold cups of tea. I rested my head on Sarah's shoulder. Outside, the day grew a little brighter. We did not say anything. After a short time I heard footsteps on the stairs, and then Charlie came into the kitchen. Sarah wiped her eyes and took a deep breath and quickly sat up straight. Charlie was wearing his Batman costume, but without the mask and without the belt that he kept his Batman tools in. It did not look as if he was expecting trouble, that morning. When he saw me he blinked. He was surprised that I was still there, I think. He rubbed his eyes sleepily and pressed the top of his head against his mother's side.

'Itch till sleep eat I'm,' he said.

'Excuse me, Batman?' said Sarah.

'I said, it's still sleepy time. Why is you awake?'

'Well, Mummy and Little Bee woke up early this morning.'

'Mmm?'

'We had a lot to catch up on.'

'Mmm?'

'Oh God, Batman, is it that you don't understand, or you don't agree?'

'Mmm?'

'Oh, I see, darling, you are like a little bat with its sonar. You'll keep sending out those "Mmms" until one of them bounces off something solid, won't you?'

'Mmm?'

Charlie stared at his mother. She looked back at him for a while, and then she turned and smiled at me. Her tears were starting to flow again.

'Charlie has extraordinary eyes, doesn't he? They're like ecosystems in aspic.'

'No they isn't,' said Charlie.

Sarah laughed. 'Well, darling, what I mean is, anyone can see there's a lot going on in there.'

She tapped the side of Charlie's head.

'Hmm,' said Charlie. 'Why is you crying, Mummy?'

Sarah gave one big sob and then waved it away. 'It's why *are you*, Charlie, not why *is you*,' she said.

'Why are you crying, Mummy?'

Sarah collapsed. It was as if all the strength went out of her bones. She sank down so that her head rested on her arms on the table top and she wept.

'Oh, Charlie,' she said. 'Mummy is crying because Mummy drank four G&Ts last night. Mummy is crying because of something Mummy has been trying not to think about. I'm so sorry, Charlie. Mummy is too grown up to feel very much any more, and so when she does, it catches her by surprise.'

'Mmm?' said Charlie.

'Oh, Charlie!' said Sarah.

She opened her arms and Charlie climbed up onto her lap and they hugged. It was not right for me to be there with them, so I went out into the garden and I sat down beside the fish-pond. I thought about my sister for a long time.

Later, when the sun was higher in the sky and the noise of the traffic on the roads had grown into a constant rumble, Sarah came out into the garden to find me.

'Sorry,' she said. 'I had to take Charlie to nursery.'

'It's okay.'

She sat down next to me and she put her hand on my shoulder. 'How are you feeling?'

I shrugged. 'Okay,' I said.

Sarah smiled, but it was a sad smile. 'I don't know what to say,' she said.

'I do not know either.'

We sat there and we watched a cat rolling on the grass on the other side of the garden, in a bright patch of sunshine.

'That cat looks happy,' I said.

'Mmm,' said Sarah. 'It's the neighbour's.'

I nodded. Sarah took a deep breath.

'Look, do you want to stay here for a while?' she said.

'Here? With you?'

'Yes. With me and Charlie.'

I rubbed my eyes. 'I do not know. I am illegal, Sarah. The men can come any minute to send me back to my country.'

'Why did they let you out of the detention centre, if you're not allowed to stay?'

'They made a mistake. If you look good or you talk good, sometimes they make mistakes for you.'

'But you're free now. They couldn't just *come for you*, Bee. This isn't Nazi Germany. There must be some procedure we can go through. Some appeal. I can *tell* them what happened to you over there. What will happen to you if you go back.'

I shook my head. 'They will tell you Nigeria is a safe country, Sarah. People like me, they can just come and drive us straight to the airport.'

'I'm sure we can work something out, Bee. I edit a magazine. I know people. We could kick up a stink.'

I looked at the ground. Sarah smiled. She put her hand on my hand.

'You're young, Bee. You don't know how the world works yet. All you've seen is trouble, so you think trouble is all you're going to get.'

'You have seen trouble too, Sarah. You are making a mistake if you think it is unusual. I am telling you, trouble is like the ocean. It covers two thirds of the world.'

Sarah flinched, as if something had struck her face.

183

'What is it?' I said.

She held her head in her hands. 'It's nothing,' she said. 'It's silly.'

I could not think of anything to say. I looked all around her garden for something to kill myself with, in case the men suddenly came. There was a shed at the far end of the garden, with a large garden fork leaning against it. That is a fine implement, I thought. If the men suddenly come, I will run with that fork and I will throw myself onto those sharp shining points.

I dug my nails into the soil of the flower-bed beside us, and I squeezed the sticky soil between my fingers.

'What are you thinking, Bee?'

'Mmm?'

'What are you thinking about?'

'Oh. Cassava.'

'Why cassava?'

'In my village we grew cassava. We planted it and watered it and when it was high – like this – we plucked its leaves so that the growing would go into the root, and when it was ready we dug it up and peeled it and grated it and pressed it and fermented it and fried it and mixed it with water and made paste out of it and ate it and ate it and ate it. When I slept at night I dreamed of it.'

'What else did you do?'

'Sometimes we played on a rope swing.'

Sarah smiled. She looked away into the garden.

'There isn't much cassava round here,' she said. 'Tons of clematis. Plenty of camellias.'

I nodded. 'Cassava would not grow in this soil.'

Sarah smiled, but she was crying at the same time. I held her hand. There were tears running down her face.

'Oh, Bee,' she said. 'I feel so bloody guilty.'

'This is not your fault, Sarah. I lost my parents and my sister. You have lost your husband. Both of us have lost.'

'I didn't lose Andrew, Bee. I destroyed him. I cheated on him with another man. That's the only reason we were in bloody Nigeria in the first place. We thought we needed a holiday. To patch things up. You see?'

I just shrugged my shoulders. Sarah sighed.

'I suppose you're going to tell me you've never taken a holiday.'

I looked down at my hands. 'Actually, I have never taken a man.'

Sarah blinked. 'Yes. Of course. I forget you're so young, sometimes.'

We sat still for a minute. Sarah's mobile telephone rang. She talked. When the call was finished, she looked very tired.

'That was the nursery. They want me to go and pick up Charlie. He's been fighting with the other children. They say he's out of control.' She bit her lip. 'He's never done that before.'

She picked up her telephone again and pressed some buttons. She held the telephone up to her ear while she looked

185

over my shoulder, over the garden. She was still chewing her lip. After a few seconds, there was the sound of another telephone ringing. It was a small, distant sound, from inside the house. Sarah's face went still. Then, slowly, she took the telephone down from her ear and pressed one of its buttons. From the house, the sound of the other telephone stopped.

'Oh, Jesus,' said Sarah. 'Oh no.'

'What? What is it?'

Sarah took a deep breath. Her whole body shuddered.

'I called Andrew. I don't know why. It was completely automatic, I didn't even think. You know . . . if there's a problem with Charlie, I always call Andrew. I just forgot he was . . . you know. Oh, God. I'm really losing it. I thought I was ready, you know, to hear what happened to you . . . and your sister. But I wasn't. I wasn't ready for it. Oh, God.'

We sat there and I held her hand while she cried. Afterwards, she passed her telephone to me. She pointed at the screen.

'He's still in my address book. Do you see?'

The screen of her telephone said ANDREW, and then a number. Just ANDREW – there was no surname.

'Will you delete him for me, Bee? I can't do it.'

I held her telephone in my hands. I had seen people speaking on mobile phones, but I always thought they would be very complicated. You will laugh at me – there she goes again, that silly little girl with the smell of tea in her skin and the stains of cassava tops still on her fingers – but I always thought there would be a frequency to find. I thought you would have to turn some dial until you found the signal of your friend, very small and faint, like tuning in to the BBC World Service on a wind-up radio. I supposed that mobile telephones were difficult like this. You would turn the dial through all the hissing and the squeaking sounds, and first you would hear your friend's voice very strange and thin and nearly drowned out by howling – like your friend had been squashed as flat as a biscuit and dropped into a metal box full of monkeys – but then you would turn the dial just one tiny fraction more and suddenly your friend would say something like, *God Save the Queen!* and tell you all about the weather in the shipping areas around the offshore waters of the United Kingdom of Great Britain and Northern Ireland. After that, you could talk.

But actually I discovered that it was much easier than this to use a mobile telephone. Everything is so easy in your country. Next to the name, ANDREW, there was a thing that said OPTIONS, and I pressed it. Option 3 was DELETE, so I pressed that, and Andrew O'Rourke was gone.

'Thank you,' said Sarah. 'I just couldn't do it myself.'

She looked down at her phone for a long time.

'I feel so bloody frightened, Bee. There's no one to call. Andrew was absolutely unbearable sometimes, but he was always so *sensible*. I suppose it was crazy of me, to send Charlie straight back to the nursery, after yesterday. But I thought it would be good for him, to get back into the routine.

There's no one to ask any more, Bee. Do you understand? I don't know if I can do this on my own. Make all the right decisions for Charlie on my own. Years of it, do you see? The right behaviour, the right schools, the right friends, the right university, the right wife. Oh, God, poor old Charlie.'

I put my hand on her hand. 'If you want, I can come to the nursery with you,' I said.

Sarah tilted her head and looked at me for a long time. Then she smiled. 'Not dressed like that,' she said.

Ten minutes later I left the house with Sarah. I was wearing a pink summer dress she lent me. It was the prettiest thing I had ever worn. Around the neck it had fine white flowers stitched in, very delicate and fancy. I felt like the Queen of England. It was a sunny morning and there was a cool breeze and I skipped along the pavement behind Sarah and every time we passed a cat or a postman or a woman pushing a pram I smiled and I said, *How do you do?* All of them looked at me like I was a crazy girl, I do not know why. I was thinking, That is no way to greet your monarch.

I did not like the nursery. It was in a big house with tall windows, but the windows were not open even though it was a fine day. Inside, the air was stuffy. It smelled of toilets and poster paint, and this was exactly the smell of the therapy room in the immigration detention centre, so I was feeling sad from the memory. In the detention centre they did not open the windows because the windows did not open. In the therapy room they gave us poster paints and brushes and they told us we must express ourselves. I used a lot of red paint. When the therapeutic assistant looked at what I painted, she said it would be good for me to try to *move on*. I said, *Yes, madam, it will be my pleasure. If you will just open a little window for me, or even better a door, I will be happy to move on right away.* I smiled, but the therapeutic assistant did not think it was a good joke.

In Charlie's nursery, the play leader did not think I was a good joke either. I knew she was the play leader because she had a badge on her green apron that said PLAY LEADER. She stared at me but she did not speak to me, she spoke to Sarah. She said, *I'm sorry, we can't have visitors, it's policy. Is this the child's carer?* Sarah looked at me and then she turned back to the play leader. She said, *Look, it's complicated, okay?* The play leader frowned. Finally she let me stand by the door while Sarah went into the room and tried to calm Charlie.

Poor Charlie. They had made him take off his Batman costume – that was what had started it. They had made him take it off because he had urinated in it. They wanted him to be clean, but Charlie did not want to be clean. He preferred to be stinking in his black mask and cape than to smell fresh in the white cotton overall they had put him in. His face was red and dirty with poster paint and tears. He was howling with rage. When anyone came near him he hit at them, with his small fists banging into their knees. He bit and he scratched and he screamed. He stood with his back pressed into the corner. He faced out into the room and he screamed, *NO NO NO NO NO!*

Sarah went up to him. She knelt down so her face was close to his. She said, *Oh, darling.* Charlie stopped shouting. He looked at Sarah. His bottom lip trembled. Then his jaw became firm again. He leaned towards his mother, and he spat. He said, *GO AWAY I WANT MY DADDY!*

They were making the other children sit cross-legged on the floor, in the far corner of the room. They were having story time. The other children were facing away from Charlie's corner, but they kept wriggling round to look over their shoulders with pale, scared faces. A woman was reading them the story. She wore blue jeans and white trainers and a turquoise sweatshirt. She was saying, *And Max tamed them by the trick of TURN AROUND AND FACE FRONT, CAITLIN, by the trick of staring straight into their eyes and saying, EMMA, PLEASE CONCENTRATE, JAMES, STOP WHISPERING, of staring straight into their eyes and saying, WILL YOU FACE FRONT, OLLIE, THERE'S NOTHING GOING ON BEHIND YOU.*

Sarah knelt on the floor and she wiped Charlie's spit off her cheek. She was crying. She was holding her arms out to Charlie. Charlie turned around and hid his face in the corner. The woman reading the story was saying, *Be still.*

I went towards Sarah. The play leader gave me a look which meant, *I told you to stay by the door.* I gave her a look back which meant, *How dare you?* It was a very good look. I learned it from Queen Elizabeth the Second, on the back of the British five-pound note. The play leader took one step back and I went up to Sarah. I touched her on the shoulder.

Sarah looked up at me. 'Oh, God,' she said. 'Poor Charlie, I don't know what to do.'

'What do you normally do when he is like this?'

'I cope. I always cope. Oh, God, Bee, I don't know what's happening to me. I've forgotten how to cope.'

Sarah covered her face with her hands. The play leader took her away and sat her down.

I went into the corner with Charlie. I stood next to him and I turned my face into the corner too. I did not look at him, I looked at the bricks and I did not say anything. I am good at looking at bricks and not saying anything. In the immigration detention centre I did it for two years, and that is my record.

I was thinking what I would do in that nursery room, if the men came suddenly. It was not an easy room, I am telling you. For example, there was nothing to cut yourself with. All the scissors were made of plastic and their ends were round and soft. If I suddenly needed to kill myself in that room, I did not know how I was going to do it.

After a long time Charlie looked up at me. 'What is you doing?' he said.

I shrugged my shoulders. 'I am thinking how to escape from this place.'

Silence. Charlie sighed. 'They tooked mine Batman costume.'

'Why did they do that?'

'Because of why I done a wee in my Batman costume.'

I knelt down and looked into Charlie's eyes. 'We are the same, you and me. I spent two years in a place like this. They make us do the things we do not want. Does it make you cross?'

Charlie nodded.

I said, 'It makes me cross too.'

From behind us I could hear that the rest of the nursery was going back to its own business. Children were talking and shouting again, and the women were helping and laughing and scolding. In our corner, Charlie looked at the ground.

'I want mine daddy,' he said.

'Your daddy is dead, Charlie. Do you know what this means?'

'Yes. In heaven.'

'Yes.'

'Where's heaven?'

'It is a place like this. Like a nursery, or a detention centre, or a strange country far away. He wants to come home to you, but he can't. Your daddy is like my Daddy.'

'Oh. Is yours daddy dead too?'

'Yes, Charlie. My Daddy is dead and my Mummy is dead and my sister is dead too. All of them are dead.'

'Why?'

I shrugged my shoulders. 'The baddies got them, Charlie.'

Charlie twisted his hands together and bent down to pick up a small scrap of red paper from the floor. He tore at it, and he put it on his tongue to see how it tasted, and then it got stuck on his fingers because of the dampness. He held his tongue between his teeth so he could concentrate on peeling the paper off his fingers. Then he looked up.

'Is you sad like me?'

I made my face go into a smile. 'Do I look sad, Charlie?'

Charlie looked at me. I tickled him under his arms and he started to laugh.

'Do we look sad, Charlie? Hey? You and me? Are we sad now?'

Charlie was laughing and wriggling finally, so I pulled him close to me and I looked in his eyes. 'We are not going to be sad, Charlie. Not you and me. Especially not you, Charlie, because you are the luckiest boy in the world. You know why this is?'

'Why?'

'Because you have a mama, Charlie, and she loves you, and that is something, no?'

I gave Charlie a little push towards his mother and he ran to her. He buried his face against her dress and they hugged each other. Sarah was crying and smiling at the same time. She was speaking into Charlie's ear, saying *Charlie, Charlie, Charlie.* Then Charlie's voice came, and it was muffled against his mother's dress. He said, *I'm NOT Charlie, Mummy, I'm Batman.*

Sarah looked at me over Charlie's shoulder and she just said, *Thank you*, not making any sound but just moving her lips.

We walked home from the nursery with Charlie swinging between us. The day was beautiful. The sun was hot and the air was buzzing with bees and the scent of flowers was everywhere. Beside the pavement there were the front gardens of the houses, full of soft colours. It was hard not to be full of hope.

'I think I shall teach you the names of all of the English flowers,' said Sarah. 'This is fuchsia, and this is a rose, and this is honeysuckle. What? What are you smiling about?'

'There are no goats. That is why you have all these beautiful flowers.'

'There were goats, in your village?'

'Yes, and they ate all the flowers.'

'I'm sorry.'

'Do not be sorry. We ate all the goats.'

Sarah frowned. 'Still,' she said. 'I think I'd rather have honeysuckle.'

'One day I will take you where I come from and you will eat only cassava for a week and then you will tell me if you would rather have honeysuckle or goat.'

Sarah smiled and leaned over to smell the honeysuckle blossom. Now I saw that she was crying again.

'Oh, I'm sorry,' said Sarah. 'I can't seem to stop. Oh, look at me, I'm all over the place.'

Charlie looked up at his mother and I rubbed the top of his head to show him everything was okay. We started to walk again. Sarah blew her nose on a tissue. She said, 'How long am I going to be like this, do you suppose?'

'It was one year for me, after they killed my sister.'

'Before you could think straight again?'

'Before I could think at all. At first I was just running, running, running – getting away from where it happened, you know? Then there was the detention centre. It was very bad. It is not possible to think clearly in there. You have not committed a crime, so all you can think of is, When will I be let out? But they tell you nothing. After a month, six months, you start to think, Maybe I will grow old in here. Maybe I will die here. Maybe I am already dead. For the first year all I could think about was killing myself. When everyone else is dead, sometimes you think it would be easier to join them, you know? But you have to move on. *Move on, move on*, they tell you. As if you are stubborn. As if you are chewing on their flowers like a goat. *Move on, move on*. At five p.m. they tell you to move on and at six p.m. they lock you back in your cell.'

'Didn't they give you any help at all in that place?'

I sighed. 'They tried to help us, you know? There were some good people. Psychiatrists, volunteers. But there was only so much they could do for us in there. One of the psychiatrists, she said to me, *Psychiatry in this place is like serving an in-flight meal in the middle of a plane crash. If I wanted to make you well, as a doctor, I should be giving you a parachute, not a cheese-and-pickle sandwich.* To be well in your mind you have first to be free, you see?'

Sarah pressed the tissue into the corners of her eyes. 'I'm not sure it's easier out here, Bee.'

'But I will help you.'

Sarah smiled. 'You're sixteen years old. You're a refugee. You're an orphan, for God's sake. I'm the one who ought to be helping you.'

I pulled on Sarah's shoulder to stop her. I took her left hand and I held it up to her. Charlie stood and looked up at us with big eyes.

'Look, Sarah. You have helped me enough already. You cut off your own finger for me. You saved my life.'

'I should have done more. I should have saved your sister too.'

'How?'

'I should have thought of something.'

I shook my head. 'You did everything you could, Sarah.'

'But we should never have been in that situation, Bee. Don't you see? We went on holiday to a place we had no right to be.'

'And what if you had not been there, Sarah? If you and Andrew had not been there, then Nkiruka and me, we would both be dead.' I turned to Charlie. 'Your mummy saved my life, did you know that? She saved me from the baddies.'

Charlie looked up at his mother. 'Like Batman?' he said.

Sarah smiled, the way I was used to now, with the tears starting to come to her eyes again. 'Like Batmum.'

'Is that why you isn't got your one finger?'

'Why I *haven't* got one finger. Yes, darling.'

'Did the baddies take it? The Penguin?'

'No, darling.'

'Was it the Puffin?'

Sarah laughed. 'Yes, darling, it was that awful Puffin.'

Charlie grinned. 'Naughty naughty Puffin,' he said, and he ran ahead of us down the pavement, shooting baddies with a gun that was not visible to my eyes. Sarah turned to me. 'Bless you,' she said.

I held tight to her arm and I placed the palm of her left hand on the back of my left hand. I arranged my fingers underneath hers, so that the only one of my fingers you could see was the one that was missing from Sarah's hand. I saw how it could be. I saw how we could make a life again. I know it was crazy to think it but my heart was pounding, pounding, pounding.

'I will help you,' I said. 'If you want me to stay then this is how it will be between us. Maybe I will only be able to stay for one month, maybe only one week. Some day, the men will come. But while I am here I will be like your daughter. I will love you as if you were my mother and I will love Charlie as if he was my brother.'

Sarah stared at me. 'Goodness,' she said.

'What is it?'

'Well, it's just that on the way home from the nursery, with the other mothers, we usually talk about potty training and cakes.'

I dropped Sarah's hand and I looked down at the ground.

'Oh, Bee, I'm sorry,' she said. 'This is all just a little bit sudden and a little bit serious, that's all. I'm so confused. I need a bit more time to think.'

I looked up at Sarah again. In her eyes I saw that it was new for her, this feeling of not knowing straight away what to do. Her eyes were the eyes of a creature who has only just been born. Before it is familiar with its world, there is only terror. I knew this expression very well. Once you have seen as many people as I have being pushed in through the doors of the immigration detention centre, it is easy to recognise this look. It made me want to remove that pain from Sarah's life as quickly as I could.

'I am sorry, Sarah. Please forget about it. I will leave. You see? The psychiatrist at the detention centre was right, she could not do anything for me. I am still crazy.'

Sarah did not say anything. She just held on to my arm and we followed Charlie down the street. Charlie was racing along and knocking the heads off the roses in the front gardens. He knocked them off with karate chops. They fell, each one with a sudden fall and a silent explosion of petals. Like my story with Nkiruka, like my story with Yevette. My feet crushed the petals as we passed over them, and I realised that my story was only made of endings.

Back at the house, we sat in Sarah's kitchen. We drank tea again and I wondered if it would be the last time. I closed my eyes. My village, my family, that disappearing taste. Everything vanishes and drains away into sand or mist. That is a good trick.

When I opened my eyes again, Sarah was watching me.

'You know, Bee, I was thinking about what you said, about you staying. About us helping each other. I think you're right. Maybe it is time to be serious. Maybe these are serious times.'

6

Serious times began on a grey, ominous day in London. I wasn't looking for serious. If I'm honest, I suppose I was looking for a bit of the other. Charlie was nearly two years old and I was emerging from the introverted, chrysalid stage of early motherhood. I fitted back into my favourite skirts. I felt like showing off my wings.

I'd decided to spend a day in the field. The idea was to remind my editorial girls that it was possible to write a feature article all on one's own. I hoped that by inspiring the staff to indulge in a little reportage, my commissioning budget would be spared. It was simply a question, I had told the office airily, of applying one's pithy remarks sequentially to paper rather than scrawling them individually on sample boxes.

Really, I just wanted my staff to be happy. At their age I'd been fresh out of my journalism degree and intoxicated with the job. Exposing corruption, brandishing truth. How well it had suited me, that absolute licence to march up to evildoers and demand *who, what, where, when,* and *why*? But now, standing in the lobby of the Home Office building in Marsham Street, waiting for a ten o'clock interview, I realised I wasn't looking forward to it. Perhaps at twenty, one is naturally curious about life but at thirty, simply suspicious of anyone who still has one. I clutched my brand-new notepad and Dictaphone in the hope that some of their youthful predisillusionment would rub off on me.

I was angry with Andrew. I couldn't focus. I didn't even look the part of a reporter – my spiral notepad was virginal white. While I waited, I besmirched it with notes from a fictitious interview. Through the lobby of the Home Office building, the public sector shuffled past in its scuffed shoes, balancing its morning coffee on cardboard carry trays. The women bulged out of M&S trouser suits, wattles wobbling and bangles clacking. The men seemed limp and hypoxic – half garrotted by their ties. Everyone stooped, or scuttled, or nervously ticked. They carried themselves like weather presenters preparing to lower expectations for the bank-holiday weekend.

I tried to concentrate on the article I wanted to write. An optimistic piece was what I needed; something bright and positive. Something absolutely unlike anything Andrew would write in his *Times* column, in other words. Andrew and I had been arguing. His copy was getting gloomier and gloomier. I think he had truly started to believe that Britain was sinking into the sea. Crime was spreading, schools were failing, immigration was creeping and public morals were slipping. It seemed as if everything was seeping and sprawling and oozing, and I *hated* it. Now that Charlie was almost two I suppose I was looking into the future my child would have to inhabit, and realising that bitching about it might possibly not be the most constructive strategy. *Why do you always have to be so bloody negative?* I asked Andrew. *If the country really is on the slide, then why not write about the people who are doing something about it?*

– *Oh yeah? Like whom?*

– *Well, like the Home Office, for example. They're the ones on the front line, after all.*

– *Oh, that's genius, Sarah, that really is. Because people really trust the Home Office, don't they? And what will you call your fine uplifting piece?*

– *You mean what's my title? Well, how about* The Battle For Britain?

I know, I know. Andrew exploded with laughter. We had a blazing row. I told him I was finally doing something constructive with my magazine. He told me I was finally growing out of my magazine's demographic. Not only was I getting old, in other words, but everything I had worked on for the last decade was puerile. How almost surgically hurtful.

I was still furious when I arrived at the Home Office building. *Always the Surrey girl, aren't you?* That had been Andrew's parting shot. *What exactly do you require the Home Office to do about this bloody country, Sarah? Strafe the chavs with Spitfires?* Andrew had a gift for deepening the incisions he began. It wasn't our first row since Charlie was born, and he always did this at the end – brought the argument back to my upbringing, which infuriated me as it was the one thing I couldn't help.

I stood in the lobby as the dowdy clerks flowed all around me. I blinked, looked down at my shoes, and had my first sensible thought for days. I realised I hadn't come out into the world today to make a point to my editorial staff. Senior editors didn't really go back to reporting to shave a few pounds from their commissioning budgets. I was there, I realised, entirely to make a point to Andrew.

And when Lawrence Osborn came down and introduced himself on the dot of ten o'clock – tall, grinning, not conspicuously handsome – I understood that the point I was making to Andrew was not necessarily going to be an editorial one.

Lawrence looked down at his clipboard. 'That's odd,' he said, 'they've marked down this interview as "non-hostile".'

I realised I was looking at him fiercely. I blushed. 'Oh, God, I'm sorry. Bad morning.'

'Don't mention it. Just tell me you'll try to be nice to me. All you journalists seem to have it in for us these days.'

I smiled. 'I am going to be nice to you. I think you people do a terrific job.'

'Ah, that's because you haven't seen the statistics we've seen.'

I laughed, and Lawrence raised his eyebrows.

'You think I'm joking,' he said.

His voice was flat and unremarkable. He didn't sound public school. There was a touch of roughness in his vowels, or a sense of some wildness reined in, as if he was making an effort. It was hard to place his voice. He took me on a tour of the building. We looked in on the Assets Recovery Agency and the Criminal Records Bureau. The mood was business-like, but relaxed. Discourage a little crime, drink a little coffee – that seemed to be the tone. We walked along unnatural galleries floored with natural materials and bathed in natural light.

'So, Lawrence,' I said, 'what do you think is going wrong with Britain?'

Lawrence stopped and turned. His face glowed in a soft yellow ray, filtered through coloured glass.

'You're asking the wrong man,' he said. 'If I knew the answer to that, I'd fix it.'

'Isn't that what you're supposed to do at the Home Office? Fix it?'

'I don't actually work in any of the departments. They tried me out here and there for a while, but I don't think my heart was in it. So here I am in the Press Office.'

'But surely you must have an opinion?'

Lawrence sighed. 'Everyone has an opinion, don't they? Maybe that's what's wrong with this country. What? Why are you smiling?'

'I wish you'd tell that to my husband.'

'Ah. He has opinions, does he?'

'On a variety of subjects.'

'Well, maybe he should work here. They love a policy debate around these parts, they really do. Your first interview, for example . . .' Lawrence looked at his clipboard, searching for a name.

'I'm sorry?' I said. 'I though *you* were my interview.'

Lawrence looked up. 'Ah, no, I'm just the warm-up guy. I'm sorry, I should have explained.'

'Oh.'

'Well, don't look so disappointed. I've fixed up a good day for you, I really have. You've got three heads of department lined up, and a real live Permanent Under-Secretary. I'm sure they'll give you more than you need for your piece.'

'But I was enjoying talking to you.'

'You'll get over it.'

'You think?'

Lawrence smiled. He had curly black hair, quite glossy but cut disconcertingly short around the back and sides. His suit, too – it was a good one, Kenzo, I think – and it fitted him well, but there was something arresting about the way he wore it.

He held his arms a little away from his body – as if the suit was the pelt of some suaver animal, recently slain and imperfectly cured so that the bloody rawness of it made his skin crawl.

'They don't really like me talking to the visitors,' said Lawrence. 'I don't think I've quite perfected the Home Office voice.'

I was surprised to find myself laughing. We walked on down the corridor. Somewhere in between the Criminal Records Bureau and the Forensic Science Service, the mood changed. People ran past us down the corridor. A crowd clustered around a television monitor. I noticed the way Lawrence put a protective hand on the small of my back as he steered me though the sudden press of people. It didn't feel inappropriate. I realised I was slowing down to feel the pressure of his hand on my back.

BREAKING NEWS, said the TV monitor. HOME SECRE-TARY RESIGNS. There was footage of the man looking haggard and climbing with his guide dog into the back seat of a torment that for the moment still resembled a ministerial car.

Lawrence inclined his head towards the others, who were staring raptly at the monitor. He spoke close to my ear.

'Look at these bastards,' he whispered. 'The man's being crucified and these people are already excited about what it means for their jobs.'

'What about you? Don't you care?'

Lawrence grinned. 'Oh, it's bad news for me,' he whispered. 'With my brilliant track record, I was next in line to be the man's guide dog.'

Lawrence took me to his office. He said he had to check his messages. I was nervous, I don't know why. There wasn't anything of Lawrence on the walls – just a generic framed photo of Waterloo Bridge, and a laminated card showing the mustering points in the event of fire. I caught myself checking my reflection in the window and then thinking, Oh, don't be so silly. I let my eyes change their focus until they rested on the flat grey wall of the neighbouring office building. I waited while Lawrence scrolled through his emails.

He looked up. 'I'm sorry,' he said. 'We're going to have to re-schedule your interviews. It'll be chaos around here for the next few days.'

The phone went and Lawrence listened for a moment. He said, 'What? Shouldn't someone more senior be doing that? Really? Oh, great. How long do I have?' He put the phone down on the table and then he put his head down on the desk. In the corridor outside the office there were sounds of laughing, shouting, doors slamming shut.

'Bastards,' said Lawrence.

'What is it?'

'That phone call? Off the record?'

'Of course.'

'I have to write a letter to the outgoing Home Secretary, expressing our department's deep regret at his leaving.'

'They don't sound particularly regretful.'

'And to think that but for your journalistic sensitivity to detail, we'd never have noticed.'

Lawrence rubbed his eyes and turned to his computer screen. He laid his fingers on the keyboard, then hesitated.

'God!' he said. 'I mean, what do you write?'

'Don't ask me. Did you know the man?'

Lawrence shook his head. 'I've been in rooms he was in, that's all. He was a twat, really, only you couldn't say that because he was blind. I suppose that's how he got so far. He used to lean slightly forward, with his hand on his guide dog's harness. He used to lean, like this, and his hand would sort of tremble. I think it was an act. He didn't tremble when he was reading Braille.'

'You don't sound as if you'll miss him much either.'

Lawrence shrugged. 'I quite admired him. He was weak and he turned that into a strength. A role model for losers like me.'

'Oh,' I said. 'You're doing self-deprecation.'

'So?'

'So, it doesn't work. Studies have shown. Women only pretend they like it in surveys.'

'Maybe I'm only pretending to do self-deprecation. Maybe I'm a winner. Maybe becoming the Home Office's press bitch was my own personal Everest.'

He said all this without facial inflection. He stared into my eyes. I didn't know where to look.

'Let's bring this back to my article,' I said.

'Yes, let's,' said Lawrence. 'Because otherwise this is going somewhere else, isn't it?'

I felt adrenaline aching in my chest. This thing that was happening, then, it had apparently slipped quite subtly over some line. It had become something acknowledged, albeit in a relatively controlled form that both of us could still step back from. Here it was, if we wanted it, hanging from a taut umbilicus between us: an affair between adults, minute yet fully formed, with all its forbidden trysts and muffled paroxysms and shattering betrayals already present, like the buds of fingers and toes.

I remember looking down at the carpet tiles in Lawrence's office. I can still see them now, with hyper-real clarity, every minute grey acrylic fibre of them, gleaming in the fluorescent light, coarse and glossy and tightly curled, lascivious, obscene, the grey pubic fuzz of an ageing administrative body. I stared at them as if I had never seen carpet tiles before. I didn't want to meet Lawrence's eyes.

'Please,' I said. 'Stop it.'

Lawrence blinked and inclined his head, innocently. 'Stop what?' he said.

And, just like that, for the moment, it was gone.

I breathed again. Above us, one of the fluorescent tubes was buzzing loudly.

'Why did the Home Secretary have to resign?' I said.

Lawrence raised an eyebrow. 'Don't tell me you don't know. I thought you were a journalist.'

'Not a serious one. *Nixie* does current affairs the way *The Economist* does shoes. On a need-to-know basis.'

'The Home Secretary had to resign because he fast-tracked a visa for his lover's nanny.'

'You believe that?'

'I don't really care one way or the other. But he never seemed that stupid to me. Oh, listen to them.'

Outside Lawrence's door there was still laughing and shouting. I heard the sound of paper being scrunched into a ball. Feet scuffed on the carpet. A paper ball clanged into a metal waste-paper basket.

'They're playing corridor football,' said Lawrence. 'They're actually celebrating.'

'You think they set him up?'

He sighed. 'I'll never know what they did to him, Sarah. I didn't go to the right schools for that. My job is just to write a goodbye letter to the man. What would you put?'

'It's hard if you didn't really know him. I suppose you'll just have to stick to generalities.'

Lawrence groaned. 'But I'm terrible at this,' he said. 'I'm the sort of person who needs to know what I'm talking about. I can't just write some spiel.'

I looked around his office.

'I'm in the same position,' I said. 'And like it or not, you seem to have become my interview.'

'So?'

'So, you're not making it easy for me.'

'In what way?'

'Well, you haven't exactly personalised this place, have you? No golf trophies, no family photos, nothing that gives me the slightest clue who you are.'

Lawrence looked up at me. 'Then I suppose you'll just have to stick to generalities,' he said.

I smiled. 'Nice,' I said.

'Thank you.'

I felt the ache of adrenaline again.

'You really don't fit in here, do you?'

'Listen, I very much doubt I'll still be working here tomorrow if I can't think of something suitably non-committal to write to the old boss in the next twenty minutes.'

'So write something.'

'But seriously, I can't think of anything.'

I sighed. 'Shame. You seemed too nice to be such a loser.'

Lawrence grinned. 'Well,' he said, 'you seemed quite beautiful enough to be so mistaken.'

I realised I was smiling back at him. 'A little blonde of me, you think?'

'Hmm. I think your roots are showing.'

'Well, I don't think you're a loser, if you must know. I think you're just unhappy.'

'Oh, do you? With your gimlet eye for emotional cues?'

'Yes, I do.'

Lawrence blinked and looked down at his keyboard. I realised he was blushing.

'Oh, sorry,' I said, 'God, I shouldn't have said that. I got carried away, I don't even know you, I'm so sorry. You look really hurt.'

'Maybe I'm just doing vulnerable.'

Lawrence drew in his elbows – drew in all of himself in fact, so that he appeared to withdraw into his body on the royal blue upholstery of his swivel chair. He paused, and tapped out a line on his computer. The keyboard was a cheap one, the kind where the keys have a high travel and they squeak on the down-stroke. He sat there so long without moving that I went behind his desk and looked over his shoulder to see what he had written.

*You tried your utmost and it has still to be seen_*

That was the unfinished sentence that stood, without resolution or caveat, on his computer screen. The cursor blinked at the end of the line. From outside in the street, police sirens screamed in and out of phase. He turned to me. The bearings squealed in his chair.

'So, tell me something,' he said.

'Yes?'

'Is it your husband who makes you unhappy?'

'What? You don't know anything about my husband.'

'It was one of the first things you said to me. About your husband and his opinions. Why would you mention him to me at all?'

'The subject came up.'

'The subject of your husband? You brought it up.'

I stopped, with my mouth open, trying to remember why he was wrong. Lawrence smiled, bitterly but without malice.

'I think it's because you're not very happy either,' he said.

I moved quickly out from behind his desk – my turn to blush now – and I went over to the window. I rolled my head on the cool glass and looked down at the ordinary life in the street. Lawrence came to stand beside me.

'So,' he said. 'Now it's me who's sorry. I suppose you'll tell me I should leave the close observation to you journalists.'

I smiled, despite myself. 'What was that line you were in the middle of writing?' I said.

'*You tried your utmost and it has still to be seen* . . . I don't know, I'm going to say, *still to be seen what great fruits your work will bear*, or, *still to be seen what the successes of your hard work will be*. Something open ended like that.'

'Or you could just leave it how it is,' I said.

'It isn't finished,' said Lawrence.

'But it's rather good,' I said. 'It's got us this far, hasn't it?'

The cursor blinked and my lips parted and we kissed and kissed and kissed. I clung to him and whispered in his ear. Afterwards I retrieved my knickers from the grey carpet tiles, and pulled them on under my skirt. I smoothed down my blouse, and Lawrence sat back at his desk.

I looked through the window at a different world from the one I had left out there.

'I've never done that before,' I said.

'No, you haven't,' said Lawrence. 'I'd have remembered.'

213

He stared at the screen for a full minute with the unfinished line on it and then, with my lipstick still on his lips, smashed down a full stop. *You tried your utmost and it has still to be seen.* Twenty minutes later, the letter was transcribed to Braille and put in the post. Lawrence's colleagues hadn't cared enough to proofread it.

Andrew called. My mobile went in Lawrence's office and I will never forget the first thing Andrew said: 'This is fuckin' fantastic, Sarah. This story is going to be full-on for weeks. They've commissioned me to write an extended feature on the Home Secretary's downfall. This is pay dirt, Sarah. They've given me a team of researchers. But I'm going to be in the office all hours on this one. You'll be all right looking after Charlie, won't you?'

I switched off the phone, very gently. It was simpler than announcing to Andrew the change in our way of life. It was easier than explaining to him: our marriage has just been mortally wounded, quite by accident, by a gang of bullies picking on a blind man.

I put down the phone and I looked at Lawrence. 'I'd really like to see you again,' I said.

Ours was an office hours affair. A long lunches in short skirts affair. A sneaked afternoons in nice hotels affair. Even the occasional evening. Andrew was pulling all-nighters in the newspaper's offices, and so long as I could find a babysitter, Lawrence and I could do what we liked. Occasionally in a lunch-hour that had extended almost to teatime, with white wine in my hand and Lawrence naked beside me, I thought about all the journalists who were not receiving guided tours, all the meet-the-media breakfasts that were not getting planned, and all the press releases that were waiting on Lawrence's computer with the cursor blinking at the end of the last unfinished sentence. *This new target represents another significant advance in the Government's ongoing programme of_*

Handing out in-flight meals in a plane crash. That's what our affair was meant to be. Lawrence and I escaped from our own tragedies and into one another, and for six months Britain slowed incrementally during normal office hours. I wish I could say that's all it was. Nothing serious. Nothing sentimental. Just a merciful interruption. A brief, blinking cursor before our old stories resumed.

But it was gorgeous. I gave myself completely to Lawrence in a way that I never had with Andrew. It happened easily, without any effort on my part. I cried when we made love. It just happened; it wasn't an act. I held him till my arms ached and I felt agonies of tenderness. I never let him know. I never let him know, either, that I scrolled through his Blackberry, read his emails, read his mind while he slept. When I started the affair, I think it could have been with anyone. It was the affair that was inevitable, not the specific man. But slowly, I started to adore Lawrence. To have an affair, I began to realise, was a relatively minor transgression. But to really escape from Andrew, to really become myself, I had to go the whole way and fall in love. And again, I didn't have to make an effort to fall in love with Lawrence. All I had to do was to permit myself to topple. *This is quite safe*, I told myself: the psyche is made to absorb the shock of such falls.

I still cried when we made love, but now I also cried when we couldn't.

It became a source of worry, hiding the affair. The actual assignations were simply concealed from Andrew, of course, and I made a point of never mentioning Andrew or his work when I was with Lawrence, in case he himself got too curious. I put up a high fence around the affair. In my mind I declared it to be another country and I policed its border ruthlessly.

Harder to disguise was the incontrovertible change in me. I felt *wonderful*. I had never felt less sensible, less serious, less Surrey. My skin started to glow. It was so blatant that I tried to conceal it with foundation, but it was no use: I simply radiated *joie de vivre*. I started partying again, as I hadn't since my early twenties. Lawrence got me in to all the Home Office events. The new Home Secretary loved to meet the media, to tell them over canapés how tough he was going to be. There were endless soirées, and always an after-party. I met a new crowd. Actors, painters, business people. I felt a thrill I hadn't felt since before I met Andrew – the thrill of realising I was attractive, of knowing myself irresistible, of being half drunk on champagne and looking around at the bright, smiling faces and giggling when I realised that suddenly anything could happen.

So I should hardly have been surprised when it did. Inevitably, at one of those parties, I finally bumped into my husband, crumpled and red eyed from the office. Andrew hated parties – I suppose he was only there on some fact-finding mission. Lawrence even introduced us. A packed room. Music – flagship British music – some band that had made it big on the internet. Lawrence, beaming, flushed with champagne, his hand resting riskily on the small of my back.

'Oh, hi! Hi! Andrew O'Rourke, this is Sarah Summers. Sarah is the editor of *Nixie*. Andrew's a columnist for *The Times*, terrific writer, strong opinions. I'm sure you two are going to get on.'

'So was the priest,' said Andrew.

'I'm sorry?'

'He was sure we were going to get on. When he married us.'

Andrew, light hearted, almost smiling. Lawrence – poor Lawrence – quickly removing his hand from my back. Andrew, noticing. Andrew, suddenly unsmiling.

'I didn't know you'd be here, Sarah.'

'Yes. Well. I. Oh. It was a last-minute thing. The magazine . . . you know.'

My body betraying me, blushing from my ankles to the crown of my head. My childhood, my inner Surrey, reawakened and vengeful, redrawing its county boundaries to annex my new life. I looked down at my shoes. I looked up. Andrew was still there, standing very still, very quiet – all the opinion, for once, drained out of him.

That night we stood on the empty foundation at the end of our garden where Andrew was planning to build his glass-house, and we talked about *saving our marriage*. Just the phrase is excruciating. Everything Andrew said sounded like his *Times* column, and everything I said could have been ripped from the agony page of my magazine.

'At what point did we forget that marriage is a commitment for life?'

'I just felt so unfulfilled, so downtrodden.'

'Happiness isn't something one can pick up off the shelf, it's something one has to work at.'

'You bullied me. I just never felt loved or supported.'

'Trust between adults is a hard-won thing, a fragile thing, so difficult to rebuild.'

It was less like a discussion and more like a terrible mix-up at the printers. It didn't stop till I threw a flowerpot at him. It glanced off his shoulder and smashed on the concrete base and Andrew flinched and walked away. He took the car and drove off and he didn't come home for six days. Later I found out he'd flown over to Ireland to get properly drunk with his brother.

Charlie started nursery that week, and Andrew missed it. I made a cake to mark the occasion for Charlie, alone in the kitchen one night. I wasn't used to being alone in the house. With Charlie asleep it was quiet. I could hear the blackbirds singing in the twilight. It was pleasant, without Andrew's constant baseline of gripes and political commentary. Like the drone note of bagpipes, one doesn't really realise it's been playing until it stops, and then the silence emerges into being as a tangible thing in its own right: a supersilence.

I remember scattering yellow Smarties over the wet icing while I listened to *Book of the Week* on Radio 4, and suddenly feeling so confused I burst into tears. I stared at my cake: three banana layers, with dried banana chips and banana icing. This was still two years before Charlie's Batman summer. At two years old, what Charlie loved most in the world was bananas. I remember looking at that cake and thinking: I love being Charlie's mother. Whatever happens now, that is the one thing I can be proud of.

I stared at the cake on its wire tray on the work surface. The phone rang.

Lawrence said, 'Shall I come over?'

'What, now? To my *house*?'

'You said Andrew was away.'

I shivered. 'Oh goodness. I mean . . . you don't even know where I live.'

'Well, where do you live?'

'I'm in Kingston.'

'I'll be there in forty minutes.'

'No, Lawrence . . . no.'

'But why? No one will know, Sarah.'

'I know but . . . wait a minute, please, let me think.'

He waited. On the radio, the continuity announcer was promising great things for the next programme. Apparently there were many misconceptions about the tax credit system, and their programme was going to clear up a good few of them. I dug my nails into the palm of my free hand and fought desperately against the part of me that was pointing out that an evening in bed with Lawrence and a bottle of Pouilly-Fumé might be more exciting than Radio 4.

'No. I'm sorry. I won't let you come to my house.'

'But why not?'

'Because my house is *me*, Lawrence. Your house is your family and my house is my family and the day you come to my house is the day our lives get more tangled up than I'm ready for.'

I put the phone down. I stood quietly for a few minutes, looking at it. I was doing this to protect Charlie, keeping the distance between me and Lawrence. It was the right thing to do. Things were complicated enough. It's something I could never have explained to my mother, I suppose: that there are circumstances in which we will allow men to enter our bodies but not our homes. My body still ached from the sound of Lawrence's voice, and the frustration rose inside me until I picked up the phone and smashed it, again and again, into my perfectly iced cake. When the cake was quite destroyed I took a deep breath, switched the oven back on, and started making another.

The next day – Charlie's first day at nursery – my train was cancelled so I was late back from work. Charlie was crying when I picked him up. He was the last child there, howling in the middle of the beeswaxed floor, smashing his little fists into the play leader's legs. When I went to Charlie, he wouldn't look at me. I pushed him home in the buggy, sat him down at the table, dimmed the lights, and brought in the banana cake with twenty burning candles. Charlie forgot he was sulking and started to smile. I kissed him, and helped to blow out the candles.

'Make a wish!' I said.

Charlie's face clouded over again. 'Want Daddy,' he said.

'Do you, Charlie? Do you really?'

Charlie nodded. His lower lip wobbled, and my heart wobbled with it. After the cake he got down from his high chair and toddled off to play with cars. A peculiar gait, toddling. A sort of teetering, really – my son at two – each step a hasty improvisation, a fall avoided by luck as much as by judgement. A sort of life on short legs.

Later, with Charlie tucked up in bed, I phoned my husband. 'Charlie wants you back, Andrew.'

Silence.

'Andrew?'

'Charlie does, does he?'

'Yes.'

'And what about you? Do you want me back?'

'I want what Charlie wants.'

Andrew's laugh down the phone – bitter, derisory. 'You really know how to make a man feel special.'

'Please. I know how badly I've hurt you. But it'll be different now.'

'You're bloody right it'll be different.'

'I can't raise our son alone, Andrew.'

'Well, I can't raise my son with a slut for his mother.'

I gripped the phone, feeling a wave of terror rise through me. Andrew hadn't even raised his voice. *A slut for his mother.* Cold, technical, as if he had also weighed up *adulteress*, *cuckolder* and *narcissist* before selecting precisely the most apposite noun. I tried to control my voice but I heard the shake in it.

'Please, Andrew. This is you and me and Charlie we're talking about. I care so much about both of you, you can't imagine. What I did with Lawrence . . . I'm so sorry.'

'Why did you do it?'

'It was never meant to mean anything. It was just sex.' The lie came out of my mouth so easily that I realised why it was so popular.

'*Just* sex? That's the convention, isn't it, these days? Sex has become one of those words you can put *just* in front of. Anything else you'd like to minimise at this time, Sarah? Just unfaithfulness? Just betrayal? Just breaking my fucking heart?'

'Stop it, please, stop it! What can I do? What can I do to make it right again?'

Andrew said he didn't know. Andrew cried down the phone. These were two things he had never done. The not knowing, and the crying. Hearing Andrew weeping over the crackling phone line, I began to cry too. When we both dried up, there was silence. And this silence had a new quality in it: the knowledge that there had been something left to cry over, after all. The realisation hung on the phone line. Tentative, like a life waiting to be written.

'Please, Andrew. Maybe we need a change of scenery. A fresh start.'

A pause. He cleared his throat. 'Yes. All right.'

'We need to get away from things. We need to get away from London and our jobs and even Charlie – we can leave him with my parents for a few days. We need a holiday.'

Andrew groaned. 'Oh, Jesus. A holiday?'

'Yes. Andrew. Please.'

'Jesus. All right. Where?'

The next day, I called him back.

'I've got a freebie, Andrew – Ibeno Beach in Nigeria, open-ended tickets. We can leave on Friday.'

'This Friday?'

'You can file your column before we leave, and you'll be back in time for the next one.'

'But *Africa*?'

'There's a beach, Andrew. It's raining here and it's dry season there. Come on, let's get some sun.'

'Nigeria, though? Why not Ibiza, or the Canaries?'

'Don't be boring, Andrew. Anyway it's just a beach holiday. Come on, how bad can it be?'

Serious times. Once they have rolled in, they hang over you like low cumulus. That's how it was with me and Andrew,

223

after we came back from Africa. Shock, then recrimination, then the two awful years of Andrew's deepening depression, and the continuing affair with Lawrence that I never could quite seem to stop.

I think I must have been depressed too, the whole time. You travel here and you travel there, trying to get out from under the cloud, and nothing works, and then one day you realise you've been carrying the weather around with you. That's what I was explaining to Little Bee on the afternoon she came with me to pick up Batman from nursery. I sat with her, drinking tea at the kitchen table.

'You know, Bee, I was thinking about what you said, about staying. About us helping each other. I think you're right. I think we both need to move on.'

Little Bee nodded. Under the table, Batman was playing with a Batman action figure. It seemed the smaller Batman was engaged in a desperate battle with an unfinished bowl of cornflakes. I started explaining to Little Bee how I was going to help her.

'What I'm going to do first is track down your case-worker – *oh, Charlie, food is not a toy* – track down your caseworker and find out where your documents are held. Then we can – *please, Charlie, don't get those flakes everywhere, don't make me tell you again* – then we can challenge your legal status, find out whether we can make an appeal, and so on. I looked this up on the web and apparently – *Charlie! Please! If I have to pick up that spoon one more time I will take away your Batman figure* – apparently if we can get you temporary resident status, I can arrange for you to take a British Citizenship Exam, which is just simple stuff, really – *Charlie! For God's sake! Right, that's it. Get out. Now! Out of the kitchen and come back when you've decided to be good* – just simple stuff about the kings and queens and the English civil war and so on, and I'll help you with the revision, and then – *oh, Charlie, oh, goodness, I'm sorry, I didn't mean to make you cry. I'm sorry, Batman. I'm so sorry. Come here.'*

Batman flinched away from my arms. His lip wobbled and his face went red and he howled, abandoning himself utterly to grief in that way only infants and superheroes have – that way that knows misery is bottomless and insatiable – that honest way. Little Bee rubbed Batman's head, and he buried his masked face in her leg. I watched his little bat cape shaking as he sobbed.

'Oh, God, Bee,' I said. 'I'm sorry, I'm just a mess at the moment.'

Little Bee smiled. 'It's okay, Sarah, it's okay.'

The kitchen tap dripped. For something to do I got up and tightened it, but the drips kept coming. I couldn't understand why that upset me so much.

'Oh, Bee,' I said. 'We've got to get a grip, both of us. We can't let ourselves be the people things happen to.'

Later, there was a knock at the front door. I pulled myself together and went in through the house. I opened the door to

225

Lawrence, suited, travel bag slung over his shoulder. I saw his relief, his involuntary smile when he saw me.

'I didn't know if I'd got the right address,' he said.

'I'm not sure you have.'

His smile disappeared. 'I thought you'd be pleased.'

'I've only just put my husband in the ground. We can't do this. What about your wife?'

Lawrence shrugged. 'I told Linda I was going on a management course,' he said. 'Birmingham. Three days. Leadership.'

'You think she believed you?'

'I just thought you might need some support.'

'Thanks,' I said. 'I've got some.'

He looked over my shoulder at Little Bee, standing in the hallway. 'That's her, is it?'

'She's staying for as long as she wants.'

Lawrence lowered his voice. 'Is she legal?'

'I don't think I give a shit. Do you?'

'I work for the Home Office, Sarah. I could lose my job if I knew you were harbouring an illegal and I didn't do anything about it. Technically, if I have the slightest doubt, I could be sacked if I even stepped through this door.'

'So . . . um . . . don't.'

Lawrence blushed, took a step back and ran his hand through his hair.

'This isn't comfortable for me either, Sarah. I don't like the way I feel about you. It'd be nice if I loved my wife and it'd be super if I didn't work for the forces of darkness. I wish I could be idealistic like you. But that's not me, Sarah. I can't afford to act as if I'm someone. I'm nothing. Even my cover story is nothing. Three days in Birmingham – *Birmingham*, fuck! On a course to learn something everyone accepts I'm hopeless at. It's so plausible it's tragic, don't you think? That's what I was thinking, even while I was making it up. I'm not ashamed of my adultery, Sarah. I'm ashamed of my fucking cover story.'

I smiled. 'I sort of remember why I like you. No one could ever accuse you of being full of yourself, could they?'

Lawrence puffed up his cheeks and blew air through his mouth, sadly. 'Not in the full light of the evidence,' he said.

I hesitated. He reached up and held my hand. I closed my eyes and felt the resolve draining out of me into the cold smoothness of his skin. I took a step back into the house. I almost staggered, really.

'Are you letting me in, then?'

'Don't get used to it,' I said.

Lawrence grinned, but then he hesitated on the threshold. He looked at Little Bee. She came up and stood just behind my shoulder.

'Do not worry about me,' she said. 'Officially you cannot even see me. You are in Birmingham and I am in Nigeria.'

Lawrence gave a quick little smile. 'I wonder which of us will get found out first,' he said.

We went in through the hall and into the living room. Batman was T-boning his red fire engine into the side of a defenceless family saloon. (In Charlie's world, I think, the emergency services are staffed by rogue elements.) He looked up when we came in.

'Batman, this is Lawrence. Lawrence is Mummy's friend.'

Batman stood and walked up to Lawrence. He stared at him. His bat senses must have told him something. 'Is you mine new Daddy?' he said.

'*No, no, no,*' I said.

Charlie looked confused. Lawrence knelt so that his face was at Charlie's level. 'No, Batman, I'm just your mummy's friend.'

Batman tilted his head to one side. The ears on his bat hood flopped over. 'Is you a goody or a baddy?' he said slowly.

Lawrence grinned and stood up. 'Honestly, Batman? I think I'm one of those innocent bystanders you see in the background in the comics. I'm just a man from a crowd scene.'

'But is you a goody or a baddy?'

'He's a goody of course,' I said. 'Come on, Charlie. Do you really think I'd let someone into our house who wasn't?'

Batman folded his arms and set his lips in a grim line. No one spoke. From outside came the evening sounds of mothers calling normal children in from gardens for tea.

Later, after I'd got Charlie to bed, I made supper while Lawrence and Little Bee sat at the kitchen table. Digging at the back of the cupboard for a refill of pepper, I found a half-full packet of the amaretto biscuits that Andrew used to love. I smelled them, secretly, holding the packet up to my nose, with my back to Lawrence and Little Bee. That sickly, sharp smell of apricot and almond – it made me think of the way Andrew used to wander around the house on his insomniac nights. He would return to bed in the small hours with that smell on his breath. Towards the end, the only thing keeping my husband going was six amaretto biscuits and one tablet of Cipralex a day.

I held Andrew's biscuits in my hand. I thought about throwing them away, and I found that I couldn't. How duplicitous grief is, I thought. Here I am, too sentimental to throw away something that gave Andrew slight comfort, even as I cook supper for Lawrence. I felt horribly traitorous, suddenly. This is exactly why one shouldn't let one's lover into one's home, I thought.

When the supper was ready – a mushroom omelette, slightly burned while I was thinking of Andrew – I sat down to eat with Lawrence and Little Bee. It was dreadful – they wouldn't talk to one another, and I realised that they hadn't spoken the whole time I'd been making supper. We ate in silence, with just the sound of the cutlery. Finally Little Bee sighed, and rubbed her eyes, and went upstairs to the bed I'd made up for her in the guest room.

I crashed the plates into the dishwasher and dumped the frying pan into the sink.

'What?' said Lawrence. 'What did I do?'

'You might have made an effort,' I said.

'Yes, well. I thought I'd be alone with you tonight. It's not an easy situation to adjust to.'

'She's my guest, Lawrence. The least you can do is be polite.'

'I just don't think you know what you're getting yourself into, Sarah. I don't think it's healthy for you to have that girl staying here. Every time you see her, you're going to be reminded of what happened.'

'I've spent two years denying what happened on that beach. Ignoring it, letting it fester. That's what Andrew did too, and it killed him in the end. I'm not going to let it kill me and Charlie. I'm going to help Little Bee, and make everything right, and then I can get on with my life.'

'Yes, but what if you can't make it right? You know the most likely outcome for that girl, don't you? They'll deport her.'

'I'm sure it won't come to that.'

'Sarah, we have an entire department consecrated to ensuring that it *will* come to that. Officially Nigeria's pretty safe, and she's got no family here, by her own admission. There's bugger all reason for them to let her stay.'

'I can't not try.'

'You'll get dragged down by the bureaucracy, and then they'll send her home anyway. You'll get hurt. It will damage you. And that's the last thing you need at the moment. You need positive influences in your life. You've got a son that you have to bring up on your own now. You need people that are going to give you energy, not drain it away.'

'And that's you, is it?'

Lawrence looked back at me, and shifted his weight forward. 'I want to be important to you, Sarah. I've wanted it from the moment you walked into my life with your reporter's notepad that you never wrote down a single word on and your Dictaphone that you didn't even switch on. And I haven't let you down, have I? Despite everything. Despite my wife and despite your husband and despite bloody well everyone. We have fun together, Sarah. Isn't that what you want?'

I sighed. 'I really don't think this is about having fun any more.'

'And do you see me running away? This is about us doing what's best for you. I'm not going to stop just because it's gone all serious. But you have to choose. I can't help you if all your focus is on that girl.'

I felt the blood draining out of my face. I spoke as quietly and calmly as I could. 'Tell me you're not asking me to choose between you and her.'

'I am absolutely not asking you to do that. But what I am saying is that you're going to have to choose between your life and her life. At some point you have to start thinking about a future for you and Charlie. Charity is lovely, Sarah, but there has to be some logical point where it stops.'

I banged my damaged hand down on the table, fingers splayed out. 'I cut off my finger for that girl. Will you tell me when is the logical point to stop something that started like that? Do you really want me to make a choice like that? I cut

231

off my own bloody finger. Do you think I wouldn't cut you off too?'

Silence. Lawrence stood up. His chair scraped. 'I'm sorry,' he said. 'I shouldn't have come.'

'No. Maybe you shouldn't.'

I sat at the kitchen table and listened to Lawrence taking his coat from the peg in the hall and picking up his travel bag. When I heard the front door opening, I stood up. Lawrence was halfway down the path by the time I got to the door.

'Lawrence?'

He turned.

'Where are you going to go? You can't go home.'

'Oh. I didn't really think about it.'

'You're meant to be in Birmingham.'

He shrugged. 'I'll get a hotel. It'll be good for me. I'll read a book on leadership. Might actually learn something.'

'Oh, Lawrence, come here.'

I held out my arms to him. I pressed my face into his neck and hugged him while he stood motionless. I breathed in the smell of him, and remembered all those hotel afternoons, high as kites on each other.

'You really are a loser,' I said.

'I just feel so bloody silly. I had it all worked out. I got the time off work, I made up the story for Linda. I even bought toys for the kids, in case I forgot on the way home. I had it all worked out. I thought it was going to be a nice surprise for you and . . . well. It was a surprise, at least, wasn't it?'

232

I stroked his face. 'I'm sorry. I'm sorry I snapped at you. Thank you for coming to see me. Please don't go to a hotel room and sit there all on your own, I can't bear it. Please stay.'

'What? Now?'

'Yes. Please.'

'I don't know if that's a good idea, Sarah. Maybe I need to take a step back and think about what we mean to each other. What you said just now, about cutting me off . . .'

'Stop it, you cunning bastard. Stop it before I change my mind.'

Lawrence almost smiled. I linked my fingers around the back of his neck.

'What I didn't say was that if I had to cut you off, it would hurt more than cutting off my finger.'

He stared at me for a long time and then he said, 'Oh, Sarah.' We went upstairs and it wasn't until we'd started that I realised we were having sex on the bed I used to share with Andrew. I was concentrating on Lawrence, burying my face in the soft hair on his chest, peeling the clothes off him, and then something happened – my bra strap snagged, Lawrence's belt buckle jammed for a second – I don't recall but it stopped the flow, anyway, and I realised that Lawrence was lying on Andrew's side of the bed, that his skin was pressing down where Andrew's had pressed, that the concave of Lawrence's back, smooth and hot with sweat, was arching proud of the depression that Andrew had made in the mattress. I hesitated

– I froze up. Lawrence sensed it, I suppose, and he kept the momentum going. He rolled over onto me. I just felt so grateful to him, I think, for getting us through that moment without thinking. I let myself dissolve into the slickness of his skin, the delicacy of his movement, the lightness of him. Lawrence was tall but he was slight. There was none of the bruising compression of my pelvis, the crushing of the breath from my lungs, the overpowering gravity of sex with Andrew that left me groaning as much in resignation as in pleasure. That was what I loved about sex with Lawrence – the glorious, giddying lightness of it. But there was something wrong, tonight. Maybe it was the presence of Andrew, so strong in the room. His books and papers were everywhere still – jamming the bookshelves, scattered in the corners of the floor – and when I thought of Andrew, I thought of Little Bee. Lawrence was making love to me and part of me was thinking, Oh! while another part was thinking, In the morn- ing I must phone the Border and Immigration Agency and start to track down her papers, and then I'll need to find her a solicitor, and start an appeal procedure, and, and . . .

I found I couldn't give myself up to Lawrence – not in that unhesitating, abandoned way I once had. Suddenly Lawrence seemed too light. His fingers barely brushed my skin, as if they were not engaging with my body but merely tracing lines in some fine and invisible dust that Africa had cloaked me in. And when his weight came onto me it was like being made love to by a summer cloud, or a winter butterfly – by some creature, in any case, that lacked the authority to bend gravity around itself and become the moment's centre.

'What's wrong, Sarah?'

I realised I was lying absolutely rigid. 'Oh, God, I'm sorry.'

Lawrence stopped, and rolled onto his back. I took hold of his penis, but already I could feel the softness returning to it.

'Please,' he said. 'Don't.'

I let go and took hold of his hand instead, but he pulled it free.

'I don't understand you, Sarah, I really don't.'

'I'm sorry. It's Andrew. It's just too soon.'

'He never stopped us while he was alive.'

I thought about that. In the darkness outside, a low jet was climbing out of Heathrow and a pair of owls were calling to each other desperately above the roar, their shrieks shrilling against the whining of the turbines.

'You're right. It isn't Andrew.'

'What is it, then?'

'I don't know. I love you, Lawrence, I really do. It's just that I've got so much to do.'

'For Little Bee?'

'Yes. I can't relax. I can't stop running it over and over in my head.'

Lawrence sighed. 'So what about *us*?' he said. 'Do you think you're going to find time for us again, one of these days?'

'Oh, of course I will. You and me, we've got plenty of time, haven't we? We'll still be here in six weeks, six months, six years. We've got time to work this out. We've got time to work out how to be together, now that Andrew's gone. But Little Bee doesn't have that time. You said it yourself. If I can't fix things for her, they'll find her and they'll deport her. And she'll be gone, and that will be that. And what sort of a future would we have then? I wouldn't be able to look at you without thinking I should have done more to save her. Is that the future you want us to have?'

'Oh, God. Why can't you be like other people and just not give a shit?'

'Leggy blonde, likes music and movies, seeks solvent man for friendship and maybe more?'

'All right. I'm glad you're not one of them. But I don't want to lose you to a refugee girl who's really got no hope of staying here anyway.'

'Oh, Lawrence. You're not going to lose me. But you might have to share me with her for a while.'

Lawrence laughed.

'What?' I said.

'Well, it's just typical, isn't it? These immigrants, they come over here, they take our women . . .'

Lawrence was smiling but there was a guardedness is his eyes, an opaqueness that made me wonder how funny he found his own joke. It was strange, to feel uncertain like this with him. Truly, he had never seemed at all complicated before. Then again, I realised, I had never invested anything complicated in him until now. Perhaps it was me. I made myself relax, and I smiled back. I kissed him on the forehead.

'Thank you. Thank you for not making this harder than it is.'

Lawrence stared at me, and his face was thin and sad in the orange glow of the street lamps filtering in through the yellow silk blinds. The flutter in my stomach surprised me, and I realised that the hairs on my arms were up.

'Sarah,' he said, 'I honestly don't think you know how hard this is.'

7

Sarah told me why she started her affair with Lawrence. It was not hard to understand. We are all trying to be free in this world. Freedom for me is a day when I am not afraid of the men coming to kill me. Freedom for Sarah is a long future where she can live the life of her choice. I do not think she is weak or foolish for living the life she was born in. A dog must be a dog and a wolf must be a wolf – that is the proverb in my country.

Actually we do not say that in my country. Why would we have a proverb with wolves in it? We have two hundred proverbs about monkeys, three hundred about cassava. We are wise to the things we know. But I have noticed, in your country, I can say anything so long as I say, *That is the proverb in my country*. Then people will nod their heads and look very serious. That is a good trick. Freedom for Sarah is a long future where she can live the life of her choice. A dog must be a dog and a wolf must be a wolf and a bee must be a bee. Freedom for a girl like me is getting through to the end of each day alive.

The future is another thing I would have to explain to the girls from back home. The future is my country's biggest export. It leaves so quickly through our sea ports, most of my people have never even seen it and they do not know what it looks like. In my country the future exists in gold nuggets hidden in the rock, or it collects in dark reservoirs far underneath the earth. Our future hides itself from the light, but your people come along with a talent for divining it. In this way, fraction by fraction, our future becomes your own. I admire your sorcery because of its subtlety and its variety. In every generation the extraction process is different. It is true that we are naïve. In my village, for example, it took us by surprise that the future could be pumped into 42-gallon barrels and shipped off to a refinery. It happened while we were preparing the evening meal, while the blue woodsmoke mixed with the thick steam of the cassava pots in the golden evening sun. It happened so quickly that the women had to grab us children and run with us into the jungle. We hid there while we listened to the screams of the men who stayed behind to fight – and meanwhile, at the refinery, by a process of distillation, my village's future was separated into its fractions. The heaviest fraction, the wisdom of our grandparents, was used to tar your roads. The middle fractions, the careful savings of our mothers from the small coins they put aside after the harvest time, these were used to power your cars. And the lightest fraction of all – the fantastical dreams of us children in the stillest hours of full-moon nights – well, that came off as a gas that you bottled and stored for winter. In this way our dreams will keep you warm. Now that they are part of your future, I do not blame you for using them. You probably do not even see where they came from.

You are not bad people. You are blind to the present and we are blind to the future. In the immigration detention centre I used to smile when the detention officers explained to me, *The reason you have to come over here, you Africans, is that you just aren't capable of good government over there.* I used to tell them that near my village there was a wide, deep river with dark caves under the banks where the fish were pale and blind. There was no light in their caves, so after a thousand generations the trick of seeing had been distilled out of their species. *Do you see what I mean?* I said to the detention officers. *Without light, how can you keep the sight of eyes? Without a future, how can you preserve the vision of government? We could try as hard as we liked in my world. We could have a most diligent Home Secretary of Lunchtime. We could have an excellent Prime Minister of the Quietest Part of the Late Afternoon. But when twilight comes – do you see? – our world disappears. It cannot see beyond the day, because you have taken tomorrow. And because you have tomorrow in front of your eyes, you cannot see what is being done today.*

The detention officers used to laugh at me, and shake their heads, and go back to reading their newspapers. Sometimes they would let me read after them. I liked to read your newspapers because it was vital for me to learn to speak your language in this way that you do. When your newspapers write about where I come from, they call it *the developing world*. You would not say *developing* unless you believed you had left us a future to be doing that in. This is how I know you are not bad people.

Actually, what you have left us with is your abandoned objects. When you think of my continent, perhaps you think of the wildlife – of the lions and the hyenas and the monkeys. When I think of it, I think of all the broken machines, of everything worn out and wrecked and shattered and cracked. Yes, we have lions. They are sleeping on the roofs of rusting containers. We also have hyenas. They are cracking the skulls of men who were too slow to run from their own troops. And the monkeys? The monkeys are out at the edge of the village, playing on top of a mountain of old computers that you sent to help in our school – the school that does not have electricity.

From my country you have taken its future, and to my country you have sent the objects from your past. We do not have the seed, we have the husk. We do not have the spirit, we have the skull. Yes, the skull. That is what I would think

241

about if I had to give a better name to my world. If the Prime Minister of the Quietest Part of the Late Afternoon telephoned me one day and said, *Little Bee, to you falls the great honour of giving a name to our ancient and much-beloved continent*, then I would say, *Sir, our world shall be called Golgotha, the place of the skull*.

That would have been a good name for my village, even before the men came to burn our huts and drill for oil. It would have been a good name for the clearing around the limba tree where we children swung on that bald old car tyre, and bounced on the seats of my father's broken Peugeot and my uncle's broken Mercedes, with the springs poking out from them, and chanted church songs from a hymn book with the covers missing and the pages held together with tape. Golgotha was the place I grew up, where even the missionaries had boarded up their mission and left us with the holy books that were not worth the expense of shipping back to your country. In our village, our only Bible had all of its pages missing after the forty-six verse of the twenty-seventh chapter of Matthew, so that the end of our religion, as far as any of us knew, was *My God, my God, why hast thou forsaken me?*

That is how we lived, happily and without hope. I was very young then, and I did not miss having a future because I did not know I was entitled to one. From the rest of the world all we knew was your old, old movies. About men who were in a great hurry, sometimes in jet planes and sometimes on motorbikes and sometimes upside down.

For news, all we had was a Golgotha TV, the kind where you have to carry the burden of programming yourself. There was just the wooden frame around where the screen used to be, and the frame sat in the red dust underneath the limba tree, and my sister Nkiruka used to put her head inside the frame to do the pictures. This is a good trick. I know now that we should have called this *reality television*.

My sister used to adjust the bow on her dress, and put a flower in her hair just so, and smile through the screen and say: *Hello, this is the news from the British BBC, today ice-cream will snow down from the sky and no one will have to walk to the river for water because the engineers will come from the city and put a stand pipe in the middle of the village*. And the rest of us children, we would all sit in a half-circle around the television set and we would watch Nkiruka announcing the news. We loved these lightest fractions of her dreams. In the pleasant afternoon shade we would gasp with delight and all of us would say, *Weh!*

One of the good things about the forsaken world is that you can talk back to television. The rest of us children, we used to shout at Nkiruka:

– This ice-cream snow, exactly what time will it occur?

– In the early evening, of course, when the day is cooler.

– How do you know this, Madam Television Announcer?

– Because the day must be cool enough or the ice-cream would melt, of course. Do you children know nothing?

And we children would sit back and nod at one another – evidently the day would need to be cool enough first. We were very satisfied with the television news.

You can play the same trick with television in your country, but it is harder because the television sets do not listen. The morning after Lawrence first stayed the night at Sarah's house, it was Charlie who wanted to turn the television on. I heard him wake up while Sarah and Lawrence were still sleeping, so I went to his room. I said, *Good morning, little brother, do you want breakfast?* He said, *No, I doesn't want breakfast, I does want TELEVISION.* So I said, *Does your mummy say it is okay for you to watch television before breakfast?* Charlie looked at me and his eyes were very patient, like a teacher who has told you the answer three times already but you have forgotten it. *Mummy is asleep, actually*, he said.

So we switched on the television. We looked at the pictures without the sound. It was the BBC morning news, and they were showing pictures of the Prime Minister making a speech. Charlie put his head on one side to watch. The ears of his Batman hood flopped over.

He said, 'That is the Joker, isn't it?'

'No, Charlie. That is the Prime Minister.'

'Is he a goody or a baddy?'

I thought to myself.

'Half the people think he is a goody and the other half think he is a baddy.'

244

Charlie giggled. 'That's silly,' he said.

'That is democracy,' I said. 'If you did not have it, you would want it.'

We sat and watched the Prime Minister's lips moving.

'What's he saying?' said Charlie.

'He is saying that he will make ice-cream snow.'

Charlie spun round to look at me. 'WHEN?' he said.

'About three o'clock in the afternoon, if the weather is cool enough. He is also saying that young people who are running away from trouble in other countries will be allowed to stay in this country so long as they work hard and do not make any fuss.'

Charlie nodded. 'I think the Prime Minisser is a goody.'

'Because he will be kind to refugees?'

Charlie shook his head. 'Because of the ice-cream snow,' he said.

There was a laugh from the door. I turned round and Lawrence was there. He was wearing a dressing-gown, and he stood there in his bare feet. I do not know how long he had been listening to us.

'Well,' he said, 'we know how to buy that boy's vote.'

I looked at the floor. I was embarrassed that Lawrence had been standing there.

'Oh, don't be shy,' he said. 'You're great with Charlie. Come and have some breakfast.'

'Okay,' I said. 'Batman, do you want some breakfast?'

Charlie stared at Lawrence and then he shook his head, so I

switched through the TV channels until we found the one that Charlie liked, and then I went into the kitchen.

'Sarah's still sleeping,' said Lawrence. 'I suppose she needs the rest. Tea or coffee?'

'Tea, thank you.'

Lawrence boiled the kettle and he made tea for both of us. He put my tea down on the table in front of me, carefully, and he turned the handle of the mug towards my hand. He sat down on the other side of the table, and smiled. The sun was lighting up the kitchen. It was thick yellow – a warm light, but not a show-off light. It did not want the glory for the illumination of the room. It made each object look as if it was glowing with a light from deep inside itself. Lawrence, the table with its clean blue cotton tablecloth, his orange tea mug and my yellow one – all of it glowing from within. The light made me feel very cheerful. I thought to myself, That is a good trick.

But Lawrence was serious. 'Look,' he said, 'I think you and I need to make a plan for your welfare. I'm going to be very clear about this. I think you should go to the local police and report yourself. I don't think it's right for you to expose Sarah to the stress of harbouring you.'

I smiled. 'She is not harbouring me. I am not a boat.'

'This isn't funny.'

'But no one is looking for me. Why should I go to the police?'

'I don't think it's right, your being here. I don't think it's good for Sarah at the moment.'

246

I blew on my tea. The steam from it rose up into the still air of the kitchen, and it glowed. 'Do you think you are good for Sarah at the moment, Lawrence?'

'Yes. Yes I do.'

'She is a good person. She saved my life.'

Lawrence smiled. 'I know Sarah very well,' he said. 'She told me the whole story.'

'So you must believe I am only staying here to help her.'

'I'm not convinced you're the kind of help she needs.'

'I am the kind of help that will look after her child like he was my own brother. I am the kind of help that will clean her house and wash her clothes and sing to her when she is sad. What kind of help are you, Lawrence? Maybe you are the kind of help that only arrives when it wants sexual intercourse.'

Lawrence smiled again. 'I'm not going to take offence at that,' he said. 'You're one of those women who has a funny idea about men.'

'I am one of those women who has seen men do things that are not funny.'

'Oh, please. This is Europe. We're a little more house trained over here.'

'Different from us, you think?'

'If you must put it that way.'

I nodded. 'A wolf must be a wolf and a dog must be a dog.'

'Is that what they say in your country?'

I smiled.

Lawrence frowned. 'I don't get you,' he said. 'I don't think you know how serious your situation is. If you did, you wouldn't smile.'

I shrugged. 'If I could not smile, I think my situation would be even more serious.'

We drank tea and he watched me and I watched him. He had green eyes, green as the eyes of the girl in the yellow sari on the day they let us out of the detention centre. He watched me without blinking.

'What will you do?' I said. 'What will you do if I do not go to the police?'

'Will I turn you in myself, you mean?'

I nodded. Lawrence tapped his fingers on the sides of his tea mug.

'I'll do what's best for Sarah,' he said.

The fear raced right through me, right into my belly. I watched Lawrence's fingers tapping. His skin was white as a seabird's egg, and fragile like it too. He held his hands around his mug of tea. He had long, smooth fingers and they were curled around the orange china mug as if it was a baby animal that might do something foolish if it was allowed to escape.

'You are a careful man, Lawrence.'

'I try to be.'

'Why is that?'

Lawrence laughed down his nose. 'Look at me. I'm hardly brilliant. I'm not strikingly good looking. All you can really say about me is I'm six foot one and not completely stupid.

Life doesn't throw a man like me many lifelines, so what I do have I try to hold on to.'

'Like Sarah?'

'I love Sarah. You can't imagine what she means to me. Apart from her, my life is utter shit. I work for the most appalling, heartless bureaucracy, my job is utterly senseless, and my boss makes me want to kill myself, he really does. I get home, and the kids are whining, and Linda is prattling on and on, endlessly, about nothing. The time I have with Sarah is the only time I feel like I'm doing something I've *chosen*. It's the only time I feel like myself. Even now, talking here with you. I mean, how weird is this, for you and me to be talking together in an ordinary English kitchen? This is incredible. This is a million miles away from anything that would happen in my life, and it's all because of Sarah.'

'You are worried I will take Sarah away from you. That is why you do not want me here. It is nothing to do with what is good for her.'

'I'm worried Sarah's going to do something silly to try to help you. Change her focus, change her life more than she needs to right at this moment.'

'And you are worried she will forget all about you in her new life.'

'Yes, all right, yes. But you can't imagine what would happen to me if I lost Sarah. I'd fall apart. I'd hit the bottle. Bam. It'd be the end of me. That terrifies me, even if you probably think it sounds pathetic.'

I took a sip of tea. I tasted it very carefully. I shook my head. 'It is not pathetic. In my world death will come chasing. In your world it will start whispering in your ear to destroy yourself. I know this because it started whispering to me when I was in the detention centre. Death is death, all of us are scared of it.'

Lawrence turned his tea mug around and around in his hands.

'Is it really death that you're running from? I mean, honestly? A lot of the people who come here, they're after a comfortable life.'

'If they deport me to Nigeria, I will be arrested. If they find out who I am, and what I have seen, then the politicians will find a way to have me killed. Or if I am lucky, they will put me in prison. A lot of people who have seen what the oil companies do, they go to prison for a long time. Bad things happen in a Nigerian prison. If people ever get out, they do not feel like talking.'

Lawrence shook his head, slowly, and he looked down into his tea. 'See, you tell me all that, but it just doesn't seem very likely to me. You'd be fine, look at you, I'm sure you'd find a way. It wouldn't be a big deal for me to report you to the police. I could just go down the road and do it. And then I'd have my life back, just like that.'

'And what about my life?'

'It isn't my problem. I can't be responsible for all the trouble in the world.'

'Even if your life kills me?'

'Listen, whatever's going to happen to you is going to happen eventually, whether I do anything or not. This isn't your country. They'll come for you, I promise you they will. They come for all of you in the end.'

'You could hide me.'

'Yeah, right, like they hid Anne Frank in the attic. Look how that worked out for her.'

'Who is Anne Frank?'

Lawrence closed his eyes and folded his hands behind his neck, and sighed.

'Another girl who wasn't my problem,' he said.

I felt a rage exploding inside me, so fierce that it made my eyeballs hurt. I banged my hand down on the table and his eyes snapped open wide.

'Sarah would hate you, if you told the police about me!'

'Sarah wouldn't know. I've seen how the immigration people work. They would come for you in the night. You wouldn't have time to tell Sarah. You wouldn't get to say a word.'

I stood up. 'I would find a way. I would find a way to tell her what you had done. And I would find a way to tell Linda too. I would break both of your lives, Lawrence. Your family life and your secret life.'

Lawrence looked surprised. He stood up and walked around the kitchen. He ran his hands through his hair. 'Yeah,' he said, 'I really think you would.'

'I would. Please do not imagine I would forgive you, Lawrence. I would make sure I hurt you.'

Lawrence looked out at the garden. 'Oh,' he said.

I waited. After a long time he said, 'It's funny. I've been lying awake all night thinking what to do about you. I thought about what would be best for Sarah, and what would be best for me. I honestly didn't even think about what *you'd* do. I suppose I should have. I just assumed you wouldn't be so switched on. When Sarah talked about you I was imagining, I don't know . . . not someone like you, anyway.'

'I have been in your country two years. I learned your language and I learned your rules. I am more like you than me now.'

Lawrence laughed down his nose again. 'I really don't think you're anything like me,' he said.

He sat down at the kitchen table again, and held his head in his hands. 'I'm a shit,' he said. 'I'm a loser, and you've got me over a barrel.'

He looked up at me. 'You won't really tell Linda, will you?'

His eyes were exhausted. I sighed and sat down opposite him.

'We should be friends, Lawrence.'

'How can we be?'

'We are not as different as you think, you and me.'

Lawrence laughed. 'I've just admitted to you that I'd sell you down the river if I could. You're the brave little refugee girl, and I'm the selfish bastard. I think our roles here are pretty clearly delineated, don't you?'

I shook my head. 'I am selfish too, you know.'

'No, you're really not.'

'Now you think I'm a sweet little girl, do you? In your mind you still don't think I really exist. It does not occur to you that I can be clever, like a white person. That I can be selfish, like a white person.'

I realised I was so angry I was shouting. Lawrence just laughed at me.

'Selfish! You? Took the last biscuit out of the tin, did you? Left the top off Sarah's toothpaste?'

'I left Sarah's husband hanging in the air,' I said.

Lawrence stared at me. 'What?'

I swallowed more tea, but it was too cold now and I put the mug down on the table. The light in the kitchen was cooling too. I watched the glow fade from all the objects in the room, and I felt the cold flow into my bones. All of the anger went out of me.

'Lawrence?'

'Yes?'

'Maybe it is better that I go somewhere else.'

'Stop. Wait. What did you just tell me?'

'Maybe you were right. Maybe it is better for Sarah and better for Charlie and better for you if I am not here. I could just run away. I am good at running, Lawrence.'

'Shut up,' said Lawrence quietly. He gripped my wrist.

'Stop it! That hurts!'

'Then tell me what you've done.'

'I do not want to tell you. I am frightened now.'

'Me too. Talk.'

I held on to the edge of the table and I breathed in and out against my fear. 'Sarah said it was strange that I came on the day of Andrew's funeral.'

'Yes?'

'It was not a coincidence.'

Lawrence let go of my arm and he stood up quickly and he put his hands on the back of his neck. He went to the kitchen window and stared out for a long time. Then he turned back to me. 'What *happened*?' he whispered.

'I don't think I should tell you. I shouldn't have said anything. I was angry.'

'Tell me.'

I looked down at the backs of my hands. I realised that I did want to tell someone, and I knew I could never tell Sarah. I looked up at him.

'I telephoned Andrew on the morning they let me out of the immigration detention centre. I told him I was coming.'

'Is that all?'

'Then I walked here from the immigration detention centre. I came in two days. I hid in the garden.' I pointed through the window. 'There,' I said, 'behind that bush where the cat is. Then I waited. I did not know what I wanted to do. I think I wanted to say thank you to Sarah for saving me, but also

I wanted to punish Andrew for letting my sister be killed. And I did not know how to do either of these things, so I waited. I waited for two days and two nights and I did not have anything to eat, so I came out when it was dark and I ate the seeds from the bird-feeder and I drank the water from the tap on the outside of the house. In the daytime I watched through the windows of the house, and I listened when they came out into the garden. I saw how Andrew talked to Sarah and Charlie. He was terrible. He was angry all the time. He would not play with Charlie. When Sarah talked, he just shrugged his shoulders or he shouted at her. But when he was alone, he did not stop shrugging or shouting. He would stand all alone at the end of the garden and talk to himself, and sometimes he would shout at himself, or hit himself on the head with the side of his fist, like this. He cried a lot. Sometimes he would fall down to his knees in the garden and weep for an hour. This is when I realised he was full of evil spirits.'

'He was clinically depressed. It was very hard for Sarah.'

'I think it was very hard for him too. I watched him for a long time. One time when he was weeping I watched him too hard and I forgot to hide myself, and he looked up and he saw me. I thought, Oh, no, now this is it, Little Bee. But Andrew did not come towards me. He stared at me and he said, *Oh, Jesus, you are not real, you are not there, just get out of my fucking head.* And then he closed his eyes tight and he rubbed them, and while he was doing this I hid myself back behind the bush. When he opened his eyes he looked again where I had just been, but he did not see me. Then he went back to talking to himself.'

'He thought he was hallucinating you? Poor bastard.'

'Yes, but I did not feel sorry for him at first. It was only later. On the third day he came out into the garden again, when Sarah was at work and Charlie was at the nursery. He was drunk, I think. His words were coming out slow and twisted.'

'That would have been his medication,' said Lawrence. His face had gone very white now, and he was still staring at me with his eyes very bright. 'Go on,' he said.

'It was still early in the morning. Andrew started shouting. He said, *Come out, come out, what do you want?* I did not say anything. *Please,* he said. *I know you are a ghost. What do you want to make you go away?* I stepped out from behind the laurel bush and he took one step back. *I am not a ghost*, I said. He started hitting himself on the side of the head. He said, *You are not real, you are in my head, you are not there.* He closed his eyes and he shook his head. While he had his eyes closed I walked right up to him, close enough to touch. When he opened his eyes and saw how close I was, he screamed and he ran inside the house. I felt sorry for him then. I followed him into the house. *Please listen,* I said. *I am not a ghost. I came because I do not know anyone else.* Then he said, *Touch me. Prove you are not a ghost.* So I moved closer and I put my hand on his hand. When he felt my hand, he closed his eyes for a long time and then he opened them again. I walked up the stairs and he walked in front of me. He walked up the stairs backwards. He was screaming, *Get out! Get out!* He ran in to his work room, his study, and he closed the door. So I stood outside the door and I shouted, *Do not be afraid of me! I am only a human being!* There was a very long silence, so I went away.'

Lawrence's hands were shaking. There were ripples on the surface of the tea in his cup.

'A little while later I came back. Andrew was standing on a chair in the middle of the room. What he had done, he had tied an electrical cable around the wooden beam in the ceiling. He had tied the other end around his neck. He looked at me and I looked at him. Then he whispered to me. He said, *It was a long time ago, okay? A long way away. Why won't you just stay over there?* So I said, *I am sorry, it is not safe over there.* And he said, *I know you died over there. I know you're only in my head.* He looked at me for a long time. His eyes were red and they were flickering around the room. I moved closer to him but he started shouting. He said, *If you come closer I will step off this chair.* So I stopped. I said, *Why are you doing this?* He answered in a very quiet voice. He said, *Because I've seen the person I am.* I said, *But you are a good person, Andrew. You care about the way the world is. I read your articles, in* The Times, *when I was learning English.* Andrew shook his head. He said, *Words are nothing. The person I am is the person you saw on that beach. He knows where the* commas go, *but he wouldn't cut off one finger to save you.* So I smiled at him and I said, *It doesn't matter. Look, I am here, I am alive.* And he thought about this for a long time. He said, *What happened to the girl who was with you?* So I said, *She is fine. She could not come here with me, that is all.* He looked into my eyes then. He looked and looked, until I could not look him in the eyes any more and I had to look down at the floor. And then he said, *Liar.* Then he closed his eyes and he stepped off the chair. The noises he made from his throat, it was like the noises my sister made while they killed her.'

Lawrence held on to the kitchen worktop.

'*Shit,*' he said.

'I tried to help him but he was too heavy. I could not lift up his body. I tried until I was exhausted and I was crying but I could not take the weight off the cord. I pushed the chair under his legs but he kicked it away. After a long time he stopped struggling but he was still alive. I could see his eyes watching me. He was spinning round on the cord. He was turning very slowly, and each time his body turned to face me, his eyes followed me until he spun around too far. His eyes were bulging out and his face was purple, but he was watching me. I thought, I have to help him. I thought, I must call for the neighbours or I must call an ambulance. I started running down the stairs to get help. But then I thought, If I call for help, the authorities will know that I am here. And if the authorities know that I am here, they will deport me, or maybe even worse. Because here is something, Lawrence:

after they let us out of the immigration detention centre, one of the other girls I was with, she hanged herself too. I ran away from that place but the police must know I was there. Two hangings, you see? The police would be suspicious. They would think I had something to do with it. I could not let them find me like that. So I ran out of Andrew's study and I held my head in my hands and I tried to think what to do, whether I should give up my life to save Andrew's life. And first I thought, Of course I must save him, whatever it costs me, because he is a human being. And then I thought, Of course I must save myself, because I am a human being too. And then after I had been standing there for five minutes thinking these things, I realised it was too late and I had saved myself. And then I went to the refrigerator and ate, because I was very hungry. After that I went back down the far end of the garden to hide, and I did not come out until the funeral.'

My hands were shaking. Lawrence took a deep breath. His hands were shaking too.

'Oh, God, this is serious,' he said. 'This is very, very serious.'

'Do you see now? Do you see why I want to help Sarah so much? Do you see why I want to help Charlie? I made the wrong choice, Lawrence. I let Andrew die. Now I must do everything I can to make things right.'

Lawrence was walking up and down the kitchen. He was holding the dressing-gown closed around him, and his fingers were twisting on the cloth. He stopped and looked at me.

'Does Sarah know any of this?'

I shook my head.

'I am scared to tell her. I think if I tell her then she will make me go away from here, and then I will not be able to help her, and then there will be no way for me to make up for the bad thing I did. And if I can not make up for it, then I do not know what I will do. I cannot run away again. There is nowhere to go. I have discovered the person I am and I do not like her. I am the same as Andrew. I am the same as you. I tried to save myself. Tell me, please, where is the refuge from that?'

Lawrence stared at me.

'What you did is a crime,' he said. 'Now I don't have a choice. I have to go to the police.'

I started to cry. 'Please, don't go to the police. They will take me away. I just want to help Sarah. Don't you want to help Sarah?'

'I love Sarah, so don't fucking well talk to me about helping her. Do you really think it was helpful to come here?'

I was sobbing now. 'Please,' I said. 'Please.'

There were tears running down my face. Lawrence slammed his hand down on the table.

'Shit!' he said.

'I'm sorry, Lawrence, I'm sorry.'

Lawrence slapped the palm of his hand against his forehead.

'Oh, you fucking bitch,' he said. 'I *can't* go to the police, can I? I can't let Sarah find out. Her head is fucked up enough about all this. If she knows you were there when Andrew died, she'll lose it. And it would be the end of me and her, of course it would. I couldn't go to the police without Linda finding out. This would be all over the newspapers. But I don't even want to think what this is going to be like, being with Sarah when I know this and she doesn't. And the police! Fuck! If I don't tell the police I'm as culpable as you are. What if it gets out and they realise I knew all along? I'm the one who's been sleeping with the dead man's wife, for fuck's sake. I've got motive. I could go to prison. If I don't pick up the phone and call the police, right now, then I could go to prison for you, Little Bee. Do you understand that? I could go to prison for you when I don't even know your real name.'

I folded my two hands over Lawrence's hand and I looked up into his face. I could not see him at all, just a pale shape against the light, blurry with tears.

'Please. I have to stay here. I have to make up for what I did. Please, Lawrence. I will tell nobody about you and Sarah, and you must tell nobody about me. I am asking you to save me. I am asking you to save my life.'

Lawrence tried to pull his hand away but I held on to it. I put my forehead against his arm.

'Please,' I said. 'We can be friends. We can save each other.'

'Oh, God,' he said quietly, 'I wish you hadn't told me any of this.'

'You made me tell you, Lawrence. I am sorry. I know what I am asking you. I know it will hurt you to keep the truth from Sarah. It is like asking you to cut off a finger for me.'

Lawrence pulled his hand out from under my hands. Then he took his hand away completely. I sat at the table with my eyes closed and I felt the skin of my forehead itching where it had rested on his arm. It was quiet in the kitchen, and I waited. I do not know how long I waited for. I waited till my tears were dry and the terror inside me was all gone and the only thing left was a quiet, dull misery that made my head and my eyeballs ache. There was no thought in my head, then. I was just waiting.

And then I felt Lawrence's hands on my cheeks. He cupped my face in his hands. I did not know if I was supposed to push his hands away or to place my hands upon his. We stayed like that for a little while and Lawrence's hands trembled on my cheeks. He turned my face up towards his, so I had to look into his eyes.

'I wish I could just make you disappear,' he said. 'But I'm nobody. I'm just a civil servant. I won't tell the police about you. Not if you keep quiet. But if you tell anyone, *ever*, about Sarah and me, or if you tell anyone, *ever*, about what happened with Andrew, I will have you on a plane to Nigeria, I swear.'

I breathed one long, deep breath.

'Thank you,' I whispered.

Sarah's voice came from upstairs. 'Who said you could watch TV, Batman?'

Lawrence took his hands away from my face and he went to make more tea. Sarah came into the kitchen. She was yawning, and her eyes were screwed up against the sunlight. Charlie came with her, holding her hand.

'I might as well tell you the rules,' said Sarah, 'since you're both new around here. Superheroes, especially dark knights, are not allowed to watch television before they've eaten their breakfast. Are they, Batman?'

Charlie grinned at her and shook his head.

'Right,' said Sarah. 'Bat flakes or bat toast?'

'Bat toast,' said Charlie.

Sarah went to the toaster and put two slices of bread into it. Lawrence and I, we both just watched her. Sarah turned around.

'Is everything all right in here?' she said. She looked at me. 'Have you been crying?'

'It is nothing,' I said. 'I always cry in the morning.'

Sarah frowned at Lawrence. 'I hope you've been looking after her.'

'Of course,' said Lawrence. 'Little Bee and I have been getting to know one another.'

Sarah nodded. 'Good,' she said. 'Because we really have to make this work. You both know that, don't you?'

She looked at each of us and then she yawned again, and she stretched her arms. 'Fresh start,' she said.

I looked at Lawrence and Lawrence looked at me.

'Now,' said Sarah. 'I'm going to take Charlie to nursery and then we can start to track down Little Bee's papers. We'll find you a solicitor first. I know a good one that we some-times use on the magazine.'

Sarah smiled, and she went over to Lawrence.

'And as for you,' she said, 'I'm going to find a little time to thank you for coming all the way to Birmingham.'

She put her hand up to Lawrence's face, but then I think she remembered that Charlie was in the room and so she just brushed her hand against his shoulder instead. I went into the next room to watch the television news with the sound turned off.

The news announcer looked so much like my sister. My heart was overflowing with things to say. But in your country, you cannot talk back to the news.

8

I remember the exact day when England became me, when its contours cleaved to the curves of my own body, when its inclinations became my own. As a girl, on a bike ride through the Surrey lanes, pedalling in my cotton dress through the hot fields blushing with poppies, freewheeling down a sudden dip into a cool wooded sanctum where a stream ran beneath the flint and brick bridge. Coming to a stop, the brakes squealing from the work of plucking one still moment out of time. Throwing my bicycle down into a pungent cushion of cow parsley and wild mint, and sliding down the plunging bank into the clear cold water, my sandals kicking up a quick brown bloom of mud from the stream bed, the minnows darting away into the black pool of shade beneath the bridge. Pressing my face into the water, with time utterly suspended, drinking in the cool shock. And then, looking up and seeing a fox. He was sunning himself on the far bank, watching me through a feathery screen of barley. I looked back at him, and his amber eyes held mine. The moment, the country: I realised it had become me. I found a soft patch of wild grass and cornflower by the side of the barley field, and I lay down with my face close to the damp earthen smell of the grass roots, listening to the buzzing of the summer flies. I cried, but I didn't know why.

The morning after Lawrence stayed overnight, I dropped off Charlie at nursery and I went home to see what I could do to help Little Bee. I found her upstairs, watching television with the sound turned off. She looked so sad.

'What's wrong?' I said.

Little Bee shrugged.

'Is everything okay with Lawrence?'

She looked away.

'What is it, then?'

Nothing.

'Maybe you're homesick. I know I would be. Do you miss your country?'

She turned to look at me and her eyes were very solemn.

'Sarah,' she said, 'I do not think I have left my country. I think it has travelled with me.'

She turned back to the television. That's all right, I thought. There'll be plenty of time to get through to her.

I tidied the kitchen while Lawrence was showering. I made myself a coffee and I realised, for the first time since Andrew died, that I had taken only one cup down from the cupboard instead of my instinctual two. I stirred in the milk, the spoon clinked against the china, and I realised I was losing the habit of being Andrew's wife. How strange, I thought. I smiled, and realised I felt strong enough to put in an appearance at the magazine.

At my usual time the commuter train was crowded with pinstripes and laptop bags, but now it was ten thirty in the morning and the train ran nearly empty. The boy opposite me stared at the carriage's ceiling. He wore an England shirt and blue jeans, white with plaster dust. Tattooed on the inside of his forearm, in a gothic typeface, were the words: THIS IS A TIME FOR HERO'S. I stared at the tattoo – at the fixity of its pride and its broken grammar. When I looked up the boy was watching me back, his amber eyes calm and unblinking. I blushed, and stared out of the window at the flickering back gardens of the semis.

The train braked as we neared Waterloo. There was a sensation of being between worlds. The brake shoes squealed against the train's metal wheels and I felt eight years old again. Here I was, converging with my magazine on unflinching rails. Soon I would arrive at a terminus and have to prove that I could step off this carriage and back into my grown-up job. When the train stopped I turned to say something to the boy with amber eyes, but he had already stood from his seat and disappeared back into the cover of the barley field beneath the shade of the sheltering woods.

I arrived on the editorial floor at eleven thirty. The place went quiet. All the girls stared at me. I smiled and clapped my hands.

'Come on, back to work!' I said. 'When a hundred thousand ABC1 urban professional women between the ages of eighteen and thirty-five lose focus then so will we, but not until.'

At the far end of the open-plan, Clarissa was sitting behind my desk. She stood when I walked over, and came round to the front. Her lip gloss was iridescent plum. She held her hands around mine.

'Oh, Sarah,' she said. 'You poor old thing. How are you coping?'

She was wearing an aubergine shirt-dress with a smooth black fishskin belt and glossy black knee-high boots. I realised I was wearing the jeans I had taken Batman to nursery in.

'I'm fine,' I said.

Clarissa looked me up and down, and furrowed her brow.

'Really?' she said.

'Really.'

'Oh. Well, that's great.'

I looked over my desk. Clarissa's laptop sat in the centre, next to her Kelly bag. My papers had been shunted to the far end.

'We didn't think you'd be in,' said Clarissa. 'You don't mind me usurping your throne, do you, darling?'

I saw the way she had plugged her Blackberry into my charger.

'No,' I said, 'of course not.'

'We thought you'd like us to get a head start on the July issue.'

I was conscious of eyes watching us from all around the office. I smiled.

'Yes, that's great,' I said. 'Really. So what have we got so far?'

'For this issue? Wouldn't you like to sit down first? Let me get you a coffee, you must feel terrible.'

'My husband died, Clarissa. I am still alive. I have a son to look after and a mortgage to pay. I'd just like to get straight back to work.'

Clarissa took a step back.

'Fine,' she said. 'Well, we've got some great stuff. It's Henley month of course so we're doing an ironic what-not-to-wear for the regatta, which is a cunning pretext for some pics of gorgeous rowers, *bien évidemment*. For fashion we're doing something called "Fuck Your Boyfriend" – see what we did there? That's going to be girls with whips snarling at boys in Duckie Brown, basically. And for the "Real Life" slot there's two choices. Either we go with this piece called "Beauty and the Budget" about a woman with two ugly daughters and only enough money to pay for cosmetic surgery for one of them. Ugh – yes – I know. *Or* – my preference – we've got a piece called "Good Vibrations" and I'm telling you, it's an eye-opener. I mean, my *God*, Sarah, some of the sex toys you can buy online these days, they're solutions to desires I had no idea *existed*, God save us all.'

I closed my eyes and listened to the hum of the fluorescent lights, the buzzing of fax machines and the fluid chatter of the editorial girls on their phones to fashion houses. It all seemed suddenly insane, like wearing a little green bikini to an African war. I breathed out slowly, and opened my eyes.

'So which piece do you want to go with?' said Clarissa. 'Cosmetic conundrum, or carnal cornucopia?'

I walked over to the window and rolled my forehead against the glass.

'Please don't do that, Sarah. It makes me nervous when you do that.'

'I'm thinking.'

'I know, darling. That's why it makes me nervous, because I know *what* you're thinking. We have this argument every month. But we have to run the stories people read. You know we do.'

I shrugged. 'My son is convinced he will lose all his powers if he takes off his Batman costume.'

'And your point is?'

'That we can be deluded. That we can be mistaken in our beliefs.'

'You think I am?'

'I don't know what to think any more, Clar. About the magazine, I mean. It all seems a bit unreal suddenly.'

'Of course it does, you poor thing. I don't even know why you came in today. It's far too early.'

I nodded. 'That's what Lawrence said too.'

'You should listen to him.'

'I do. I'm lucky to have him, I really am. I don't know what I'd do otherwise.'

Clarissa came and stood next to me at the window.

'Have you spoken with him much, since Andrew died?'

'He's at my house,' I said. 'He showed up last night.'

'He stayed *overnight*? He's married, isn't he?'

'Don't be like that. He was a married man before Andrew died.'

Clarissa shivered. 'I know. It's just a bit creepy, that's all.'

'Is it?'

Clarissa blew a strand of hair out of her eyes. 'Sudden, I suppose I mean.'

'Well, it wasn't my idea, if you must know.'

'In which case I revert to my original choice of word. *Creepy*.'

Now we both stood with our foreheads against the glass, looking down at the traffic.

'I actually came here to talk about work,' I said after a while.

'Fine.'

'I want us to go back to the kind of article we did while we were making our name. Let's just, for once, put a real life feature in the "Real Life" slot. That's all I'm saying. I won't let you talk me out of it this time.'

'What, then? What kind of a feature?'

'I want us to do a piece on refugees to the UK. Don't worry, we can do it in the style of the magazine. We can make it about women refugees if you like.'

Clarissa rolled her eyes.

'And yet something in your tone tells me you're not talking about women refugees with sex toys.'

I smiled.

'What if I said no?' said Clarissa.

'I don't know. Technically, I suppose, I could sack you.'

Clarissa thought for a moment.

'Why refugees?' she said. 'Is this because you're still cross we didn't go with the Baghdad woman in the June issue?'

'I just think it's an issue that isn't going to go away. May, June, or any time soon.'

'Fine,' said Clarissa. Then she said, 'Would you really sack me, darling?'

'I don't know. Would you really say no?'

'I don't know.'

We stood for a long time. In the street below, an Italian-looking boy was cycling past the traffic queue. Mid-twenties, shirtless and tanned in short white nylon shorts.

'Five,' said Clarissa.

'Out of ten?'

'Out of five, darling.'

I laughed. 'There are days when I would cheerfully swap lives with you, Clar.'

Clarissa turned to me. I noticed the very slight mark of foundation left on the window-pane where her forehead had been. It hovered like a light flesh-toned cloud over the bone-white spire of Christ Church Spitalfields.

'Oh, Sarah,' said Clarissa. 'We go too far back to let one another down. You're the boss. Of course I'll get you a feature on refugees, if you really want it. But I really don't think you understand how quickly people's eyes will glaze over. It isn't an issue that affects anyone's own *life*, that's the problem.'

I felt a lurching vertigo and I took a step back from the glass.

'You'll just have to find an angle,' I said shakily.

Clarissa stared at me. 'You're bereaved, Sarah. You're not thinking straight. You're not ready to be back at work yet.'

'You want my job, is that it, Clar?'

She reddened. 'You didn't say that,' she said.

I sat down on the edge of the desk and massaged my temples with my thumbs.

'No, I didn't. God. I'm so sorry. Anyway, maybe you *should* have my job. I'm losing the plot, I really am. I don't see the point in it any more.'

Clarissa sighed. 'I don't want your job, Sarah.'

She waved her long nails in the direction of the editorial floor.

'They're still hungry for it, Sarah. Maybe you should move on and let one of them have the job.'

'Do you think they really deserve it?'

'Did we deserve it, at their age?'

'I don't know. All I remember is how badly I wanted it. Didn't it seem so thrilling, back then? I thought I could take on the world, I really did. Make real life issues sexy. Be challenging, remember? The bloody name of our magazine, Clar. Remember why we chose it? *Nixie*, for heaven's sake. We were going to bring them in with sex and then immerse them in the issues. We weren't going to let anyone teach us how to run a magazine. We were going to teach them, remember? Whatever happened to us *wanting* that?'

'What happened to wanting, Sarah, was getting a few of the things we wanted.'

I smiled, and sat down at my desk. I scrolled through the mocked-up pages on Clarissa's screen.

'These are actually pretty good,' I said.

'Of course they're good, darling, I've been doing the exact same story every single month for ten years. Cosmetic surgery and sex toys I can do with my eyes closed.'

I leaned back in the chair and closed my eyes. Clarissa put her hand on my shoulder.

'But seriously, Sarah?'

'Mmm?'

'Please just give yourself a day to think about it, will you? The refugee piece, I mean. You're in a state at the moment, with everything that's happened. Why don't you take tomorrow off, just to make sure you're sure, and if you are sure then of course I'll make it happen for you. But if you're not sure, then let's not throw away our careers over it right now, okay, darling?'

I opened my eyes. 'Okay,' I said. 'I'll take a day.'

Clarissa sagged with relief. 'Thank you, doll. Because it's not so bad, what we do. Really. No one dies when we write about fashion.'

I looked out over the editorial floor and saw the girls watching me back: speculative, excited, predatory.

I took another half-empty train back to Kingston and arrived home at two in the afternoon. It was hot and hazy, with a stillness and a heaviness to the day. We needed some rain to break it.

Lawrence was in the kitchen when I got back home. I put the kettle on.

'Where's Bee?'

'She's in the garden.'

I looked out and saw her, lying on the grass, at the far end of the garden beside the laurel bush.

'She seem okay to you?'

He just shrugged.

'What is it? You two really haven't hit it off, have you?'

'It's not that,' said Lawrence.

'There's a tension though, isn't there? I can feel it.'

I realised I had stirred one of the teabags until it burst. I drained the mug into the sink and started again.

Lawrence stood behind me and put his arms around my waist.

'It's you who seems tense,' he said. 'Is it work?'

I leaned my head backwards onto his shoulder and sighed.

'Work was hideous,' I said. 'I lasted forty minutes. I'm wondering if I should quit.'

He sighed into the back of my neck.

'I knew it,' he said. 'I knew something like this was coming.'

I looked out at Little Bee, lying on her back, watching the hazy sky filling in with grey.

'Do you remember what it felt like to be her age? Or Charlie's age? Do you remember back when you felt you could actually *do* something to make the world better?'

'You're talking to the wrong man. I work for central government, remember? Actually *doing* something is the mistake we're trained to avoid.'

'Stop it, Lawrence, I'm being serious.'

'Did I ever think I could change the world? Is that your question?'

'Yes.'

'A bit, maybe. When I first joined the civil service, I suppose I was quite idealistic.'

'When did it change?'

'When I realised we weren't going to change the world. Certainly not if that involved implementing any computer systems. Round about lunchtime on the first day.'

I smiled and put my mouth close to Lawrence's ear. 'Well, you've changed my world,' I said.

Lawrence swallowed. 'Yes,' he said. 'Yes, I suppose I have.'

Behind us the icemaker dropped another cube. We stood for a while and looked out at Little Bee.

'Look at her,' I said. 'I'm so scared. Do you really think I can save her?'

Lawrence shrugged. 'Maybe you can. And don't take this the wrong way, but so what? Save her and there's a whole world of them behind her. A whole swarm of Little Bees, coming here to feed.'

'Or to pollinate,' I said.

'I think that's naïve,' said Lawrence.

'I think my features editor would agree with you.'

Lawrence massaged my shoulders and I closed my eyes.

'What's eating you?' said Lawrence.

'I can't seem to use the magazine to make a difference,' I said. 'But that's how it was conceived. It was meant to have an edge. It was never meant to be just another fashion rag.'

'So what's stopping you?'

'Every time we put in something deep and meaningful, the circulation drops.'

'So people's lives are hard enough. You can see how they might not want to be reminded that everyone else's lives are shit too.'

'I suppose so. Maybe Andrew was right after all. Maybe I need to grow up and get a grown-up's job.'

Lawrence held me close.

'Or maybe you should relax for a little while and just enjoy what you've got.'

I looked out at the garden. The sky was darker now. It seemed the rain couldn't be far off.

'Little Bee has changed me, Lawrence. I can't look at her without thinking how shallow my life is.'

'Sarah, you're talking absolute shit. We see the world's problems every day on television. Don't tell me this is the first time you've realised they're real. Don't tell me those people wouldn't swap lives with you if they could. Their lives are fucked up. But fucking up your life too? That isn't going to help them.'

'Well, I'm not helping them now, am I?'

'How could you possibly do more? You cut off a *finger* to save that girl. And now you're sheltering her. Food, lodging, solicitor . . . none of that comes cheap. You're taking down a good salary and you're spending it to help.'

'Ten per cent. That's all I'm giving her. One finger in ten. Ten pounds in every hundred. Ten per cent is hardly a wholehearted commitment.'

'Re-evaluate that. Ten per cent is the cost of doing business. Ten per cent buys you a stable world to get on with your life in. Here, safe in the West. That's the way to think of it. If everyone gave ten per cent, we wouldn't need to give asylum.'

'You still want me to kick her out, don't you?'

Lawrence spun me round to look at him. There was something in his eyes that looked almost like panic, and at that moment it troubled me for reasons I could not fathom.

'No,' he said. 'Absolutely not. You keep her and you look after her. But please, please don't throw your own life away. I care about you too much for that. I care about us too much.'

'Oh, I don't know, I really don't.' I sighed. 'I miss Andrew,' I said.

Lawrence took his hands from my waist, and took a step back.

'Oh, please,' I said. 'That came out all wrong. I just mean, he was so good with the ordinary things. He was no nonsense, you know? He would just say to me, *Don't be so bloody foolish, Sarah. Of course you shall keep your job.* And I would feel awful because of the way he would talk to me, but I *would* keep my job and then of course he'd turn out to be right, which was even worse in a way. But I miss him, Lawrence. It's funny how you can miss someone like that.'

Lawrence stood against the opposite counter, watching me.

'So what do you want from me?' he said. 'You want me to start getting on my high horse like Andrew did?'

I smiled. 'Oh, come here,' I said.

I hugged him, and breathed in the soft, clean smell of his skin.

'I'm being impossible again, aren't I?'

'You're being bereaved. It's going to take a while for all the pieces to fall into place. It's good that you're taking a look at your life, really it is, but I don't think you should rush into anything, you know? If you still feel like quitting your job in six months' time, then do it by all means. But right now your job is paying for you to do something worthwhile. It is possible to do good things with an imperfect situation. God knows, I should know.'

I blinked back tears. 'Compromise, eh? Isn't it sad, growing up? You start off like my Charlie. You start off thinking you can kill all the baddies and save the world. Then you get a little bit older, maybe Little Bee's age, and you realise that some of the world's badness is inside you, that maybe you're a part of it. And then you get a little bit older still, and a bit more comfortable, and you start wondering whether that badness you've seen in yourself is really all that bad at all. You start talking about ten per cent.'

'Maybe that's just developing as a person, Sarah.'

I sighed, and looked out at Little Bee.

'Well,' I said, 'maybe this is a developing world.'

9

Sarah had this very big decision to make at work, so she took a day off. She said to me and Lawrence and Charlie in the morning, *Come on, we are going on an adventure.* I was happy because Sarah was smiling. Also I was glad because it was many years since the last time I went on an adventure.

What is an adventure? That depends on where you are starting from. Little girls in your country, they hide in the gap between the washing machine and the refrigerator and they make believe they are in the jungle, with green snakes and monkeys all around them. Me and my sister, we used to hide in a gap in the jungle, with green snakes and monkeys all around us, and make believe that we had a washing machine and a refrigerator. You live in a world of machines and you dream of things with beating hearts. We dream of machines, because we see where beating hearts have left us.

When we were children, me and Nkiruka, there was a place we went in the jungle near our village, a secret place, and that was where we played houses. The last time we went on that adventure my big sister was ten years old and I was eight. We were already too old for the game and both of us knew it, but we agreed to dream our dream one last time so that we could fix it into our memories, before we awoke from it forever.

We crept out of our village in the quietest part of the night. It was the year before the trouble first began with the oil, and four years before my sister started smiling at the older boys, so you can see that it was a peaceful time for our village. There were no sentries guarding the road where the houses ended, and we walked out with no one to ask us where we were going. We did not walk out straight away, though. First we had to wait until the rest of the village was asleep. It took longer than usual because the moon was full, and so bright that it gleamed on the metal roofs and sparkled on the bowl of water that me and my sister kept in our room to wash our faces with. The moon made the dogs and the old people restless, and there were long hours of barking and grumbling before silence came to the last of the houses.

Me and Nkiruka, we watched through the window until the moon grew to an extraordinary size, so big that it filled the window-frame. We could see the face of the man in the moon, so close that we could see the madness in his eyes. The moon made everything glow so brightly it felt like day, and not an ordinary day at all but a baffling day, an extra day, like the sixth toe of a cat or like a secret message that you find hidden between the pages of a book you have read many times before and found nothing. The moon shone on the limba tree and it gleamed on the old broken Peugeot and it sparkled on the ghost of the Mercedes. Everything glowed with this pale dark brightness. That is when Nkiruka and I walked out into the night.

The animals and the birds were acting strangely. The monkeys were not howling and the night birds were quiet. We walked out through such a silence, I am not joking, it was as if the little silver clouds that drifted across the face of the moon were leaning down to the earth and whispering, *Shhh*. Nkiruka's eyes when she looked over at me, they were scared and excited at the same time. We held hands and we walked the mile through the cassava fields to the place where the jungle started. The paths of red earth between the rows of cassava, they gleamed in the moonlight like the rib bones of giants. When we reached the jungle, it was silent and dark.

We did not speak, we just walked in before we got too scared. We walked for a long time, and the path got narrower, and the leaves and the branches closed in on us tighter and tighter until we had to walk one behind the other. Branches began closing in on the path so that we had to crouch down. Soon we could not carry on at all. So Nkiruka said, *This is not the right path, now we must turn around*, and we turned around. But that is when we realised that we were not on a path at all, because the branches and the plants were still very tight all around us. We carried on for a little way, weaving around the plants, but very soon we realised we had missed the path and we were lost.

Under the jungle it was so dark we could not see our own hands, and we held on to each other very close so we would not get separated. All around us now we could hear the noises of the jungle animals moving in the undergrowth, and of course they were very small animals, just rats and shrews and jungle pigs, but in the dark they became huge for us, as big as our fear and growing with it. We did not feel like pretending we had a refrigerator or a washing machine. It did not seem like the kind of night where such appliances would help.

I started to cry because the darkness was complete and I did not think it would ever end. But Nkiruka, she held me close and she rocked me and she whispered to me, *Do not be sad, little sister. What is my name?* And through my sobs I said, *Your name is Nkiruka*. And my sister rubbed my head and she said, *Yes, that is right. My name means 'the future is bright'. See? Would our mother and our father have given me this name if it was not true? As long as you are with me, little sister, the darkness will not last forever*. I stopped crying then, and I fell asleep with my head on my sister's shoulder.

I woke up before Nkiruka. I was cold, and it was dawn. The jungle birds were waking up and there was a pale light all around us, a thin grey-green light. All around us there were low fern plants and ground creepers, and the leaves were dripping with the dew. I stood up and took a few steps forwards, because it seemed to me that the light was brighter in that direction. I pushed aside a low branch, and that is when I saw it. There was a very old Jeep in the undergrowth. Its tyres had rotted away to nothing and the creepers and the ferns were growing out through the arches of its wheels. The black plastic seats were tattered and the short rusty springs were poking out through them. Fungus was growing on the doors. The Jeep was pointed away from me, and I walked closer.

I saw that the jungle and the Jeep had grown together, so that there was no telling where the one ended and the other began – whether the jungle grew out of the Jeep or the Jeep grew out of the jungle. The footwells of the Jeep were filled with the rotted leaves of many seasons, and all the Jeep's metal had become the same dark colour as the fallen leaves and the earth. Lying across the front seats there was the skeleton of a man. At first I did not see it because the skeleton was dressed in clothes the same colour as the leaves, but the clothes were so torn and ragged that the white bones shone through them in the early morning light. It looked as if the skeleton had become tired from driving and he had laid himself down across the two front seats to sleep. His skull lay on the dashboard, a little way apart from the rest of the skeleton. He was looking up at a small bright patch of sky, high above us through a gap in the forest canopy. I know this because the skull was wearing sunglasses and the sky was reflected in one of the lenses. A snail had crawled across this lens and eaten all the green mould and dirt off it, and it was in the glistening trail of this creature that the glass reflected the sky. Now the snail was halfway along one arm of the sunglasses. I went closer to look. The sunglasses had thin gold frames. On the corner of the lens that reflected the sky, the snail had crawled across the place where the glasses said *Ray-Ban*. I supposed that this had been the man's name, because I was young and my troubles had still not found me and I did not yet understand that there could be reasons for wearing a name that was not one's own.

I stood and looked down at Ray Ban's skull for a long time, watching my own face reflected in his lenses. I saw myself fixed in the landscape of my country: a young girl with tall dark trees and a small patch of sunlight. I stared for a long time, and the skull did not turn away and neither did I, and I understood that this is how it would always be for me.

After a few minutes, I walked back to my sister. The branches closed behind me. I did not understand why the Jeep was there. I did not know that there had been a war in my country nearly thirty years before. The war, the roads, the orders – everything that had brought the Jeep to that place had been overgrown by the jungle. I was eight years old and I thought that the jeep had grown up out of the ground, like the ferns and the tall trees all around us. I thought it had grown

286

up quite naturally from the red soil of my country, as native as cassava. And I knew that I did not want my sister to see it.

I followed my steps back to the place where Nkiruka was still sleeping. I stroked her cheek. *Wake up*, I said. *The light is back. We can find the way home now.* Nkiruka smiled at me and sat up. She rubbed the sleep out of her eyes. *There*, she said. *Didn't I tell you that the darkness would not last forever?*

'Is everything all right?' said Sarah.

I blinked and I looked around at the kitchen. From the clean white walls and the kitchen table, I saw the jungle creepers shrink back into the darkest corners of the room.

'You seemed miles off.'

'Sorry,' I said. 'I still have not quite woken up.'

Sarah smiled. 'I was just saying, let's go for an adventure.'

Charlie looked up at her.

'Is we going to Gotham City?' he asked.

Sarah laughed. '*Are we* going. No, Batman, we're just going to the park.'

Charlie slumped down to the floor. 'Don't want to go to the park.'

I knelt down beside him. 'Batman,' I said. 'In the park there are trees, and lots of old branches on the ground.'

'So?'

'So, we can build Gotham City there, out of branches.'

Charlie scratched his head, behind one of his bat ears. 'With mine bat crane?'

'And your special powers.'

Charlie grinned. 'I want to go to the park NOW!' he said.

'Come on then, my little crusader,' said Sarah. 'Let's get into the Batmobile.'

Lawrence sat in the front of the car with Sarah, and I went in the back with Charlie. We drove through the gate of Richmond Park, and up a steep hill. On both sides of the narrow road, tall green grasses swayed in the breeze and deer held their heads up to look at us. Sarah stopped in a car park, next to an ice-cream van.

'No, Batman,' said Sarah. 'Before you ask, the answer is not yet.'

Charlie dragged on her hand as we walked, looking back at the ice-cream van. The park was not crowded and we walked along a dirt path to an enclosure called the Isabella Plantation. Inside there were great jungles of a coiling, tangling bush.

'Lovely rhododendrons,' said Sarah.

Underneath their smooth, curling branches, the shade was dark and cool. In the open it was hot. We stopped on a neat grass lawn, beside a small lake with ducks swimming on it. Sarah spread out a blanket in the shade of a tree with red, peeling bark and a brass label to say what it was. In the Isabella Plantation there was no wind. The surface of the lake was oily and smooth. The sky was reflected in it. The water and the sky stretched out to meet one another and the line where they met was hazy and uncertain. Large fish swam in the lake but they did not break the surface. All you could see was the swirls in the water where they had been. I looked at Sarah and she looked back at me and we found that we could not smile.

'I'm sorry,' she said. 'This is reminding you of the beach, isn't it?'

'It's okay,' I said. 'It is only water.'

We sat on the blanket. In the shade it was cool and peaceful. All over the grass lawn there were families arriving and settling down to enjoy the day. One of those families, they made me look twice. There was a father and a mother and a little girl, and the father was doing tricks with a coin to make his daughter laugh. He flipped the coin high in the air and I saw it tumbling through the bright blue sky with the sunshine flashing upon it and the Queen of England's face upon the coin – with her lips moving and saying, *Good lord, we appear to be falling* – and it fell all the way back into the man's hand, and the man's hand closed around it, and the colour of his hand was very dark, darker even than my skin. And his daughter was laughing and trying to open up the fingers of his hand, and her skin was much lighter that her father's – it was the colour of the sticks that Charlie was racing around and collecting. And the mother, she was laughing too, and helping her daughter to get the father's hand open, and the mother's skin was as white as Sarah's.

I would not even try to explain this to the girls from my village because they would not believe it. If I told them that there were in this place children that were born of black and white parents, holding hands in the park and laughing together, they would only shake their heads and say, *Little miss been-to is making up her tales again.*

But I looked around that place and I realised that there were other families like this. Most were white but some were black, and as many as were black were mixed. I smiled when I saw this. I was thinking to myself, Little Bee, there is no *them* in this place. These happy people, these mixed-up people who are one thing and also another thing, these people are *you.* Nobody will miss you and nobody is looking for you. So what is stopping you from just stepping out into this mixed-up country and becoming a part of it? I thought to myself, Little Bee, maybe that is just what you should do.

Charlie was pulling my hand. He wanted to build Gotham City straight away, so we went together to the edge of the rhododendron jungle. There were many pale, smooth sticks of wood that had fallen there. We worked for a long time. We built towers and bridges. We built roads, railway lines and schools. Then we built a hospital for injured superheroes and a hospital for injured animals, because Charlie said his city needed these things. Charlie was concentrating very hard. I said to him, 'Do you want to take off your Batman costume?' But he shook his head.

'I am worried about you. You will be exhausted by this heat. Come on, aren't you too hot in your costume?'

'Yes, but if I is not in mine costume then I is not Batman.'

'Do you need to be Batman all the time?'

Charlie nodded. 'Yes, because if I is not Batman *all the time* then mine daddy dies.'

Charlie looked down at the ground. In his hands he was holding a stick, so tight that I could see the small white bones of his knuckles through the skin.

'Charlie,' I said. 'You think your daddy died because you were not Batman?'

Charlie looked up. Through the dark eyeholes of his bat mask, I could see the tears in his eyes.

'I was at mine nursery,' he said. 'That's when the baddies got mine daddy.'

His lip trembled. I pulled him towards me and I held him while he cried. I stared over his shoulder at the cold black tunnels that loomed between the tangled rhododendron roots. I stared into the black but all I could see was Andrew spinning slowly round on the electrical cable, with his eyes watching me each time he revolved. The look in his eyes was the look of those black tunnels: there was no end to them.

'Listen, Charlie,' I said. 'Your daddy did not die because you were not there. It is not your fault. Do you understand? You are a good boy, Charlie. It is not your fault at all.'

Charlie pulled himself out of my arms and looked at me.

'Why did mine daddy die?'

I thought about it.

'The baddies got him, Charlie. But they are not the sort of baddies Batman can fight. They are the sort of baddies that your daddy had to fight in his heart and I have to fight in my heart. They are baddies from inside.'

Charlie nodded. 'Is there lots?'

'Of what?'

'Of baddies from inside?'

I looked at the dark tunnels, and I shivered.

'I think everyone has them,' I said.

'Will we beat them?'

I nodded. 'Of course.'

'And they won't get me, will they?'

I smiled. 'No, Charlie, I don't think those baddies will ever get you.'

'And they won't get you either, will they?'

I sighed. 'Charlie, there are no baddies here in the park. We are on holiday here. Maybe you can take one day off from being Batman.'

Charlie pointed his stick at me and he frowned, as if this was a trick of his enemies.

'Batman is *always* Batman,' he said.

I laughed, and we went back to building houses out of sticks. I put a long, bone-white one on top of a pile that Charlie said was a multistorey Batmobile park.

'Sometimes I wish I could take one day off from being Little Bee,' I said.

Charlie looked up at me. A drop of sweat fell from inside his bat mask. 'Why?'

'Well, you see, it was hard to become Little Bee. I had to go through a lot of things. They kept me in detention and I had to train myself to think in a certain way, and to be strong, and to speak your language the way you people speak it. It is even an effort now just to keep it going. Because inside, you know, I am only a village girl. I would like to be a village girl again and do the things that village girls do. I would like to laugh and smile at the older boys. I would like to do foolish things when the moon is full. And most of all, you know, I would like to use my real name.'

Charlie paused with his spade in the air.

'But Little Bee *is* yours real name,' he said.

I shook my head. 'Mmm-mmm. Little Bee is only my superhero name. I have a real name too, like you have *Charlie.*'

Charlie nodded.

'What is yours real name?' he said.

'I will tell you my real name if you will take off your Batman costume.'

Charlie frowned. 'Actually, I have to keep mine Batman costume on forever,' he said.

I smiled. 'Okay, Batman. Maybe another time.'

Charlie started to build a wall between the jungle and the suburbs of Gotham City.

'Mmm,' he said.

After a while, Lawrence came over to us.

'I'll take over here,' he said. 'Go and see if you can talk some sense into Sarah, will you?'

'Why, what is wrong?'

Lawrence held his hands out with the palms upwards, and he sent air upwards out of his mouth so that his hair blew. 'Just go and see her, will you?' he said.

I walked back to the blanket in the shade. Sarah was sitting there with her arms around her knees.

'Honestly,' she said when she saw me, 'that *bloody* man.'

'Lawrence?'

'Sometimes I'm not so sure I wouldn't be better off without him. Oh, I don't mean that, of course I don't. But honestly. Don't I have the right to talk about Andrew?'

'You were arguing?'

Sarah sighed.

'I suppose Lawrence still isn't happy about you being around. It's putting him on edge.'

'What did you say, about Andrew?'

'I told him I was sorting out Andrew's office last night. You know, looking through his files. I just wanted to see what bills I'm meant to pay now, check we don't owe money on any of our cards, that sort of thing.'

She looked at me. 'The thing is, it turns out Andrew didn't stop thinking about what happened on the beach. I thought he'd put it out of his mind, but he hadn't. He was researching it. There must have been two dozen folders in his office. Stuff about Nigeria. About the oil wars, and the atrocities. And . . . well, I had no idea how many people like you ended up in the UK after what happened to your villages. Andrew had a whole binder full of documents about asylum and detention.'

'Did you read it?'

Sarah chewed her lip. 'Not much of it. He had enough in there to read for a month. And he had his own notes attached to each document. It was very meticulous. Very Andrew. It was too late at night to really sit down and start reading through it. How long did you say they kept you in that place, Bee?'

'Two years.'

'Can you tell me what it was like?'

'It is best that you do not know. It is not your fault that I was there.'

'Tell me. Please?'

I sighed, because the memory of that place made my heart heavy again.

'The first thing was that you had to write down your story. They gave you a pink form to write down what had happened to you. This was the grounds for your asylum application. Your whole life, you had to fit it onto one sheet of paper. There was a black line around the edge of the sheet, a border, and if you wrote outside the line then your application would not be valid. They only gave you enough space to write down the very saddest things that had happened to you. That was the worst part. Because if you cannot read the beautiful things that have happened in someone's life, why should you care about their sadness? Do you see? That is why people do not like us refugees. It is because they only know the tragic parts of our life, so they think we are tragic people. I was one of the only ones who could write in English, so I wrote the applications for all the others. You have to listen to their story and then fit their whole life inside the line, even for the women who are bigger than one sheet of paper, you know? And after that, everyone was waiting for their appeal. We did not have any information. That was the worst thing. No one there had committed a crime, but you did not know if you would be released tomorrow, or next week, or never. There were even children in there, and they could not remember their life before detention. There were bars on the windows. They let us exercise outdoors for thirty minutes a day, unless it was raining at exercise time. If you got a headache you could ask for one paracetamol, but you had to apply for it twenty-four hours in advance. There was a special form to fill in. And there was another form if you wanted a sanitary towel. Once there was an inspection of the detention centre. Four months later we saw the inspectors' report. It was pinned to a board that said STATUTORY NOTICES, at the end of a corridor that nobody used, because it led to the exit and the exit was locked. One of the other girls found the notice board when she was trying to find a window to look out of. The report said, *We find the humiliating procedures excessive. We do not see how anybody can abuse an excess of sanitary towels.'*

Sarah looked over to where Lawrence and Charlie were laughing and kicking sticks at each other. When she spoke again, her voice was quiet. 'I suppose Andrew was planning a book,' she said. 'I think that's why he was collecting all that material. It was too much research to do if he was only going to write an article or something.'

'And you told this to Lawrence?'

Sarah nodded. 'I said I thought maybe I should carry on Andrew's work. You know, read through his notes. Find out a bit more about the detention centres. Maybe even, I don't know, write the book myself.'

'That is why he got angry?'

'He went ballistic.' Sarah sighed. 'I think he's jealous of Andrew.'

I nodded slowly and I said, 'Are you certain it is Lawrence you want to be with?'

She looked at me with sharp eyes.

'I know what you're going to tell me. You'll tell me he cares more about himself than he cares about me. You'll tell me to watch out for him. And I'll tell you that's just what men are like, but you're too young to know it yet, and so you and I will argue too, and then I really will be utterly miserable. So don't say it, okay?'

I shook my head. 'It is more than that, Sarah.'

'I don't want to hear it. I've chosen Lawrence. I'm thirty-two, Bee. If I want to make a stable life for Charlie, I have to start sticking with my choices. I didn't stick with Andrew, and now I know I should have. He was a good man – you know that and I know that – and I should have worked at it, even though it wasn't perfect. But now there's Lawrence. And he isn't perfect either, you see? But I can't just keep walking away.' Sarah took a deep and shaking breath. 'At some point you just have to turn around and face your life head on.'

I pulled my knees up to my chest and I watched Lawrence playing with Charlie. They were walking through the streets of Gotham City like giants, stomping along between the tall towers, and Charlie was laughing and shouting. I sighed. 'Lawrence is good with Charlie,' I said.

'There,' said Sarah. 'Thank you, for making an effort. You're a good girl, Bee.'

'If you knew everything I have done, you would not think I am good.'

Sarah smiled. 'I'll get to know you better, I suppose, if I write this book of Andrew's.'

I put my hands on the top of my head. I looked at the dark tunnels underneath the rhododendron forest. I thought about running away and hiding. In the bushes of the park. In the full-moon night in the jungle. Under the planks of an upside-down boat. *Forever*. I closed my eyes tight shut and I wanted to scream, but no sound came out.

'Are you all right?' said Sarah.

'Yes. I am fine. I am tired, that is all.'

'Right,' said Sarah. 'Look, I'm going to go back to the car and call work. I can't get a signal here.'

I walked back to where Charlie and Lawrence were playing. They were throwing sticks into the bushes. When I got close, Charlie carried on with his sticks but Lawrence stopped and turned to me.

'Well?' he said. 'Did you talk her out of it?'

'Out of what?'

'Her book. She had some idea she was going to finish a book Andrew was writing. Didn't she tell you?'

'Yes. She told me. I did not talk her out of the book but I did not talk her out of you either.'

Lawrence grinned. 'Good girl. See? We're going to get along after all. Is she still upset? Why hasn't she come down here with you?'

'She is making a phone call.'

'Fair enough.'

We stood there for a long time, looking at one another.

'You still think I'm a bastard, don't you?'

I shrugged. 'It does not matter what I think. Sarah likes you. But I wish you would stop telling me I am a *good girl*. Both of you. That is something to say to a dog when it brings back a stick.'

Lawrence looked at me, and I felt a great sadness because there was such an emptiness in his eyes. I looked away over the water of the lake where the ducks swam. I looked and I saw the blue reflection of the sky. I stared for a long time now, because I understood that I was looking into the eyes of death again, and death was still not looking away and neither could I.

Then there was the barking of dogs. I jumped, and my eyes followed the sound and for one second I felt relief, because I saw the dogs at the other end of the lawn that we were on, and they were only fat yellow family dogs, out for a walk with their master. Then I saw Sarah, hurrying back along the path towards us. Her arms were hanging by her sides, and in one of her hands she held her mobile phone. She stopped next to us, took a deep breath, and smiled. She held out her hands to both of us, but then she hesitated. She looked all around the place where we were standing.

'Um, where's Charlie?' she said.

She said it very quietly, then she said it again, louder, looking at us this time.

I looked all across the wide grass lawn. In one direction there were the two yellow dogs, the ones who had barked. Their master was throwing sticks into the lake for them. In the other direction, there was the thick rhododendron jungle. The dark tunnels through the branches looked empty.

'Charlie?' Sarah shouted. 'Charlie? Oh, my God. CHAR-LIE!'

I span around under the hot sun. We ran up and down. We called his name. We called again and again. Charlie was gone.

'Oh my God!' said Sarah. 'Someone's taken him! Oh my God! CHARLIE!'

I ran across to the rhododendron jungle and I crawled into its cool shade and I remembered the darkness under the forest canopy on the night I walked out to the jungle with Nkiruka. While Sarah screamed for her son I widened my eyes into the blackness of those tunnels and I stared into them. I looked for a long time. I saw that the nightmares of all our worlds had somehow mingled together, so that there was no telling where the one ended and the other began – whether the jungle grew out of the Jeep or the Jeep grew out of the jungle.

10

I left Charlie playing happily with Lawrence and Little Bee. I was halfway back to the car park before I could get my phone to find a network. I climbed to a high point on the dirt path and I looked down from a hazy sky and saw two bars of signal. My tummy lurched and I thought, Right, I'll do it now, before I calm down and change my mind. I called the publisher and told him I didn't want to edit his magazine any more.

What the publisher said was, *Fine.*

I said, *I'm not sure you heard me. Something extraordinary has happened in my life, and I really need to run with it. So I need to quit the job.* And he said, *Yeah, I heard you, that's fine, I'll get someone else.* And he hung up.

And I said, *Oh.*

I stood there for a minute, shocked, and then I just had to smile.

The sun was lovely. I closed my eyes and let the breeze airbrush away the traces of the last few years. One phone call: I realised it was as simple as that. People wonder how they are ever going to change their lives, but really it is frighteningly easy.

I was already thinking about how I might carry on with Andrew's book. The trick, of course, would be to keep it impersonal. I wondered if that had been a problem for Andrew. The first thing they teach us in journalism school is, don't put yourself in the story.

But what if the story is that we are in the story? I started to understand how Andrew must have agonised over it. I wondered if that was why he had kept so quiet.

Dear Andrew, I thought. How is it that I feel closer to you now than I did on the day we were married? I just told Little Bee I didn't want to hear what she had to say because I know I need to stick with Lawrence, but at the same time here I am talking to you in my head. This is the forked tongue of grief again, Andrew. It whispers in one ear: *return to what you once loved best*, and in the other ear it whispers, *move on*.

My phone went, and my eyes snapped open. It was Clarissa.

'Sarah? They told me you resigned. Are you *crazy*?'

'I told you I was thinking about it.'

'Sarah, I spend a lot of time *thinking* about bedding Premiership footballers.'

'Maybe you should try it.'

'Or maybe you should come in to the office, right now, and tell the publishers you're very sorry, and that you're going through a bereavement at the moment, and please – pretty please – could you have your nice job back.'

'But I don't want that job. I want to be a journalist again. I want to make a difference in the world.'

'Everyone wants to make a difference, Sarah, but there's a time and place. Do you know what you're doing, honestly, if you throw your toys out of the pram like this? You're just having a mid-life crisis. You're no different from the middle-aged man who buys a red car and shags the babysitter.'

I thought about it. The breeze seemed colder now. There were goosebumps on my arms.

'Sarah?'

'Oh, Clarissa, you're right, I'm confused. Do you think I've just chucked my life away?'

'I just want *you* to think about it. Will you, Sarah?'

'All right.'

'And call me?'

'I will. Clarissa?'

'Darling?'

'Thank you.'

I hung up and walked slowly back along the path. Behind me the wild grasses rose to a stand of oaks, feral and lightning blasted, and in front of me the Isabella Plantation stood within its wrought-iron palisades, docile, lush and circumscribed. It is hard, when it comes right down to the actual choice, to know what you want out of life.

It seemed like a long walk. When I saw Lawrence and Little Bee, I rushed to be with them. They looked so forlorn, standing there, looking away from each other, not speaking. I thought, Oh gosh, how foolish I've been. I have always struck myself as a very practical woman, capable of adaptation. I immediately thought, If I turn around now, and walk back to where I can get a signal, I can phone the publisher and tell him I made a mistake. And not just a little mistake but a great, elemental, whole-life mistake. During one whole week of grace I utterly forgot, you see, that I was a sensible girl from Surrey. It was something about Little Bee's smile, and her energy, that made me sort of fall in love with her. And thus love makes fools of us all. For a whole week I actually thought I was a better person, someone who could make a difference. It completely slipped my mind that I was a quiet, practical, bereaved woman who focused very hard on her job. I unaccountably forgot that nobody is a hero, that everyone is so bloody *tainted*. Isn't that odd? And now might I please have my old life back?

From further along the grass lawn, carried up by the breeze, came the sound of barking dogs. Little Bee looked across and saw me. I went right up to her and Lawrence.

I held out my hands to both of them, but then I noticed that Charlie was no longer with them.

'Um, where's Charlie?'

It is painful to think about this, even now. I looked all around, of course I did. I ran up and down. I began screaming Charlie's name. I raced around the perimeter of the lawn, looking into the gloom under the edge of the rhododendrons, scanning the reed beds at the side of the lake. I shouted myself hoarse. My son was nowhere. A aching panic took me over. The sophisticated parts of my mind shut down, the parts that might be capable of thought. I suppose the blood supply to them had been summarily turned off, and diverted to the eyes, the legs, the lungs. I looked, I ran, I screamed. And all the time in my heart it was growing: the unspeakable certainty that someone had taken Charlie.

I ran along one of the paths and came across a picnicking family, installed in a clearing. The mother – long auburn hair with rather frazzled ends – sat cross-legged and barefoot on a tartan rug, surrounded by the peelings and the uneaten segments of satsumas. She was reading *BBC Music Magazine*. She had it spread out on the rug, pinned down with one foot to stop the pages blowing. There was a slender silver ring on her second toe. Beside her on the rug, two flame-haired girls in blue gingham dresses were eating Kraft cheese slices straight from the packet. The husband, blond and stocky, stood a few feet away and talked into his mobile. *Lanzarote's just a tourist trap these days*, he was saying. *You should go somewhere off the beaten track, like Croatia or Marrakech. Your money goes further there in any case.* I ran deeper into the clearing, looking all around. The mother looked up at me.

'Is everything all right?' she called out.

'I've lost my son,' I said.

She looked at me blankly. I smiled idiotically. I didn't know what to do with my face. My mind and my body were keyed up to fight with paedophiles and wolves. Confronted with these ordinary people, spread out across their picnic rug in this absurdly pleasant tableau, my distress seemed desperate and vulgar. My social conditioning fought against my panic. I felt ashamed. Instinctively, I also knew that I needed to speak to the woman calmly, in her register, if I was to communicate clearly and get across the information I needed without wasting any time. I struggled – maybe I had been struggling all my life – to find the correct point of balance between nicety and hysteria.

'I'm very sorry,' I said, 'I've lost my son.'

The woman stood up and looked around the clearing. I couldn't understand why her movements were so slow. It seemed that I was operating in air, while she occupied some more viscous medium.

'He's about this high,' I said. 'He's dressed as Batman.'

'I'm sorry,' she said in slow motion. 'I haven't seen any-thing.'

Each word took forever to form. It felt like waiting for the woman to engrave the sentence in stone. I was already halfway out of the clearing before she finished speaking. Behind me I heard the husband saying, *You could always go for the cheapest package tour and just use the flights. Then you can find some nicer accommodation once you're out there.*

I ran through a labyrinth of small, dark paths between the rhododendrons, shouting Charlie's name. I crawled through dark tunnels between the branches, utterly at random. My forearms bled from the scratches, but I felt no pain. I don't know how long I ran for. Perhaps for five minutes, or perhaps for the time it takes for a divine being to create a universe, make humanity in its image but find no solace in it, and then preside in horror over the slow grey death of the thing, knowing itself to still be utterly alone and unconsoled. Somehow I arrived back at the place where Charlie had built his city of sticks. I tore the structures apart, shouting his name. I looked for my son under piles of sticks as little as six inches high. I scrabbled through drifts of dead leaves. Of course I knew my son wasn't underneath. I knew, even as I was scrabbling away at anything that protruded. I found an old crisp packet. The broken wheel of a pushchair. My nails bled into a barely submerged history of family days out.

Across the expanse of grass I saw Little Bee and Lawrence, who'd returned after their own searches through the rhododendrons. I ran over to them, but when I was halfway across the grass I remember the last rational thought that went through my mind: He isn't on the grass, and he isn't in the bushes, so he must be in the lake. Even as I thought it, I could feel the second stage of my mind shutting down. The panic simply rose up out of my chest to engulf me. I swerved away from Lawrence and Little Bee and I ran down to the edge of the lake. I splashed out into it, knee high, then waist high, staring down into the muddy brown water, screaming Charlie's name at the waterlilies and the startled mandarin ducks.

I saw something under the water, lying on the muddy sludge of the lake's bottom. Underwater, glimpsed between lilies and distorted by ripples, it looked like a bone-white face. I reached down and grabbed for it. I lifted it up into the light. It was the cracked half-skull of a rabbit. As I held it up, dripping muddy water, I realised that my phone had been in the hand I held the skull in. My phone was gone, somewhere – my life was gone, somewhere – lost in the bushes or the lake. I stood in the water, holding a skull. I didn't know what to do now. I heard a whistling sound and I looked down sharply. I understood that the breeze was whistling through the empty eye socket of the skull, and that is when I truly began to scream.

Charlie O'Rourke. Four years old. Batman. What went through my mind? His perfect little white teeth. His look of fierce concentration when he was dispatching baddies. The way he hugged me, once, when I was sad. The way, since Africa, that I had been running between worlds – between Andrew and Lawrence, between Little Bee and my job – running everywhere except to the world where I belonged. Why had I never run to Charlie? I screamed at myself. My son, my beautiful boy. Gone, *gone*. He had disappeared as he had lived, while I was looking the other way. Towards all my own selfish futures. I looked at the empty days before me, and there was no end to them.

Then I felt hands on my shoulders. It was Lawrence. He led me out of the lake and stood me on the bank. I was shivering in the breeze.

'We need to be systematic about this now,' he said. 'Sarah, you stay here and keep calling for him, so he knows where to come back to if he's wandering. I'll go and ask everyone inside the plantation to start looking, and I'll keep looking myself. And Bee, you take my phone and you go to where you can get reception and you call the police. Then you wait at the plantation gate for the police, so you can show them where we are when they arrive.'

Lawrence handed his phone to Little Bee, and turned back to me.

'I know it sounds extreme,' he said, 'but the police are good at this. I'm sure we'll find Charlie before they get here, but just on the off-chance that we don't, it makes sense for us to bring them in sooner rather than later.'

'Okay, do it,' I said. 'Do it now.'

Little Bee was still standing there, holding Lawrence's phone in her hand, staring at Lawrence and me with large and frightened eyes. I couldn't understand why she wasn't already running.

'Go!' I said.

She still stared at me. 'The police . . .' she said.

Understanding buzzed dully in my mind. *The number. Of course! She didn't know the emergency number.*

'The number is 999,' I said.

She just stood there. I couldn't work out what the problem was.

'The *police*, Sarah,' she said.

I stared at her. Her eyes were pleading. She looked terrified. And then, very slowly, her face changed. It became firm, resolved. She took a deep breath, and she nodded at me. She turned, slowly at first and then very fast, and she ran off in the direction of the plantation gate. When she was halfway across the grass, Lawrence raised a hand to his mouth.

'Oh shit, the *police*,' he said.

'What?'

He shook his head.

'Never mind.'

Lawrence ran off into the maze of paths between the rhododendrons. I went to the middle of the grass lawn and began shouting again for Charlie. I called and called, while the ducks paddled cautiously back into their accustomed circuits on the lake, and the breeze left me shivering in my wet jeans. At first I called out Charlie's name as a sound for him to home in on, but as my voice began to go I realised that another line had been crossed and I was shouting the name just to hear it, to ensure its continuing existence in the world. I realised that the name was all I had. My voice sank to a whisper. I breathed Charlie's name.

When Charlie came, he came all on his own. He trotted out from beneath the dark tangle of rhododendrons, filthy with dirt, trailing his bat cape behind him. I ran to him, took him into my arms and held him. I pressed my face into his neck and I breathed in his smell, the sharp salt of his sweat and the acid tang of the soil. The tears streamed down my face.

'Charlie,' I whispered. 'Oh, my world, my whole world.'

'Get off, Mummy! You're squashing me!'

'Where were you?'

Charlie held out his hands to the sides, palms upwards, and answered me as if I was simple. 'In mine bat cave, of course.'

'Oh, *Charlie*. Didn't you hear us all shouting? Didn't you see us all looking for you?'

Charlie grinned beneath his bat mask.

'I was hiding,' he said.

'Why? Why didn't you come out? Couldn't you see how worried we all were?'

My son looked forlornly at the ground. 'Lawrence and Bee was all cross and they wasn't playing with me. So I went into mine bat cave.'

'Oh, Charlie. Mummy's been so confused. So terribly silly and selfish. I promise you, Charlie, I'll never be so silly again. You're my whole world, you know that? I'll never forget that again. Do you know how much you mean to me?'

Charlie blinked at me, sensing an opportunity.

'Can I have an ice-cream?' he said.

I hugged my son. I felt his warm, sleepy breath on my neck, and through the thin grey fabric of his costume I felt the gentle, insistent pressure of the bones beneath his skin.

11

The policemen came after fifteen minutes. There were three of them. They came slowly, in a silver car with bright blue and orange stripes along the sides and a long bar of lights on the roof. They drove right along the dirt path to the gate of the Isabella Plantation where I was standing. They got out of the car and they put on their hats. They were wearing white short-sleeved shirts and thick black vests with a black-and-white chequered stripe. The vests had many pockets, and in them there were batons and radios and handcuffs and other things I could not guess the names of. I was thinking, Charlie would like this. These policemen have more gadgets than Batman.

If I was telling this story to the girls from back home, I would have to explain to them that the policemen of the United Kingdom did not carry guns.

– *Weh! No pistol?*

– *No pistol.*

– *How come they carry all those gadgets but forget the most important thing? How do they shoot the bad men?*

– *They do not shoot the bad men. When they start shooting they usually get in trouble.*

– *Weh! That is one topsy-turvy kingdom, where the girls can show their bobbis but the police cannot show their guns.*

And I would have to nod and tell them again, *Much of my life in that country was lived in such confusion.*

The policemen slammed the police car doors behind them: *thunk.* I shivered. When you are a refugee, you learn to pay attention to doors. When they are open; when they are closed; the particular sound they make; the side of them that you are on.

One of the policemen came close, while the other two stood with their heads leaning over to listen to the radios attached to their vests. The policemen who came, he was not much older than me, I think. He was tall, with orange hair under his hat. I tried to smile at him, but I couldn't. I was so worried about Charlie, my head was spinning. I was scared that my Queen's English would fail me. I tried to calm myself.

If this policeman began to suspect me, he could call the immigration people. Then one of them would click a button on their computer and mark a check box on my file and I would be deported. I would be dead, but no one would have fired any bullets. I realised, this is why the police do not carry guns. In a civilised country, they kill you with a click. The killing is done far away, at the heart of the kingdom in a building full of computers and coffee-cups.

I stared at the policeman. He did not have a cruel face. He did not have a kind face either. He was young and he was pale and there were no lines on his face yet. He was nothing. He was innocent, like an egg. This policeman, if he opened the door of the police car and made me get inside, then to him it was only the interior of a car he was showing me. But I would see things he could not see in it. I would see the bright red dust on the seats. I would see the old dried cassava tops that had blown in to the footwells. I would see the white skull on the dashboard and the jungle plants growing through the rusted cracks in the floor and bursting through the broken windscreen. For me, that car door would swing open and I would step out of England and straight back into the troubles of my country. This is what they mean when they say, *It is a small world these days.*

The policeman looked carefully at me. On his vest, his radio was saying, 'CHARLIE BRAVO, PROCEED.'

'He is not called Charlie Bravo,' I said. 'His name is Charlie O'Rourke.'

The policeman looked at me with no expression.

'Are you the lady who made the emergency call?'

I nodded. 'I will take you to where we are,' I said.

I started to walk into the plantation.

'Just a few details first, madam,' said the policeman. 'What is your relationship to the missing person?'

I stopped and turned round.

'It is not important,' I said.

'It's procedure, madam.'

'Charlie is missing,' I said. 'Please, we cannot waste time. I will tell you everything later.'

'It's a ring-fenced plantation, madam. If the child is in there, he's not going anywhere. No harm in getting some basic details.'

The policeman looked up and down at me.

'We're looking for a Caucasian male child, am I right?'

'Sorry?'

'Caucasian male child. White boy.'

'Yes, that is right. His mother is inside the plantation.'

'And are you the child's carer?'

'No. No I am not. Please, I do not see why . . .'

He took a step towards me and I stepped back, I could not help myself.

'You seem unusually nervous of me, madam. Is there something I should know?'

He said this very calmly, looking into my eyes all the time.

I stood up as straight and tall as I could, and I closed my eyes for a moment, and when I opened them again I looked at the policeman very coldly and I spoke with the voice of Queen Elizabeth the Second.

'How dare you?' I said.

The policeman took half a step back, as if I had hit him. He looked down at the ground and he blushed.

'I'm sorry, madam,' he mumbled.

Then he looked back at me. At first he looked embarrassed, but slowly an expression of anger came over his face. I realised I had gone *over the top* again. I had made him ashamed, and that is one thing I would not need to explain to the girls from my country or the girls from your country: when you make a man ashamed, you make him dangerous. The policeman looked in my eyes for a long time, and I began to feel very afraid. I did not think I could hide it, so I had to look down. That is when the policeman turned to one of the others.

'Keep this one with you and run her details,' he said. 'I'll go in with Paul and locate the mother.'

'Please,' I said. 'I need to show you the way.'

The policeman gave me a cold smile. 'We're big boys, we'll find our way.'

'I do not understand why you need my details.'

'I need your details, madam, because you quite clearly do not want to give me your details. That is generally the point at which I decide I need them. Nothing personal, madam. You'd be amazed how often in missing persons cases, the member of the public who puts in the call is the one who holds the key to the disappearance.'

I watched him walk through the gate of the plantation with the one called Paul. The other policeman came up to me and shrugged.

'Sorry,' he said. 'If you could just step this way, madam, we'll get you comfortable in the patrol car and I'll just run your personals. It won't take a minute and then I won't detain you any longer. Meanwhile my colleagues will locate the child if he's there to be found, I can assure you.'

He opened the back door of the police car and he made me sit down. He left the door open while he talked into his radio. He was thin, with pale slim wrists and a little pot belly, like the detention officer who was on duty on the morning they released us. The police car smelled of nylon and cigarettes.

'What is your name, madam?' said the policeman after a while.

'Why do you need to know?'

'Look, we do two or three missing persons a week and we always come to the situation cold. We're here to help, and the situation may be very clear in your mind but for us we don't know what we're dealing with until we ask a few questions. Scratch the surface and there's usually a right old story underneath. Families are the strangest. Often you ask a few questions and you start to get a pretty good idea why the missing person made themselves scarce, if you see what I mean.' He grinned. 'It's all right,' he said, 'you're not a suspect or anything.'

'Of course.'

'All right then, so if we could just start with your name.'

I sighed, and I felt very sad. I knew it was all over for me now. I could not give the policeman my real name, because then they would find out what I was. But I did not have a false name to give him either. Jennifer Smith, Alison Jones – none of these names are real when you have no documents to go with them. Nothing is true unless there is a screen that says it is, somewhere in that building full of computers and coffee-cups, right at the exact centre of the United Kingdom. I sat up very straight in the back seat of the police car, and I took a breath and I looked the policeman straight in the eye.

'My name is Little Bee.'

'Spell that for me please?'

'L-I-T-T-L-E-B-E-E.'

'And is that a first name or a surname, madam?'

'It is my whole name. That is who I am.'

The policeman sighed, then he turned away and spoke into his radio.

'Charlie Bravo to control,' he said, 'Send out a unit, will you? I've got one to bring in for a mug match and dabs.'

He turned back to me, and he was not smiling any more.

'Please,' I said. 'Please let me help to find Charlie.'

He shook his head. 'Wait here.'

He closed the car door. I sat for a long time. Without the breeze it was very hot in the back of the police car. I waited there until another set of policemen came and took me away. They put me into a van. I watched the Isabella

Plantation disappearing in the back window, through a bare metal grille.

Sarah and Lawrence came to visit me that evening. I was in a holding cell at the police station in Kingston-upon-Thames. The police guard, he banged open the door without knocking and Sarah walked in. Sarah was carrying Charlie. He was asleep in her arms with his head resting on her shoulder. I was so happy to see Charlie safe, I cried. I kissed Charlie on the cheek. He twitched in his sleep, and he sighed. Through the holes in his bat mask, I could see that he was smiling in his sleep. That made me smile too.

Outside the cell, Lawrence was arguing with a police officer.

'This is ridiculous. They can't deport her. She has a home to go to. She has a sponsor.'

'They're not my rules, sir. The immigration people are a law unto themselves.'

'But surely you can give us a bit of time to make a case. I work for the Home Office, I can get an appeal together.'

'If you don't mind my saying so, sir, if I worked for the Home Office and I knew all along this lady was illegal, I'd keep my mouth shut.'

'Just one day, then. Twenty-four hours, *please*.'

'I'm sorry, sir.'

'Oh for fuck's sake, it's like talking to a robot.'

'I'm flesh and blood like you, sir. The thing is, as I say, I don't make the rules.'

Inside my cell, Sarah was crying.

'I didn't understand,' she said. 'I'm so sorry, Bee, I had no idea. I thought you were just being obtuse. When Lawrence sent you to call the police, he didn't even think . . . and I didn't think . . . and now . . . oh God. You knew what might happen, and you did it without a word or a thought for yourself.'

I smiled. 'It was worth it,' I said. 'It was worth it to find Charlie.'

Sarah looked away.

'Don't be sad, Sarah. The police found Charlie, that is right?'

She turned back to me, slowly, and she looked at me with very bright eyes.

'Yes, Bee, there was a big search, and they found him. All thanks to you. Oh, Bee, I have never met a kinder . . . or a braver . . . oh God . . .'

She moved her face very close to my ear.

'I *won't* let them do it,' she whispered. 'I'll find a way. I won't let them send you back to be killed.'

I tried very hard to smile.

To survive, you have to look good or talk good. Me, I learned the Queen's English. I learned everything I could learn about your language, but I think I went *over the top*. Even now, I did not have the right words. I took Sarah's left hand in my hands, and I lifted it up to my lips, and I kissed the smooth joint that was all that was left of her missing finger.

That night I wrote a letter for Sarah. The officer on duty gave me a pencil and paper, and he promised to post it for me. *Dear Sarah. Thank you for saving my life. We did not choose for our worlds to come together. For a while I thought they had joined, but that was just a beautiful dream. Do not be sad. You deserve for your life to be simple again. I think they will come for me soon. Our worlds are separate, and now we must be separate too. Love, Little Bee.*

They came for me at four o'clock in the morning. There were three uniformed immigration officers, one woman and two men. I heard their shoes banging on the linoleum of the corridor. I had been awake all night, waiting for them. I was still wearing the summer dress that Sarah had given me, with the pretty lace around the neck, and in my hand I carried my things in the see-through plastic bag. I stood up, so I was waiting for them when they banged open the door. We walked out of the cell. The door closed behind me. *Boom*, went the door, and that was it. Out in the street it was raining. They put me in the back of a van. The road was wet and the headlights pushed streaks of light along it. One of the back windows was half open. The back of the van had a smell of vomit, but the air that blew in smelled of London. All along the streets the windows of the apartments were silent and blind, with their curtains closed. I disappeared without anyone to see me go. The female officer handcuffed me to the back of the seat in front.

322

'It is not necessary to handcuff me,' I said. 'How could I run away?'

The female officer looked back at me. She was surprised.

'You speak pretty good English,' she said. 'Most of the people we bring in don't speak a word.'

'I thought if I learned to speak like you people do, I would be able to stay.'

The officer smiled.

'It doesn't matter how you talk, does it?' she said. 'You're a drain on resources. The point is, you don't *belong* here.'

The van turned the corner at the end of the street. I looked through the metal grille on the back window of the van and I watched two long rows of semi-detached houses disapear. I thought about Charlie, fast asleep under his duvet, and I thought of his brave smile, and my heart ached that I would never see him again. There were tears in my eyes.

'But please, what does it mean?' I said. 'What does it mean, to belong here?'

The female officer turned to look at me again.

'Well, you've got to be British, haven't you? You've got to have our values.'

I turned away from the woman and looked out at the rain.

Three days later a different group of officers took me from another holding cell and they put me in a minibus with one other girl. They took us to Heathrow Airport. They took us straight through the queue at the airport terminal and they put us in a small room. We were all wearing handcuffs. They told us to sit down on the floor – there were no chairs there. There were twenty others in the room, men and women, and it was very hot in there. There was no fresh air and it was difficult to breathe. A guard was standing at the front of the room. She had a truncheon and a can of pepper spray in her belt. I asked her, *What is happening here?* The guard smiled. She said, *What is happening here is that a large number of flying machines that we call AEROPLANES are taking off and landing on a long stretch of tarmac that we call a RUNWAY, because this is a place that we call an AIRPORT, and soon one of those aeroplanes is going to set off for UM-BONGO LAND, where you come from, and you're going to be on it. Yeah? Whether you like it or bloody not. Now has anyone else got any questions?*

We waited for a long time. Some of the others were taken out of the room. One of them cried. Another, a thin man, he was angry. He tried to resist the guard, and she hit him twice in the stomach with her truncheon. After that he was quiet.

I fell asleep sitting down. When I woke up, I saw a purple dress and long brown legs in front of me.

'Yevette!' I said.

The woman turned around to look at me, but it was not Yevette. At first I was sad not to see my friend, and then I understood that I was happy. If this was not Yevette, then there was a chance that Yevette was still free. I thought of her walking down the street in London, in her purple flip-flops with her eyebrows painted in pencil, buying a pound of salt fish and laughing, WU-ha-ha-ha-ha! into the bright blue sky. And I smiled.

The woman who was not Yevette, she made an angry face at me. *What is wrong with you?* she said. *You think they are sending us on holiday?*

I smiled. *Yes,* I said. *It is the holiday of a lifetime.*

She turned around and she would not talk to me any more, and when they called her to stand up for her flight, she walked away without making any trouble and she did not once look back at me.

When I saw her go, my situation became real for me and I was scared now, for the first time. I was scared of going back. I cried and I watched my own tears soaking away into the dirty brown carpet.

They gave us no food or water, and I became faint. After a few more hours they came for me. They walked me straight onto the aeroplane. The other passengers, the paying passengers, they made them stand back while I went first up the aeroplane steps. Everybody was staring at me. They took me to the back of the aeroplane, to the last row of seats before the toilets. They put me in the seat next to the window and a guard sat down beside me, a big man with a shaved head and a gold earring. He wore a blue Nike T-shirt and black Adidas trousers. He took off my handcuffs, and I rubbed my wrists to bring the blood back into my hands.

'Sorry,' said the man. 'I don't like this shit any more than you do.'

'Then why do you do it?'

The man shrugged and did up his seatbelt.

'It's a job, isn't it?' he said.

He pulled a magazine out of the seat pocket in front of him, and opened it up. There were men's wristwatches there for sale, and also a fluffy model of the aeroplane that could be given to children.

'You should do a different job, if you do not like this one.'

'No one chooses this job, love. I don't have qualifications, do I? I used to do labouring, casual, but you can't compete with the Polskis now. The Poles will do a full day's work for a kind word and a packet of fags. So here I am, chaperoning girls like you on the holiday of a lifetime. Waste, really, isn't it? I bet you're more employable than I am. You should be escorting me, really, shouldn't you? Back to this place we're going, whatever the name of it is again.'

'Nigeria.'

'Yeah, that was it. Hot there, is it?'

'Hotter than England.'

'Thought so. These places usually are, where you people come from.'

He went back to his magazine and he turned a few pages. Each time he turned the page, he licked his finger to make it stick. There were tattoos on the knuckles of his fingers, small blue dots. His watch was big and gold but the gold was wearing off. It looked like one of the watches from the aeroplane magazine. He turned a few more pages and then he looked up at me again.

'Don't say much, do you?'

I shrugged.

'That's all right,' he said. 'I don't mind. Rather that than the waterworks.'

'The waterworks?'

'Some of them cry. Some of the people I escort back. The women aren't the worst, believe it or not. I had this bloke once, Zimbabwe we were going to, sobbed away for six hours straight. Tears and snot everywhere, like a baby, I kid you not. It got embarrassing after a while. Some of the other passengers, you know? Giving it the looks, and all of that. I was like, *Cheer up, mate, it might never happen*, but it wasn't no good. He just kept crying and talking to himself in foreign. Some of you people, I'm sorry to see you go, but this one, I tell you, I couldn't wait to sign him over. Good money though, that job was. There was no flight out for three days so they put me up at the Sheraton. Watched Sky Sports for three days, scratched my arse, got paid time-and-a-half. Course the people who really make the money are the big contractors. The ones I'm working for now, Dutch firm, they run the whole show. They run the detention centres and they run the repatriations. So they're earning either way, whether we lock you up or whether we send you back. Nice, eh?'

'Nice,' I said.

The man tapped his finger against the side of his head.

'But that's how you've got to think, these days, isn't it? It's the global economy.'

The plane began to roll backwards on the tarmac and some television screens came down from the ceiling. They started to show us a safety film. They said what we should do if the cabin filled with smoke, and they also said where our life-jackets were kept in case we landed on water. I saw that they did not show us the position to adopt in case we were deported to a country where it was likely that we would be killed because of events we had witnessed. They said there was more information on the safety card in the seat pocket in front of us.

There was a huge and terrifying roar, so loud that I thought, *They have tricked us. I thought we were going on a journey, but actually we are being destroyed.* But then there was a great acceleration, and everything started shaking and rising up to a terrifying angle, and suddenly all the vibration was gone and the sound died down and my stomach went crazy. The man beside me, my guard, he looked at me and laughed.

'Relax, love, we're in the air.'

After the take-off, the captain came on the intercom. He said it was a fine, sunny day in Abuja.

I understood that, for a few hours, I was not in anyone's country. I said to myself, *Look here, Little Bee – finally, you are flying. Buzz, buzz*. I pressed my nose against the aeroplane window. I watched the forests and the fields and the roads with their tiny cars, all those tiny precious lives. Me, I felt that my own life was already over. From very high up in the sky, all alone, I could see the curve of the world.

And then I heard a voice, a kind and gentle voice that was familiar.

'Bee?' said the voice.

I turned from the window and saw Sarah. She was standing in the aisle and she was smiling. Charlie was holding her hand and he was smiling too. He was wearing his Batman outfit and he was grinning as if he had just killed all the baddies.

'We is in the sky, isn't we?' he said.

'No, darling,' said Sarah. 'We *are* in the sky, *aren't* we?'

I did not understand what I was seeing. Sarah reached over the guard and she put her hand on my hand.

'Lawrence found out what flight they were putting you on,' she said. 'He knows a few useful people, at the end of the day. We couldn't let you go back alone, Bee. Could we, Batman?'

Charlie shook his head. Now he looked very solemn.

'No,' he said. 'Because you is our friend.'

The guard, he did not know what to do.

'I've seen bloody everything now,' he said.

Finally he stood up and made room for Sarah and Charlie to sit beside me. They hugged me while I cried, and the other passengers turned around in their seats to stare at this miracle, and the aeroplane flew all of us into the future at five hundred and fifty miles per hour.

After some time they brought us peanuts, and Coca Cola in tiny cans. Charlie drank his too quickly, and the Coca Cola came out of his nose. After Sarah cleaned him up, she turned to me.

'I did wonder why Andrew didn't leave a note,' she said. 'And then I thought about it. It wasn't Andrew's style. He didn't really like to write about himself.'

I nodded.

'Anyway, he left me something better than a note.'

'What?'

Sarah smiled. 'A story.'

At Abuja they opened the aeroplane doors, and heat and memory rolled in. We walked across the tarmac through the shimmering air. In the terminal building my guard signed me over to the authorities. *Cheerio*, he said. *Best of luck, love.*

The military police were waiting for me in a small room, wearing uniforms and gold-framed sunglasses. They could not arrest me because Sarah was with me. She would not leave my side. *I am a British journalist*, she said. *Anything you do to this woman, I will report it.* The military police were uncertain, so they called their commander. The commander came, in a camouflage uniform and a red beret, with tribal scars on his cheeks. He looked at my deportation document, and he looked at me and Sarah and Charlie. He stood there for a long time, scratching his belly and nodding.

'Why is the child dressed in this fashion?' he said.

Sarah looked straight back at him. She said, 'The child believes he has special powers.'

The commander grinned. 'Well, I am just a man,' he said. 'I will not arrest any of you at this time.'

Everybody laughed, but the military police followed our taxi from the airport. I was very frightened but Sarah gripped my hand. *I will not leave you*, she said. *So long as Charlie and I are here, you are safe*. The police waited outside our hotel. We stayed there for two weeks, and so did they.

The window of our room looked out over Abuja. Tall buildings stretched back for miles, tall and clean, some covered in silver glass that reflected the long, straight boulevards. I watched the city as the sunset made the buildings glow red, and then I watched all night. I could not sleep.

When the sun rose it shone between the horizon and the base of the clouds. It blazed on the golden dome of the mosque while the four tall towers were still lit up with electric lights. It was beautiful. Sarah came out onto the balcony of our room, and she found me standing there and staring.

'This is your city,' she said. 'Are you proud?'

'I did not know such a thing existed in my country. I am still trying to feel that it is mine.'

I stood there all morning while the heat of the day grew stronger and the streets grew busy with car taxis and scooter taxis and walking sellers with their swaying racks of T-shirts and headscarves and medicine.

Charlie sat inside, watching cartoons with the air conditioning on, and Sarah laid out all of Andrew's papers on a long, low table. On each pile of papers we placed a shoe, or a lamp or a glass, to stop them blowing in the breeze from the big mahogany fans that spun on the ceiling. Sarah explained how she was going to write the book that Andrew had been researching. *I need to collect more stories like yours*, she said. *Do you think we can do that here? Without going down to the south of the country?*

I did not answer. I looked through some of the papers and then I went and stood on the balcony again. Sarah came and stood beside me.

'What is it?' she said.

I nodded my head down at the military police car waiting on the street below. Two men leaned against it, in green uniforms with berets and sunglasses. One of them looked up. He said something when he saw us, and his colleague looked up too. They stared up at our balcony for a long time, and then they lit cigarettes and sat in the car, one in the front seat and one in the back seat, with the doors open and their heavy boots resting on the tarmac.

'You know it is not a good idea to collect stories,' I said.

332

Sarah shook her head. 'I don't agree. I think it's the only way we'll make you safe.'

'What do you mean?'

Sarah lifted her eyes up from the street.

'Our problem is that you only have your own story. One story makes you weak. But as soon as we have one hundred stories, you will be strong. If we can show that what happened to your village happened to a hundred villages, then the power is on our side. We need to collect the stories of people who've been through the same things as you. We need to make it undeniable. Then we can send the stories to a lawyer and we'll let the authorities know, if anything happens to you, those stories will go straight to the media. Do you see? I think that was what Andrew hoped to do with his book. It was his way of saving girls like you.'

I shrugged. 'What if the authorities are not afraid of the media?'

Sarah nodded, slowly. 'That's a possibility,' she said. 'I don't know. What do you think?'

I looked out across the towers of Abuja. The great buildings shimmered in the heat, as if they were insubstantial, as if they could be awoken from and forgotten with a splash of cold water to the face.

'I do not know,' I said. 'I do not know how things are in my country. Until I was fourteen years old my country was three cassava fields and a limba tree. And after that, I was in yours. So do not ask me how my country works.'

333

'Hmm,' said Sarah. She waited for a minute, and then she said, 'So what do you want us to do?'

I looked again at the city we saw from that balcony. I saw for the first time how much space there was in it. There were wide gaps between the city blocks. I thought these dark green squares were parks and gardens, but now I saw that they were just empty spaces, waiting for something to be built. Abuja was a city that was not finished. This was very interesting for me, to see that my capital city had these green squares of hope built into it. To see how my country carried its dreams in a see-through bag.

I smiled at Sarah. 'Let us go and collect the stories.'

'You're sure?'

'I want to be part of my country's story.' I pointed out into the heat. 'See? They have left space for me.'

Sarah held on to my hand, very tight.

'All right,' she said.

'But Sarah?'

'Yes?'

'There is one story I must tell you first.'

I told Sarah what happened when Andrew died. The story was hard to hear and it was hard to tell. Afterwards I went back inside the hotel room and she stayed out on the balcony on her own. I sat down on the bed with Charlie and he watched cartoons while I watched Sarah's shoulders shaking.

The next day we started our work. Early in the morning Sarah walked out into the street and she gave a very large amount of money to the military policemen waiting outside the hotel. After this, their eyes were the eyes of the faces on the banknotes that Sarah gave them. They saw nothing but the inside of the military police car's glove box and the lining of the policemen's uniform pockets. The policemen's only rule was, we had to be back at the hotel before sunset each evening.

My job was to find people who would normally be scared to talk to a foreign journalist, but who talked to Sarah because I promised them that she was a good person. These were people who believed what I told them, because my story was the same as theirs. I discovered there were a lot of us in my country, people who had seen things the oil companies wished we had not seen. People the government would prefer to be silent. We went all around the south-east of my country in an old white Peugeot, just like the one that my father used to have.

I sat in the passenger seat and Sarah drove, with Charlie smiling and laughing in the back. We listened to the music on the local radio stations, turned up very loud. The red dust from the road blew everywhere, even inside the car, and when we took off Charlie's Batman suit to wash him at the end of each day, his white skin had two bright red diamonds on it, where the eyeholes of his mask had been.

Sometimes I got scared. Sometimes when we arrived in a village, I saw the way some of the men looked at me and I remembered how me and my sister were hunted. I wondered if there was still money from the oil companies, for anyone who would shut my mouth for once and all. I was scared of the village men, but Sarah just smiled. *Relax*, she said. *Remember what happened at the airport. Nothing's going to happen to you so long as I'm here.*

And I did begin to relax. In each village I found people with stories, and Sarah wrote them down. It was easy. We started to be happy. We thought we had done enough to save ourselves. We thought, This is a good trick.

One night when we had been in my country for two weeks, I dreamed of my sister Nkiruka. She walked up out of the sea. First the surface of the water swirled from the movement of something unseen and then, in the hollow between two waves, I saw the top of her head with white foam dancing around it. Then my sister's face rose above the water and slowly she walked up the beach towards me and she stood there smiling and wearing the Hawaiian shirt that I was wearing when they released me from detention. It was soaked with salt water. My sister spoke my name once, and then she waited.

When Sarah woke up, I went to her. *Please*, I said, *we have to go to the sea. I must say goodbye to my sister.* Sarah looked at me for a long time, and then she nodded. We did not say anything. That morning Sarah gave the policemen much more money than before. We drove south to Benin City and we got there in the late afternoon. We stayed overnight in another hotel that was just the same, and the next morning we drove south again, to the coast. We left early, when the sun was still low in the sky and the light shining into the car windows was warm and golden. Charlie sighed and banged his heels on the back seat.

'Is we nearly there yet?' he said.

Sarah smiled at him in the rear-view mirror.

'Nearly, darling,' she said.

The road ran out at one of the fishing villages they have in that place, and we stepped down onto the sand. Charlie laughed and ran down the beach to make sand castles. I sat on the beach next to Sarah and we looked out over the ocean. There was no sound except for the waves breaking on the beach. After a long time, Sarah turned to me.

She said, 'I'm proud we've come this far.'

I took her hand. 'You know, Sarah, since I left my country, often I think to myself, *How would I explain these things to the girls back home?*'

Sarah laughed and stretched her hands along the beach in both directions.

'Well?' said Sarah. 'How would you explain this to the girls back home? I mean, this would take some explaining, wouldn't you say?'

I shook my head. 'I would not explain this to the girls back home.'

'No?'

'No, Sarah. Because today I am saying goodbye to all that. We are the girls back home now. You and me. There is nothing else for me to go back to. I do not need to tell this story to anyone else. Thank you for saving me, Sarah.'

When I said this I saw that Sarah was crying, and then I was crying too.

When the day became hotter, the beach filled up with people. There were fishermen who walked out into the waves and sent wide bright nets spinning out before them, and there were old men who came to sit and look at the sea, and mothers who brought their children to splash in the water.

'We should go and ask these people if anyone has a story,' I said.

Sarah smiled and pointed at Charlie. 'Yes, but it can wait,' she said. 'Look, he's having such fun.'

Charlie was running and laughing and I can tell you that a dozen of the local children were running with him, and laughing and shouting because if there is one thing you do not see very often on the beach in my country it is a white superhero less than one metre in height, with sand and salt water on his cape. Charlie was laughing with the other children, running and playing and chasing.

It was hot, and I dug my toes down into the cooler sand.

'Sarah,' I said. 'How long do you think you will stay?'

'I don't know. Do you want to try coming with me to England? We could try to get you papers this time.'

I shrugged. 'They do not want people like me.'

Sarah smiled. 'I'm English and I want people like you. Surely I'm not the only one.'

338

'People will say you are naïve.'

Sarah smiled. 'Let them,' she said. 'Let them say whatever gives them comfort.'

We sat for a long time and watched the sea.

In the afternoon the sea breeze blew and I fell asleep for a little while, half in and half out of the shade of the trees at the top of the beach. The sun warmed my blood until I could not keep my eyes open, and the sea roared in and out, in and out, and my breathing slipped into time with the waves as I began to dream. I dreamed we all stayed together in my country. I was happy. I dreamed I was a journalist, telling the stories of my country, and we all lived in the same house – me and Charlie and Sarah – in a tall, cool three-storey house in Abuja. It was a very beautiful home. It was the sort of place I never even dreamed of, back in the days when our Bible ended at the twenty-seventh chapter of Matthew. I was happy in this house that I dreamed of, and the cook and the housekeeper smiled at me and called me 'princess'. Early each morning the garden boy brought me a scented yellow rose for my hair, trembling on its fine green stem with the dew of the night still on it. There was a carved wood veranda, painted white, and a long curved garden with bright flowers and dark shade. I travelled through my country and I listened to stories of all kinds. Not all of them were sad. There were many beautiful stories that I found. There was horror, yes, but there was joy in them too. The dreams of my country are no different from yours – they are as big as the human heart.

In my dream Lawrence telephoned Sarah to ask when she was coming home. Sarah looked across the veranda at Charlie, playing with his building blocks, and she smiled and she said, What do you mean? We *are* home.

It was the sound of the surf pounding on the beach that woke me. Crash, like the drawer of a cash register springing open and all the coins inside it smashing against the edge of their compartments. The surf pounded and ebbed, the cash drawer opened and closed.

There is a moment when you wake up from dreaming in the hot sun, a moment outside time when you do not know what you are. At first, because you feel absolutely free, as if you could transform yourself into anything at all, it seems that you must be money. But then you feel the hot breath of something on your face and it seems that no, you are not money, you must be that hot breeze blowing in from the sea. It seems that the heaviness you feel in your limbs is the weight of the salt in the wind, and the sweet sleepiness that bewitches you is simply the weariness that comes from the day-and-night pushing of waves across the ocean. But next you realise that no, you are not the breeze. In fact you can feel sand drifting up against your bare skin. And for an instant you are the sand that the breeze blows up the beach, just one grain of sand among the billions of blown grains. How nice to be inconsequential. How pleasant to know that there is nothing to be done. How sweet simply to go back to sleep, as the sand does, until the wind thinks to awaken it again. But then you understand that no, you are not the sand, because this skin that the sand drifts up against, this skin is your own. Well, then, you are a creature with skin – and what of it? It is not as if you are the first creature that fell asleep under the sun, listening to the sound of waves pounding. A billion fishes have slipped away like this, flapping on the blinding white sand, and what difference will one more make? But the moment carries on, and you are not a fish dying – in fact you are not even truly sleeping – and so you open your eyes and look down on yourself and you say, *Ah, so I am a girl, then, an African girl. This is what I am and this is how I will stay*, as the shape-changing magic of dreams whispers back into the roar of the ocean.

I sat up and blinked and looked around. A white woman was sitting next to me on the beach, in the thing called *shade*, and I remembered that the white woman's name was Sarah. I saw her face, with her wide eyes staring away down the beach. She looked – I searched for the name of her expression in your language – she looked *frightened*.

'Oh my God,' Sarah was saying. 'I think we need to get away from here.'

I smiled sleepily. *Yes yes*, I was thinking. *We always need to get away from here. Wherever here is, there is always a good reason to get away from it. That is the story of my life. Always running, running, running, without one single moment of peace. Sometimes, when I remember my mother and my father and my big sister Nkiruka, I think I will always be running until the day I am reunited with the dead.*

Sarah grabbed my hand and tried to pull me up.

'Get up, Bee,' she said. 'There are soldiers coming. Up the beach.'

I breathed in the hot, salty smell of the sand. I sighed. I looked in the direction Sarah was staring. There were six soldiers. They were still a long way away, along the beach. The air above the sand was so hot that it dissolved the men's legs into a shimmer, a green confusion of colours, so that the soldiers seemed to be floating towards us on a cloud made of some enchanted substance, free as the thoughts of a girl waking up from dreams on a hot beach. I screwed up my eyes against the glare and I saw the light gleaming on the barrels of the soldiers' rifles. These rifles were more distinct than the men who carried them. They held their firm, straight lines while the men beneath them shimmered. In this way the weapons rode their men like mules, proud and gleaming in the sun, knowing that when a beast beneath them died, they would simply ride another one. This is how the future rode out to meet me in my country. The sun shone on its rifles and it pounded on my bare head too. I could not think. It was too hot and too late in the afternoon.

'Why would they come for us here, Sarah?'

'I'm sorry, Bee. It's those policemen in Abuja, isn't it? I thought I'd paid them enough to close their eyes for a few days. But someone must have put the word out. I suppose they must have seen us in Sapele.'

I knew it was true, but I pretended that it was not. That is a good trick. That is called, *Saving one minute of the quietest part of the late afternoon while the whole of time is ending.*

'Maybe the soldiers are just going for a walk by the sea, Sarah. Anyway, this is a long beach. They will not know who we are.'

Sarah put her hand on my cheek and she turned my head until I was looking in her eyes.

'Look at me,' she said. 'Look how bloody *white* I am. Do you see any other women on the beach this colour?'

'So?'

'They'll be looking out for a girl with a white woman and a white boy. Just walk away from us, okay, Bee? Go down to the point down there, where those other women are, and don't look around till the soldiers have gone. If they take me and Charlie, don't worry. There's no way they'll do anything to us.'

Charlie held on to Sarah's leg and looked up at her.

'Mummy,' he said, 'why is Little Bee got to go?'

'It's not for long, Batman. Just until the soldiers have gone.'

Charlie put his hands on his hips. 'I don't want Little Bee to go,' he said.

'She has to hide, darling,' said Sarah. 'Just for a few minutes.'

'Why?' said Charlie.

343

Sarah stared out to sea, and the expression on her face was the saddest thing I ever saw. She answered Charlie, but she turned to me when she spoke.

'Because we still haven't done enough to save her, Charlie. I thought we had, but we need to do more. And we will do more, darling. We will. We won't ever give up on Little Bee. Because she is part of our family now. And until she is happy and safe, then I don't think we will be either.'

Charlie held on to my leg.

'I want to go with her,' he said.

Sarah shook her head. 'I need you to stay and look after me, Batman.'

Charlie shook his head. He was not happy. I looked away down the beach. The soldiers were half a mile away. They came slowly, looking left and right, checking the faces of the people on the beach. Sometimes they stopped and did not continue on their way until someone showed them papers. I nodded, slowly.

'Thank you, Sarah.'

I walked down the slope of the beach to the hard sand where the waves were breaking. I looked out at the hazy horizon and I followed the deep blue-and-indigo of the ocean from that distant line all the way to the beach where it crashed into waves of white spray and sent its last thin sheets of water foaming and hissing up the sand to sink away to nothing in the place where my feet were standing. I saw how it ended there. The wet sand under my feet made me think of how it was when the men took me and Nkiruka away, and for the first time I began to be fearful. I was fully awake now. I knelt down in the shorebreak and I splashed the cold salt water over my head and my face until I could think clearly. Then I walked quickly along the beach to the point that Sarah had shown me. The point was two or three minutes away. A tall ridge of dark grey rock came out of the jungle there at the height of the treetops, and it ran across the sand and then out into the sea, getting shorter as it went but still as high as two men at the point of the rock, where it stuck out into the surf. The waves crashed against it and sent explosions of white foam into the silver-blue sky. In the shade of the rock it was suddenly cold, and my skin shivered when it touched the dark stone. There were some local women resting in the shade there, sitting on the hard sand with their backs against the rock while their children played all around them, jumping over their mothers' legs and running into the shorebreak, laughing and daring each other to go out into the white roaring foam where the great waves crashed against the point of the rock.

I sat down with the other women and smiled at them. They smiled back and talked in their language, but I did not understand it. The women smelled of sweat and woodsmoke. I looked back along the beach. The soldiers were close now. The women around me, they were watching the soldiers too. When the soldiers were close enough to notice the colour of Sarah's skin, I saw them start to walk faster. They stopped in front of Sarah and Charlie. Sarah stood very straight and she stared at the soldiers with her hands on her hips. The leader of the soldiers stepped forward. He was tall and relaxed, with his rifle riding high on his shoulder and his hand scratching the top of his head. I could see he was smiling. He said something and I watched Sarah shaking her head. The head soldier stopped smiling then. He shouted at Sarah. I heard the shout but I could not hear what he said. Sarah shook her head again, and she pushed Charlie behind her legs. Around me the local women were staring and saying, *Weh*, but the children were still playing in the shorebreak and they had not noticed what was occurring further down the beach.

The leader of the soldiers, he took the gun down from his shoulder and he pointed it at Sarah. The other soldiers gathered in close and they unslung their weapons too. The leader shouted again. Sarah just shook her head. The leader pulled back the barrel of his gun then and I thought he was going to push it into Sarah's face, but just then Charlie broke away and he started to run down the beach towards the rocky point where we were sitting. He ran with his head down and his Batman cape fluttering behind him, and at first the soldiers just laughed and watched him go. But the leader of the soldiers, he was not laughing. He shouted something at his men, and one of them raised his rifle and swung it round to point at Charlie. The women around me, they gasped. One of them screamed. It was a crazy, shocking sound. At first I thought it was a seabird right beside me and my head snapped

346

round to look, and when I turned back towards where Charlie was running, I saw a jet of sand flying up from the hard beach beside him. At first I did not know what it was, but then I heard the rifle shot that had made it. Then I screamed too. The soldier was swinging the barrel of his rifle, taking aim again. That was when I stood up and I started to run towards Charlie. I ran so hard my breath was burning and I screamed at the soldiers, *Don't shoot, don't shoot, I AM THE ONE THAT YOU WANT*, and I ran with my eyes half closed and one hand spread out in front of my face as if that would protect me from the bullet that would come for me. I ran, cringing like a dog from the whip, but the bullet did not come. The leader of the soldiers, he shouted out an order and his man put down his rifle. All of the soldiers stood there then, with their hands at their sides, watching.

Charlie and me, we came together halfway between the rocky point and the soldiers. I knelt and I held out my arms to him. His face was twisted with terror and I held him while he cried against my chest. I waited for the soldiers to come and get me, but they did not. The leader stood there and he watched, and I saw the way he slung his rifle back on his shoulder and lifted his hand to scratch his head again. I saw Sarah, with her hands behind her head, pulling at her hair and screaming to be let go while one of the soldiers restrained her.

After a long time Charlie stopped sobbing and he turned his face up towards mine. I peeled back his Batman mask a little, so I could see his face, and he smiled at me. I smiled back at him, in that moment that the soldiers' leader gave me, that one minute of dignity he offered me as one human being to another before he sent his men across the hard sand to fetch me. Here it was, then, finally: the quietest part of the late afternoon. I smiled down at Charlie, and I understood that he would be free now even if I would not. In this way the life that was in me would find its home in him now. It was not a sad feeling. I felt my heart take off lightly like a butterfly and I thought, *Yes*, this is it, something has survived in me, something that does not need to run any more, because it is worth more than all the money in the world and its currency, its true home, is the living. And not just the living in this particular country or in that particular country, but the secret, irresistible heart of the living. I smiled back at Charlie and I knew that the hopes of this whole human world could fit inside one soul. This is a good trick. This is called, *globalisation*.

'Everything will be all right for you, Charlie,' I said.

But Charlie was not listening – already he was giggling and kicking and struggling to be put down. He stared over my shoulder at the local children, still playing in the shorebreak around the rocky point.

'Let me go! Let me go!'

I shook my head. 'No, Charlie. It is a very hot day. You cannot run around in your costume like that or you will boil, I am telling you, and then you will be no good to us at all to fight the baddies. Take off your Batman costume, right now, and then you will just be yourself and you can go to cool off in the sea.'

'No!'

'Please, Charlie, you must. It is for your health.'

Charlie shook his head. I stood him in the sand and I knelt down beside him and I whispered in his ear.

'Charlie,' I said, 'do you remember when I promised you, if you took off your costume, that I would tell you my real name?'

Charlie nodded.

'So do you still want to know my real name?'

Charlie tilted his head to one side so that both of the ears of his mask flopped over. Then he tilted it to the other side. Then finally he looked straight at me.

'What is yours real name?' he whispered.

I smiled. 'My name is Udo.'

'Ooh-doh?'

'That is it. Udo means *peace*. Do you know what peace is, Charlie?'

Charlie shook his head.

'Peace is a time when people can tell each other their real names.'

Charlie grinned. I looked over his shoulder. The soldiers were walking across the sand towards us now. They were walking slowly, with their rifles in their hands pointing down at the sand, and while the soldiers walked, the waves rolled in to the beach and crashed upon the sand one by one at this final end of their journey. The waves rolled and rolled and there was no end to the power of them, cold enough to wake a young girl from dreams, loud enough to tell and retell the future. I bent my head and I kissed Charlie on the forehead. He stared at me.

'Udo?' he said.

'Yes, Charlie?'

'I is going to take off mine Batman costume now.'

The soldiers were almost on us.

'Hurry then, Charlie,' I whispered.

Charlie pulled off the mask first, and the local children gasped when they saw his blond hair. Their curiosity was greater than their fear of the soldiers and they ran with their skinny legs straining towards the place where we were, and then when Charlie took off the rest of his costume and they saw his skinny white body they said, *Weh!* because such a child had never before been seen in that place. And then Charlie laughed, and he slipped out from my arms and I stood up and stayed very still. Behind me I felt the soft shocks of the soldiers' boots in the sand and in front of me all of the local children ran with Charlie down to the crashing water by the rocky point. I felt the hard hand of a soldier on my arm but I did not turn around. I smiled and I watched Charlie running away with the children, with his head down and his happy arms spinning like propellers, and I cried with joy when the children all began to play together in the sparkling foam of the waves that broke between worlds at the point. It was beautiful, and that is a word I would not need to explain to the girls from back home, and I do not need to explain to you, because now we are all speaking the same language. The waves still smashed against the beach, furious and irresistible. But me, I watched all of those children smiling and dancing and splashing each other in salt water and bright sunlight, and I laughed and laughed and laughed until the sound of the sea was drowned.

Acknowledgements and thanks

'However long the moon disappears, someday it must shine again' is taken from www.motherlandnigeria.com

The 'Ave Maria' in the Ibo language is taken from the Christus Rex et Redemptor Mundi website at www.christusrex.org

Some Nigerian English idioms are from 'A Dictionary of Nigerian English [Draft]' by Roger Blench and *A Dictionary of Nigerian English Usage* by Herbert Igboanusi, Enicrownfit Publishers, 1 Jan 2001.

Some Jamaican English idioms are from *A Dictionary of Jamaican English* by F.G. Cassidy and R.B. Le Page, University of the West Indies Press, 31 Jan 2002.

353

Some four-year-old English idioms are from my son, Batman.

The rather brilliant line, 'We do not see how anybody can abuse an excess of sanitary towels' is taken verbatim from the transcript of the Bedfordshire County Council special report of 18 July 2002 into the fire at the Yarl's Wood Immigration Detention Centre on 14 February 2002, where it is attributed to Loraine Bayley of the Campaign to Stop Arbitrary Detention at Yarl's Wood.

Details of the UK immigration detention system were provided by Christine Bacon, whose direction of *Asylum Monologues* with the Actors for Refugees groups in the UK and Australia was an inspiration for this project. Christine also kindly read my manuscript and disabused me of some of my misconceptions. For those interested, I recommend her eye-opening working paper for the University of Oxford Refugee Studies Centre, 'The Evolution of Immigration Detention in the UK: The Involvement of Private Prison Companies', at www.rsc.ox.ac.uk/PDFs/RSCworkingpaper27.pdf

Background on the medical and social aspects of immigration and asylum was provided by Dr Mina Fazel, Bob Hughes and Teresa Hayter. Many thanks also to Bob and Teresa for their hospitality, their encouragement, and for reading my manuscript and offering suggestions. The novel's accuracy is down to them; the inevitable errors are mine.

Thanks to Andy Paterson and Olivia Paterson for excellent notes on my early draft.

Thanks to Sharon Maguire and Anand Tucker for their warmth and support.

I owe a great deal to Suzie Dooré, Jennifer Joel, Maya Mavjee, Marysue Rucci and Peter Straus, whose several patient readings and insightful editorial notes on my drafts have been invaluable. Thank you.

Chris Cleave, London, 18 February 2008
www.chriscleave.com

If your face is swollen from the severe beatings of life, smile and pretend to be a fat man.

Nigerian proverb

"I went into a room in Paris with a coffee maker and a radio and I came out six weeks later with a beard and a manuscript, not really knowing how I'd done it ..."

read more from
CHRIS CLEAVE...

- Q and A
- Why he writes
- Reviews and prize news
- His Guardian column
- Film and TV news
- Short stories for free
- Charity links

www.chriscleave.com

Follow Chris on Twitter: twitter.com/chriscleave

And you can find Chris Cleave and many other Sceptre authors on www.sceptrebooks.co.uk

You aren't stupid. You know there's no such thing as a perfect mother. Plenty of other books will tell you there is, but this one won't lie to you.

I was weak and I cheated and I was punished, but my god I loved my child through all of it. Love means you never break, and it means you're stronger than the things they do to you. I know this is true because I have been through fire, and I am the proof that love survives.

I am not a perfect mother but I will tell you the perfect truth, because this is you and me talking. This is my story.

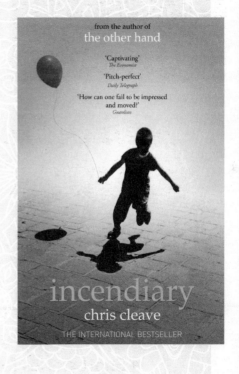

from the author of
the other hand

'Captivating'
The Economist

'Pitch-perfect'
Daily Telegraph

'How can one fail to be impressed and moved?'
Guardian

incendiary
chris cleave
THE INTERNATIONAL BESTSELLER

'Stunning'   – *New York Times*

'Chris Cleave has the ability to create moving and beautiful scenes within a terrifying backdrop. I couldn't put it down; it's subversive, thought-provoking and well written' – *Observer*, Books of the Year

SCEPTRE